PRAISE FOR

# where the truth lies

"Warman sensitively portrays the sibling-like tensions
and intimacy of boarding-school friendships. . . . Memorable."
—*Booklist*

"A smart, sensitive melodrama."
—*BCCB*

PRAISE FOR

# breathless

An ALA Best Book for Young Adults

"Poignantly honest and real. . . . Exudes authenticity
and is told with depth, intelligence, humor, and affection."
—Todd Strasser, bestselling author of *Give a Boy a Gun*

★ "Achingly realistic . . . with rare, refreshing honesty
and flashes of wry humor."—*Booklist*, **starred review**

★ "Vivid and exquisite. Katie is achingly real, and her
relationship with her ferocious, guarded, and superbly faithful
roommate, Mazzie, is one of the most tender and intimate
platonic friendships in YA lit."—*BCCB*, **starred review**

where
the
truth
lies

BOOKS BY JESSICA WARMAN

*Breathless*
*Where the Truth Lies*
*Between*

# where the truth lies

jessica warman

Walker & Company  New York

First published in the United States of America in September 2010
by Walker Publishing Company, Inc., a division of Bloomsbury Publishing, Inc.
Paperback edition published in August 2011
www.bloomsburyteens.com

For information about permission to reproduce selections from this book, write to
Permissions, Walker BFYR, 175 Fifth Avenue, New York, New York 10010

The Library of Congress has cataloged the hardcover edition as follows:
Warman, Jessica.
Where the truth lies / Jessica Warman.
p.    cm.
Summary: Emily, whose father is headmaster of a Connecticut boarding school,
suffers from nightmares, and when she meets and falls in love with the handsome
Del Sugar, pieces of her traumatic past start falling into place.
ISBN-13: 978-0-8027-2078-8 • ISBN-10: 0-8027-2078-1 (hardcover)
[1. Nightmares—Fiction. 2. Memory—Fiction. 3. Boarding schools—Fiction.
4. Schools—Fiction. 5. Dating (Social customs)—Fiction.
6. Family life—Connecticut—Fiction. 7. Connecticut—Fiction.] I. Title.
PZ7.W2374Whe 2010        [Fic]—dc22        2010000782

ISBN 978-0-8027-2292-8 (paperback)

Book design by Danielle Delaney
Typeset by Westchester Book Composition
Printed in the U.S.A. by Quad/Graphics, Fairfield, Pennsylvania
2  4  6  8  10  9  7  5  3  1

All papers used by Bloomsbury Publishing, Inc., are natural, recyclable products
made from wood grown in well-managed forests. The manufacturing processes
conform to the environmental regulations of the country of origin.

*For my girls, Estella and Esmé.*
*And, of course, for Colin.*

"Two dogs live within me.
The one that grows the largest
is the one I feed the most."
—*Native American folktale*

where
the
truth
lies

part one

# chapter one

I have insomnia. Actually, I have something called night terrors. So it's not that I *can't* sleep—it's more like I'm afraid to sleep. And when I finally do, it's almost always that kind of half-awake struggle, a fight to find some rest in between the real world and the part of my subconscious where nightmares unfold and wrap themselves around me. It's always hard to tell the difference, to know where I really am. Most of the time, I wake up gasping for air. Sometimes—but not very often—I'll find my breath and wake up screaming. My nightmares are always about the same things: fire or water. Never both at once.

It's an unseasonably warm October in Connecticut. Usually, it's not uncommon to have snow by now. But this year we're having a warm snap; the leaves have turned already, but suddenly it's in the eighties again. My parents' house isn't air-conditioned, so I'm lying in my bed on top of the sheets, wearing just a bra and underwear, sweating like crazy. I could swear I'm awake until I see my mother's face above me, and I kind of brace myself for what's coming: smoke, flames—then she'll disappear. In my sleep, I blink and blink, trying to will her out of danger, to help her breathe. I don't know why she's in my dreams sometimes, why she would ever be in the middle of a fire, her face obscured by smoke as I reach for her, unable to grasp at anything but thick air.

My attempts to save her never work. I can't speak or help in any way; all I can do is hope. I don't know how the dreams end; I always wake up while everybody is still struggling.

"Emily. It's time to get up."

But I can't *move*. You know that kind of nightmare? Where you need to run away, or wake up—anything for a breath, an escape. It's a mystery to everyone why I have these dreams. I've never been in a fire. I've never even come close to drowning, though water has always scared me. I've been having these dreams for as long as I can remember, and I don't think they'll ever stop.

"Wake up, sleepy girl . . ." My mother leans over, shakes me, her long brown hair brushing my cheeks. Her hands are cool, her slim fingers touching my cheek in concerned irritation. She and my dad have had to wake me like this a thousand times before. When I was younger, sometimes I used to fight them when they tried to rouse me. I've pulled hair, clawed at their faces, smacked and kicked. One time I even gave my dad a bloody nose.

"Emily. I'm really here. Wake up, sweetie. Em!"

And like *that*—it's over. I sit upright, staring, eyes wide. I try to catch my breath. My body goes from hot to cold in an instant, my flesh rising in goose bumps as I look at her.

I put a hand to my mouth. "It's you? I'm awake?"

Mom shakes her head. "This never stops scaring me. The pills still aren't helping?"

My shrink has me on sleeping pills. My parents don't know this, but I hardly ever take them. Even though it's never happened, I'm afraid that, if I *were* to start having a nightmare after taking a pill, I'd be too out of it to wake myself up. And then what?

"I didn't mean to fall asleep." My precalc book is open on the floor beside my bed. "What time is it?"

Mom gives me a frown. Even though I've been a boarding student for years now—I'm a junior—she always gets sad at the end of the weekend. "About that time. Dinner's in less than two hours."

My dad is the headmaster here. He likes to pretend that he holds me to exactly the same rules as everyone else, and one of the rules is that *everybody* has to be at the formal Sunday dinner at six o'clock sharp.

But it's not really like that. I mean, I'm his only daughter. He's my *dad*. No matter how many years I've been at his school, it's almost impossible to take him seriously, especially when most of his orders are followed by a wink. My friends call me a Daddy's Girl, and they're right.

"Don't forget your backpack," my mom says, as I stand to smooth the wrinkles in my uniform, getting ready to go back to my dorm.

"I've got it." My eyes still feel heavy, a little unfocused. Because it's so warm outside, the whole day has been like a fog.

My mother and I are eye to eye now, close enough that when she leans forward, our foreheads touch.

She kisses me on the tip of my nose. "Have a good week, Emily."

"I will."

"Don't forget you have an appointment with Dr. Miller on Thursday afternoon."

Dr. Miller is my shrink, the school psychiatrist. Leave it to Stony-brook to have a school *psychiatrist*.

"I won't forget." Not that it matters if I do; Dr. Miller will just come to my dorm room and get me. She is caring to the point of annoyance.

My mom glances at my clock again. "You should go. I'm sure you have homework to finish before dinner."

I nod. "I've got, like, hours of precalc." Math is my academic kryptonite. Actually, it's one of my many intellectual weaknesses. For someone with two reasonably intelligent parents, I've always struggled in school. I can recite the notes on my quarterly reports from memory, because they all say practically the same thing: *Emily is a bright girl, but she seems unable to stay focused in class.* You'd be unable to focus, too, if you were up half the night most nights, too scared to fall asleep, dreading what might happen in your dreams.

Mom nods. She pushes her hair away from her face in a gesture that I've witnessed countless times before. But it never gets old; she always looks beautiful, youthful, like an ordinary woman trying to collect herself. Even if it's just for an instant.

"Okay, Em. See you later."

"Is Daddy home?"

She shakes her head. "Golf."

"Oh. Right." My dad goes golfing almost every Sunday afternoon. It's kind of like part of his job; usually he goes with a few members of Stonybrook's board of directors. Still, sometimes he comes home early, just to see me off before the start of the week. We're close like that. My dad is the nicest guy I know.

I walk back to my dorm alone, sweating as I trudge uphill. For a moment, I wonder what my mom will do with her time alone before dinner. I want to know what happens in those unseen

moments—there are so few of them on campus—but at the same time, I'm glad she has them to herself.

Sometimes I think life would be easier if my family lived far away, like every other student's. Because even though my parents are here, I seem to miss them all the time, aching for something I've never had, something just out of reach, even though it's always been present. My parents and I are as close as can be, but the difference is that I have to share them with everyone. I'm used to it by now; it's just how life has always been, how it's always going to be. But, still, sometimes I wish it could be just the three of us.

That's why it's important to have friends. They make you laugh. They help you forget, even when you don't know what it is you're trying not to remember.

Campus is laid out on a hillside, with my parents' house at the very bottom, the dorms in the middle, and the school all the way at the top. It's beautiful, picturesque New England, the kind of place that you can take one look at and fall in love with. To me, the whole place is like home. I've been here for as long as I can remember—even before I went to school here, I lived with my parents and could look out my window at night to see lights glowing in the dorms, and I'd imagine what life would be like when I got older and would finally live in the dorms myself.

It is a dream. It is a slumber party every night. I mean, it's not perfect, but it's close. I know I'm lucky. When I'm here on campus, surrounded by all my friends, with my parents so nearby, I often feel like nothing can hurt me. That's why the nightmares are so perplexing. How am I so terrified, when there is nothing to be afraid of? And why do they make me feel so desperately alone, when I have everyone I could ever want right here with me?

# chapter two

Stonybrook Academy is tiny; there are only about three hundred students from grades seven through twelve. So even if you don't know everyone, you still kind of know them. There are only ten girls in my dorm, split up among five bedrooms on the second floor, since the first floor is just a great room and kitchenette. The fourth and fifth bedrooms on the second floor are joined together, so you have to walk through the fourth to get to the captive fifth. The two rooms combined are known as the quad, and I share it with three girls: Grace Paulsen-Taylor, Francine Bingham (who everybody calls Franny), and my best friend, Stephanie Prince. Franny and I have the front room, while Stephanie and Grace share the back.

I can tell something's the matter as soon as I walk in. Stephanie and Grace aren't around. Their door is open, unmade bunk beds visible through the beads hung in their doorway. Franny is alone, curled into the tiny ledge of the windowsill, staring at the hazy sky. She doesn't notice when I walk in. She's tugging at her blond hair, pulling strands out one by one. Franny has trichotillomania. It's a kind of compulsion—I've looked it up online. It means that she pulls her hair out like crazy, but with

Franny it's always only one strand at a time. The room reeks of weed.

"Franny," I whisper, shutting the door as fast as possible, cringing as it slams behind me. "What the hell are you doing?"

"Hmmm?" she asks, not even looking at me. The window is open; all that separates my roommate from a fifty-foot drop is a flimsy screen. As usual, Franny appears tired, bored, and lonely.

*Tug. Tug.* After she pulls out each single hair, she gives it a long look of quiet satisfaction before carefully feeding it through the screen, like she's threading a needle. One of these days, she'll start getting bald spots.

I fan the air with my hand—like that's going to do anything. "It reeks in here! Since when do you get high? And would you get off the windowsill?" I feel like I've been teleported to an after-school special, as though at any moment she might lose her balance and tumble to her death. What's the lesson we've all learned? Weed *kills kids*, kids.

Franny gets up, wordlessly strips down to her underwear, and lies on her bed. "I'm so tired," she says, curling onto her side to gaze at me. "Turn the light out. Let's take a nap before dinner." She gives me a lazy smile, followed by a yawn. "Come on, Emily. Come cuddle." And she pats the spot beside her. "Sleepy time."

For as long as I've known her, Franny has been a cuddlebug. Normally, I'd probably take her up on it. I mean, who doesn't love cuddles? But I'm worried and angry, and not in the mood for playing.

"Where are Grace and Stephanie?"

She yawns again. *Tug.* This time, she lets the hair drift aimlessly into the air; it rises upward in the densely hot room and wafts past me, like the remnants of a cobweb. "I dunno. Probably over at Winchester." Winchester is one of the upper-school boys' dorms.

"Where did you get the smoke, Franny?"

Franny and I have been roommates since the seventh grade. At first, we didn't have a choice; roommates are randomly assigned so that people don't get too cliquey. But my roommates and I are kind of a clique anyway. It's no secret to anyone that the four of us only scored the quad because I'm the headmaster's daughter.

Over the years, I've grown more than a little bit protective of Franny. Stonybrook Academy is the kind of place where . . . well, kids get sent here for a few reasons, none of which are mutually exclusive. Tuition is high, one of the highest in the country for boarding schools, so of course we've got plenty of rich kids, particularly some children of high-profile people. For instance, Franny's mom is a senator. Grace's father owns the golf course where they've held the US Open more than once. Stephanie's dad is a lawyer, and apparently he's a pretty good one. Steph has told me plenty of times that it's impossible to win an argument with him.

There are the kids who come here because they're supersmart, and a diploma from Stonybrook is pretty much a ticket into any college you want. There are the bad kids whose parents just can't deal with them. And then there are the kids who aren't necessarily bad at all, but their parents just can't deal, period. Those are the kids who show up on the first day of seventh grade and don't even go home for most of the holidays.

Franny is one of those kids. I can't count the number of holidays she's shared at my house. By the time she was eleven, her mom was on her second husband, who turned out to be *very* affectionate with his stepdaughter. Instead of facing the fact that she'd married a perv and putting Franny in therapy, her mom opted for a quick divorce, boarding school for her only daughter, and a heavy case of denial. Senator Bingham (R-California) is on her third husband now, and Franny tells me that she refers to the time leading up to her second divorce as Franny's "Lolita phase."

Sitting beside Franny on the bed, I pull up the sheet to cover

her frail body. She reaches under her pillowcase and fishes out a crushed pack of cigarettes and a lighter. "Will you get me some water?" she asks. *Tug.* One at a time: controlled, neurotic, minimal. So totally Franny.

I sigh. "Yes. You shouldn't smoke in here, though. It's gross."

"I'm *stoned*. I want a cigarette."

"The cleaning ladies don't come till tomorrow. You can't blame the smell on them. You could get caught."

"Whoopee." She lights up, exhaling smoke through her tiny nostrils. "Nobody cares."

*I* care; I hate cigarettes. But aside from how I feel, Franny is kind of right. On paper, Stonybrook Academy has a zero-tolerance drug and alcohol policy. Supposedly, if you get caught smoking or drinking or doing anything illicit on campus, you're immediately expelled. I've never heard of it happening, though. The thing is, Stonybrook relies so heavily on private funding—donations, specifically—that it can't afford to go kicking out everyone who gets caught doing something they shouldn't be, especially since most of those kids are the children of rich people. Not only would we not be able to operate without all that money coming in, but we wouldn't be able to attract such plush donors if we didn't already have a reputation as a Posh Boarding School. My dad tells me that it's just the way the world works, and I guess maybe he's right. At least, I've never seen it work any other way.

But, oh, poor Franny. I want to protect her so badly. She and I are friends, sure, but we're so different that it's always been hard for me to get through to her. She's shy and kind of dull and always, always throws up at parties after just one or two drinks, and is irretrievably sad—but I love her like a sister.

It's really true: everybody here is like brother and sister. And even though people know that Franny has a miserable home life, and though I've never told anyone the specifics of her situation,

it's tough to keep a secret here, especially when a person never goes home and her own *mother* never comes to visit. So everybody ought to know better than to go getting her stoned, all by herself on a weekend, when she literally could have slipped away, out the window, her weak, tiny frame shattered against the sandy dirt below.

She sits up to drink the water, taking it in huge gulps, letting the sheet slip away from her body. For as long as I've known her, Franny has worn matching day-of-the-week bra and underwear. She's worn them every day for over four years, always on the correct day. She has *dozens* of sets.

"All right," I say, sighing, wrinkling my nose as the smoke from her cigarette wafts past me. "Spill. Who got you stoned?"

*Tug. Gaze. Let go.* Then she crosses her arms. "Why?"

"Because, Franny, you could have fallen out the window. You're kind of delicate, you know?" I put my hands on her arms. All I can feel is bone under her skin. "Tell me."

Franny rolls her eyes. Her left eye gets lazy when she's tired, like right now, giving her a kind of sad look, her long hair—it reaches almost to her butt—greasy and in dire need of a trim, her underwear announcing to anyone who might happen to walk in that it's SUNDAY!

I don't know why I even bothered asking. As soon as her gaze flickers toward the hallway, before she has a chance to open her mouth, the answer is obvious.

"Renee," we both say at the same time.

I glare at the doorway. "Ohhh . . . she's gonna get it."

"Can I take a nap now?" Franny asks. She grinds out her cigarette against the side of a coffee cup that she keeps beneath her bed specifically for use as an ashtray.

"Yes." I tuck her in tightly, as though the sheet might be enough to keep her in place. I sit on the side of the bed and smooth the

hair away from her sweaty brow, leaning over to give her a kiss on the forehead. Then I get up, turning off the light on my way out. "Just promise me you'll stay away from the windowsill." I pause. "And quit tugging your hair out."

"Um-hmmm. I'll quit breathing while I'm at it, *Mom*."


Renee Graham: a sophomore at Stonybrook and the only child of three-time Oscar winner Amy Wallace. Her last name comes from her mom's second husband, Bruce Graham, who is a Tony, Golden Globe, *and* Academy Award winner. I've never met Amy Wallace in real life, although I've seen plenty of her movies, and Renee looks exactly like her. Bruce Graham, however, is around plenty: he comes to all of the parent weekends, picks Renee up for vacation, and even shows up out of the blue sometimes to take her out for dinner. He hasn't been her stepfather since she was ten, but from what I've heard, Renee doesn't even live with her mom; when she goes home for the holidays, she stays with Bruce in Manhattan.

Even though she lives directly across the hall, Renee and I aren't what you'd call friends. She's nice enough, I guess, and we aren't enemies or anything. We've just never bothered with each other much. First of all, there's the fact that I'm a year older than she is. Besides that, I have Stephanie and Grace and Franny, and Renee has . . . whoever. Besides, Renee is so aloof, so casual and cool, that it's impossible not to feel intimidated by her. Even at a school with so many celebrities' kids and overachievers, and even though she's only a sophomore, Renee has a quality to her that's almost magical. I guess it's what you call charisma.

Like when she answers her door, after I've been banging on it for a good thirty seconds. "Hola, babycakes," she says, batting her long brown eyelashes at me. "What's up?"

13

She's just gotten out of the shower; a short, white silk bathrobe clings to her still-damp body, which is lanky and flawless. Her dark hair is wrapped tightly in a towel, her widow's peak exposed on her forehead. I know for a *fact* that Renee, with all her money, does not own a blow-dryer. She just lets her hair air-dry, runs a comb through it, and voilà: tousled perfection. I don't know why, but I'm infinitely annoyed by this factoid. I mean, who doesn't own a hair dryer? It's like not owning a toothbrush or something.

Personally, I don't know what I'd do without one; I have long red hair that is thick and wavy and will not respond to a hairbrush without a heavy spraying of detangler beforehand. Nobody knows where the color came from; both of my parents have brown hair. I'm also covered in freckles. You'd think that, being a redhead and all, I'd have one of those fiery, feisty personalities, but I don't; most people would probably describe me as quiet and somewhat shy. Standing across from Renee, I feel impossibly strange looking. Not exotic strange, like she is, just *weird* strange.

"Do you have to ask what's up?" I say, trying my best to sound imposing.

She blinks. There's no sarcasm in her voice; it's just matter-of-fact. "I just did."

"Franny," I tell her. "I found her practically unconscious against the screen on our windowsill. She could have fallen out. I could be staring at her dead body right now."

Renee shakes her head. "Don't be so dramatic, Emily. That seems unlikely. She was fine when I left her."

I look around; we shouldn't be talking about this in the hallway. "Can I come in?"

Renee's roommate, Hillary Swisher, is gone; there's no doubt in my mind she's over at her boyfriend's dorm, making out on the common-room sofa. Instead, there are a few other girls in the

room. They all look younger, and I don't recognize any of them, which means they're probably—

"Seventh graders," Renee explains, nodding at them with a sincere smile.

Right.

Of the three, it's obvious two of them have been crying. They sit cross-legged on Renee's bed, legs and elbows touching, kind of holding on to each other. They look lost. The first few weeks at *any* new school are tough, but I can't imagine going away to boarding school at age twelve. I mean—I *did* go to boarding school at twelve, but my dad was just down the hall in his office. I could walk to my parents' house whenever I wanted. These girls are alone, parents probably hundreds of miles away. Sometimes I think it is kind of a cruel thing to do to your own child, but pretty much everyone starts at Stonybrook in seventh grade. It's just the way things happen for some people.

Renee gives them another demure smile. Despite their homesickness, they're clearly in awe of her. I mean, everyone who's been to the movies or stood in line at a supermarket browsing the tabloids knows who Renee is. She leans over her bed and puts her arms around them in a group hug. She takes a moment to kiss each of them on the forehead. I find the gesture surprisingly sweet and touching, and it takes me a little off guard. I'd always imagined that Renee was too cool to be overly sensitive or caring, but she certainly seems that way now.

"I have to talk to Emily in private for a few minutes," she says, "but why don't the three of you come get me when you're ready to go up to dinner?"

They nod. They give me hesitant, tearful smiles on their way out. For a minute I forget all about Franny, but as soon as the door closes I remember why I'm here: because that *was* Franny, four years ago. And in a lot of ways, it still is.

As I step farther into the room, Renee says in a sarcastic tone, "Be careful to stay on my side."

This is the first year Renee and Hillary have been roommates, and I hear they've already been bickering nonstop.

Right now, a thick line of duct tape divides the room into two halves.

"It creates kind of a problem," Renee says as I stare at the tape, "because, as you can see, our closet is on Hillary's side of the room, and the door is on my side."

"Uh-huh. And this was whose idea?"

"Not mine." With a wicked little grin, Renee strolls pointedly across the line to Hillary's bed, takes her wet hair out of the towel, and tosses the towel onto her roommate's side of the floor. Then she lies down on Hillary's bed, her hair getting the pillowcase all wet. "God, I miss Madeline."

I sigh. "No kidding." Madeline Moon-Park was Renee's old roommate. She didn't come back to school this year. "Where did she go?" I ask.

Renee shrugs. "I don't know. I can't get ahold of her. She changed her e-mail address, and her home phone doesn't work. All I know is that I came back expecting to room with Madeline, and she didn't show up, so they put me with Hillary instead." She pauses. "Don't *you* know where she went? Didn't your dad say anything?"

I shake my head. "Just that she wasn't coming back. I figured you would have talked to her by now."

"Well, I haven't. You know what she's like. If she doesn't want to talk, she's not going to talk."

I almost smile. There was *nobody* else like Madeline. I never understood how she and Renee got to be so close, but their relationship was practically telepathic. For a moment, I imagine how I'd feel if Franny or Steph or Grace suddenly disappeared, never to be heard from again. I'd be heartsick.

"Want to know why she did it?" Renee asks, her tone shifting from nostalgia to bitterness.

"You know why Madeline left?"

"No. Want to know why Hillary put the tape down?"

"Oh. Sure." With the room split in two, it's obvious this is a mismatched pair of individuals. Renee's side is a mess: piles of clothing and shoes litter the floor; the bed is unmade; Renee's desk is covered with books and papers and a coffeepot that is half-full, definitely *not* fresh—there's fuzzy white mold climbing the sides of the pot, growing on the surface of the sludge. Amidst the mess on her desk, there are several framed photographs of Renee with Bruce Graham. In one of them, she's standing beside him on the red carpet at, like, age twelve, his "date" to the Academy Awards. I remember that so vividly from eighth grade; Renee going to the Oscars for spring break was the talk of the school.

Hillary's side of the room is spotless—at least it was, until Renee threw her towel on the floor and got into the bed. There isn't a stitch of clothing in sight; all of Hillary's schoolbooks are stacked neatly on a small bookshelf. Above her bed, there's a collage of photos, mostly of her and her boyfriend and a few other friends. I don't see Renee in any of them.

"Last Saturday, I came home early from the city, and Hillary was gone—off somewhere with Max, of course."

Max Franklin is Hillary's boyfriend. The two have been insep-arable since the ninth grade. They're the kind of couple who makes everyone, including me, want to gag. They'll probably get married someday.

"So Hillary rolls in around midnight, drunk as a skunk, and she starts puking everywhere, right?" Renee sits up, getting angry all over again. "I mean *everywhere*. I was asleep, and she woke me up with . . . well, let's just say it was disgusting."

"But you said *she's* the one who put down the tape?"

Renee's tone is calm. "Would you listen to me, Emily? I'm trying to explain something to you. After she passed out, I was so . . .
I don't know, so *kertwanged* over the whole mess. But somebody
had to clean it up, right? I mean, we've gotta live in this room,
obviously."

I glance at the moldy coffeepot again. "Uh-huh."

"So I cleaned it up all by myself," she finishes.

"And that's what made Hillary so mad?" I give her a doubtful
look. "Really?"

Renee shrugs. She tries to hold back a smile without success.
"Well . . . I used her clothes to clean up the . . . mess."

"You used her *clothes*?"

"Right. But not her uniforms—I mean, we had school the next
day. Hillary's a clotheshorse—she's all about couture and whatever, you know?"

I do know.

"I used her *real* clothes. Some of them got ruined." She sighs,
looks around the room. "I might have gone a little too far. Hence
the tape. We're still adjusting to each other."

"So I take it Hillary's still mad?"

Renee shrugs. "She'll be over it soon."

That's what it's like here: things flare up and diffuse, flare up
and diffuse. You get really good at conflict resolution. Ten girls
in a dorm—you can't be mortal enemies with anyone, especially
your roommate. It would make life miserable.

But we're way off track. I cross my arms and try to glare at her.
"Listen, I don't want you getting Franny stoned anymore."

Renee raises one thick, perfect eyebrow. "What are you,
her mom?"

*Good thing I'm not*, I think.

"You two aren't even friends," I say. "Why were you hanging out
in the first place?"

It occurs to me that Renee is probably stoned, too. I can't even tell. That's another thing about her. She's the kind of person who's so self-assured, she'd never be the type to get paranoid or weird when she's high.

"I'm sorry," she says. "Sincerely. I just wanted to help."

"By getting her high? How was that helping?"

"I was trying to get her to eat. You know—the munchies?"

I shake my head. "Yeah, I know all about the munchies. But that makes no sense. Why were you trying to get her to eat?"

"Emily, have you seen the girl naked? We were in the bathroom together, okay, and she was walking around in her shower shoes and those *weird* underwear of hers, and I could see the divot in her sternum. With her hair pulled up, I could see the outline of her skull. She has fuzzy hair on her arms—did you know that happens to people when they're starving themselves? And then I was thinking about it, and I couldn't remember the last time I'd seen her eat."

"You think she's anorexic?" I frown. "Listen, I know Franny. She's got plenty of problems, but that's not one of them."

Renee takes a long moment to consider me. "You seem so certain. The girl is so stressed that she's literally pulling her hair out. It's called—"

"I know what it's called. And she's seeing a therapist for it," I lie. Franny's mother is very antitherapy, very much "everything's happy and great as long as we don't talk about it." She's a very popular politician.

"So you aren't worried?" Renee asks.

"No," I say. "I see her eat. Franny's always been too skinny."

Renee shrugs. "If you say so. I thought stuffing her face might do her some good. I was only trying to help." She gets up, smooths the sheets on Hillary's bed, and flips the pillow to hide the wet spot. With her back to me, she says, "I stay up really late sometimes."

When I don't respond, she turns around, steps deliberately across the tape to her side of the room, and adds, "Sometimes I hear you. What do you dream about?"

I'm not sure how to answer her. Why is she bringing this up? "I don't remember. Everyone has nightmares sometimes. We're, you know"—I borrow one of Dr. Miller's favorite reassuring phrases, trying to hide my sarcasm—"in a time of great transition from childhood to adulthood."

Renee shakes her head, damp hair landing perfectly across her shoulders. "You're lying to me, Emily."

"Oh yeah? Who are you all of a sudden, Sigmund Freud? My roommate's anorexic, I've got issues with my dreams . . . you're like a real Svengali, aren't you?"

She seems genuinely sorry, almost confused. "I was just trying to help Franny. And sometimes when you scream . . ." She shudders. "It's horrible."

I'm at a total loss for words. I've never had a conversation remotely this intimate with Renee before.

"Well . . . I'm sorry I wake you up."

She blinks. "I didn't say you woke me. I said I heard you. I'm already awake."

"Oh."

". . ."

". . ."

"Just . . . let me worry about Franny, okay? She'll be all right. We'll both be fine." I attempt a smile. "Worry about your territory war over here, okay? You'll get used to Hillary."

"Hillary Swisher," Renee declares, "will never be Madeline Moon-Park."

I giggle. Everybody misses Madeline—she was obnoxious to the point of hilarity, a tiny bundle of energy with the foulest

mouth I'd ever heard—and it's just like her to disappear without a word to anyone.

"If you leave Franny alone," I say, "I'll try to find out what happened to Madeline."

Renee shrugs. "If we don't know by now, we probably never will." Her expression grows serious. "Emily—you can knock, you know? If you can't sleep. I have tranquilizers. They're prescription. They'll knock you out. Or we could stay up . . ."

All of a sudden, I've had my fill of Renee. I stare at the duct tape, unwilling to meet her gaze. "I should check on my roommate."


Back in the quad, I find Franny snoring softly into her pillow, fast asleep. The sheet beside her is covered in a tiny bundle of hairs. Even though it's only late afternoon, she'll likely stay this way until morning if I don't wake her up. She sleeps *a lot*.

Grace and Stephanie's door is closed. They're back.

I walk in without knocking. Both of them are on the bottom bunk—Stephanie's bed—sitting cross-legged atop the covers in their bras and underwear. Because their room is captive, it's always like ten degrees hotter than everywhere else in the dorm. The heat is incredible; it's gotta be close to ninety. Both of them are sweating, sipping mineral water, having a lazy conversation.

"I'm going to cheat on my Latin quiz," Stephanie murmurs to nobody in particular. Her gaze flickers to me and she gives me a bright smile. "Emily! Yay!" She pats the space beside her on the bed. "Come. Sit."

"How are you gonna do *that*? You'll get caught. You'll get kicked *out*." Grace is the most excitable person I've ever met. She's constantly making wild predictions about everybody's future. She's almost always wrong.

21

Stephanie hooks her arm around me as soon as I'm seated beside her, my head resting on her shoulder. "I will not get caught. She uses the same quizzes for every class. Ethan took his last week, and he kept it for me. I'm just going to memorize his answers. Would you relax already?"

Oh, Ethan Prince. Ethan is Stephanie's twin brother, and they're superclose. He's a prefect and an all-around good guy. He even looks like Clark Kent, except not in an "I can't tell that Clark Kent is Superman" kind of way, but in a "Clark Kent is obviously Superman" way. The only reason he'd ever help his sister cheat is because Steph has taken Latin for almost four years and can still barely conjugate.

Stephanie has been my best friend since about the first week of seventh grade. We had all the same classes together, and the friendship just kind of fell into place. We've been inseparable ever since. But Stephanie and Ethan are completely different. While Ethan doesn't have a mean bone in his body, Stephanie is much more . . . spirited. She says what's on her mind all the time, even if it hurts someone. A lot of people think she's a bitch. I like to think she provides balance to my personality—I've always been so quiet, I can use someone outspoken sometimes. But lately, especially since school started this year, something feels different about our relationship. Stephanie seems more callous, more defensive somehow, and it bothers me more than it used to.

But she's been my best friend since we were *twelve*. I'm not going to let things just slip away. So I rest my head on her shoulder again, and feel content knowing that, for right now, life is good.

"Hey, Em." Grace turns her head lazily in my direction. She sighs. "It's a freaking *oven* in here."

I undo the top few buttons of my own shirt. The windows are open, but the air outside is stagnant; there's no cross-breeze. "We could go into my room."

Stephanie yawns. "Franny's practically comatose. Besides, your room stinks. Is she stoned?"

"Yup." I give them a quick rundown of the afternoon's events.

Stephanie digs a Latin quiz with a big A+ at the top out of her book bag, stares at it blankly for a few moments, and then tosses it aside. It glides to the floor like there's a thickness to the air; that's how hot it is in here.

"So Madeline isn't coming back for sure?" Stephanie asks. "Emily, ask your dad already. He's gotta know *something*."

"I can try." If I'm supersneaky, I can probably get my dad to tell me what he knows—maybe. Like I said, he thinks it's important to treat me like any other student . . . most of the time.

"He might not be able to tell you," Steph murmurs. "You know, student confidentiality laws and all that." Her long, curly blond hair is pulled into a messy ponytail. She and Ethan are fraternal twins, obviously, and they're both good-looking as hell, but they don't even seem related in lots of ways. Aside from the differences in their personalities, Stephanie looks just like her dad, while Ethan looks like their mom. "Ooh, Grace!" Stephanie is suddenly excited. "Show her! Show her what we got at the mall!"

"Yes!" Grace hops out of bed. Her muscles are visible everywhere beneath her tan skin; she's a cross-country runner. She goes to a bag beside her bed, leans over to dig inside, and emerges looking triumphant. "Look. What. We. Got." She adds, as though I wouldn't know, "It's for your dad's car. Think we can sneak it onto the Escalade somewhere?"

My roommates call my father "Dad." You'd think it would bother me, but it really doesn't. After all, I'm his real daughter; we both know that. I'm so used to sharing him, and besides, my roommates all have strained, sad relationships with their parents, whereas my own father is loving and kind and . . . well, wonderful.

23

I love my roommates like sisters; they deserve someone like him in their lives.

Grace is holding up an airbrushed license plate that says "Dadmobile" in hot pink letters.

I clap a hand to my mouth. "Oh my God. He'll die."

"I was thinking we could switch it with his real license plate," Grace says.

I nod. "Yes! We should do it after dinner, when he's still up at school."

For a split second, Stephanie frowns. "You don't think Dad will be mad?" She rolls her eyes. "*My* dad would flip." Her father is a total jerk. We have nicknames for him, too, but none of them are very nice.

I shake my head. "Come on. You're talking about Headmaster John Meckler. He's a teddy bear."

"I don't mean to change the subject," Grace says, "but we need to tell her about the *other* thing, Steph."

Stephanie picks up the Latin quiz from the floor. She peers at it for another few seconds, sighs, and tosses it away again. "Right. So let's tell her."

"Tell me what?"

"Oohhhh . . ." Grace, who is petite with curly chestnut hair and a pixie's face to match, rubs her hands together in excitement. "We were over at Winchester, right?"

I nod.

"And there's a *new boy*. He's a junior like us. He said his parents enrolled him over the weekend."

This is beyond unusual for Stonybrook. There's a long wait list and an exhaustive admissions process; nobody *ever* starts after the beginning of the school year.

"A new boy?" I repeat. *A boy! A boy a boy aboy!*

"Is he *ever*." Grace reaches out, grasps my wrist. Her hands are clammy. "Emily. He has a *tattoo*."

I feel a tingle of excitement in my spine. "He does? Where?"

"On his wrist," Stephanie interrupts. "It's right over his veins." She shudders. "I didn't even want to ask him about it. Must have hurt like *hell*."

"Oh, you could barely talk to him," Grace says. "She let Ethan do all the talking. Steph could hardly look Del—that's his name—in the eye."

Stephanie flicks Grace on the ear. "Shut up, Grace."

"*You* shut up!"

"His name is Del?" I ask, ignoring the bickering. "That's not a name."

"Del Sugar," Grace finishes. "What do you mean, it's not a name? It's his name, isn't it?" She pauses. "Okay, it's a little bit weird. But Emily, he's *so* cute."

"What does his tattoo look like? What does *he* look like?"

"Emily," Stephanie says, "calm down. You'll see him at dinner." She pauses. Then, trying to be nonchalant, she adds, "It's not like it's a big deal that he has a tattoo. People have tattoos, Em. You know, my brother and I are getting matching tattoos once we turn eighteen."

Grace and I share a quick glance. We're both trying not to smile.

"What, um, what tattoo are you getting, Stephanie?" I ask, winking at Grace.

Steph narrows her eyes at us. "You *know*. You both know."

"I forgot," Grace says. "Why don't you tell us again?"

Everyone calls Ethan "The Prince." Mostly because that's his last name, but also because it's just too perfect. He's something like six feet five, really well built with dark hair and a coolness to

him that isn't a bit intimidating. He plays baseball. He loves music, and is really good at percussion instruments. Aside from my father, he's just about the nicest person I've ever met.

His constant kindness is what I'd say is Ethan's only downfall: he's so nice, he gives people the benefit of the doubt too much. It's like he has blinders on when it comes to other people—especially his sister. I mean, sure, Stephanie is my best friend, but I'm not oblivious to the finer points of her personality. Ethan, however, *does* seem oblivious. He thinks she can do no wrong. He doesn't even acknowledge that she smokes cigarettes, and more often than not, she reeks unmistakably.

Anyway, for *years* Stephanie has been trying to give herself the nickname "The Princess." But as much as she's tried, it just hasn't stuck. Sometimes Ethan calls her Princess—but Ethan calls lots of girls Princess. Mostly, he calls his sister Stephie.

But the plot gets thicker. Last year, Ethan went out with Lindsey Cole for about six months. They were like the golden couple. Since everyone calls Ethan the Prince already, they started calling *Lindsey* the Princess. To say that Stephanie didn't like it *at all* is a major understatement. After Ethan and Lindsey broke up, Stephanie got the idea that she and Ethan should get matching Prince and Princess tattoos someday. And she made sure nobody ever called Lindsey the Princess again.

I know Steph better than I know Ethan, so I can't really say how he feels about the idea. But I know how Grace and I and pretty much everybody else feels, and as her closest friend, I haven't held back in sharing my opinion with Stephanie.

"Please stop talking about that," I say. "It's so gross."

Grace nods. "You need to let it go. Just imagine how your *husband* will feel someday."

Stephanie has full, pouty lips, which she presses together now in agitation. "I don't know what you mean."

"Well, then you need to have a talk with Dr. Miller. I think there's a name for it." Grace glances at the clock. "We have to go to dinner. Somebody wake up Franny."

Steph glares at both of us. "You two go ahead."

"I'll spray some perfume on her," I say.

"Uh-huh." She continues to pout. "Don't save me a seat." For a second, I think she might really be mad. But when she remembers to slip the Dadmobile plate into her backpack as she's getting ready to leave, I know she's mostly joking.

Grace and I head out together. Franny peers at us with sleepy eyes as we walk into my room, but she doesn't say anything. Her frame is so tiny that I can barely make it out beneath the sheets.

I go over to her bed and kneel beside her. "Hey, my little waif. Time to wake up."

"Mmmm . . . ," she murmurs. "I want *cuddles*, Emily."

"Later. It's time for dinner."


Once we get outside, we join the threads of students leaving their dorms to head up to dinner, everyone eventually forming a thick cluster of bodies that winds up the hill.

Just ahead of us, Renee walks with the seventh-graders from earlier. They're almost tripping over each other as they try to stay close to her, hanging on her every word.

At one point, when she turns around to say something, she catches my eye. She raises her right hand and wiggles her fingers in an easy wave.

"You know how her mother's a cocaine addict?" Grace murmurs under her breath.

I nod. It's been in the tabloids, on and off, for years.

Grace hooks her arm through mine, leans closer to whisper, "I heard she relapsed."

Grace can be a major gossip sometimes. But I still feel bad for Renee. I can't imagine what it would be like to grow up with a mother like that.

Before I have a chance to respond to the wave, Renee turns around to lead the way again. She isn't wearing her school blazer. The back of her white shirt is untucked from her plaid skirt. Her hair is pulled into two messy braids that trail down her back, leaving wet spots that make it obvious she isn't wearing a bra.

"I don't know how she gets those groupies," Grace says. "For someone so rich, she's awfully . . . disheveled."

I'm wondering if she has a blow-dryer back in New York; if she let her hair air-dry when she went to the Oscars with Bruce Graham. "I don't know, Grace," I say. "If you were in seventh grade, wouldn't you want to be just like her?"

Grace doesn't say anything; she just shakes her head.

"Tell me if you see the new boy," I say.

"Oh, I will."

We walk silently, both of us staring at Renee.

Even now—even though we don't have a single thing in common, besides Franny—I can't stop feeling disappointed that she didn't wait for me to wave back before she turned around.

# chapter three

Tonight we're having ham for dinner, carved on a marble slab by Digger, the head of the dining hall staff. He's a tall, quiet guy in his late sixties whose wielding of a carving knife makes everyone somewhat uncomfortable. The ham is cloyingly sweet, its smell thick enough to make me want to gag in this heat.

We can sit anywhere we want. Since I know Steph was a little miffed by all the joking about her and Ethan, I decide to sit with just Grace tonight. I can see my parents across the dining hall; Stephanie and Franny are at their table, along with Ethan and a few other boys from his dorm.

Even though the room isn't that big, Grace can't spot Del Sugar.

"He must not be here," she says, shrugging. "Oh well. You'll see him tomorrow, I'm sure."

I nibble at the edge of a dinner roll, unwilling to touch my ham, which appears to actually be *sweating*. "Then where is he?"

She shrugs again. The topic feels old already, like the whole thing might have been a misunderstanding or exaggeration, like maybe he's not really here at all. As I said, nobody ever comes after the beginning of the year. If he were here, *everyone* would be looking at him.

"I heard he's some kind of prodigy," Grace says, "and that's why Dad let him in."

"Really?" I don't even flinch when she calls my father "Dad."

"Yes."

A prodigy. There are plenty of those here already. It doesn't make any sense.

After dinner, I kind of forget about Del. I've got more important things on my mind.

It's already pitch-dark, but still hot. Outside the dining hall, it smells like warm ham and autumn. There's just a twinge of the smell of the ocean, which is always present in Connecticut, no matter how far inland you go.

Grace and I wait for Steph and Franny outside the dining hall. Once the four of us are standing alone together, I say, "Okay. How are we going to do this?"

Stephanie still wants to sulk a little. "I just want to say again," she announces, "that plenty of people get matching tattoos."

Franny wasn't in on our conversation earlier, but she's heard about Steph's whole "matching tattoos" idea already. She snorts. *Tug.* "Husbands and wives. Rock stars and gold diggers. Not *brothers and sisters*, Stephanie."

"I don't want to fight," Grace says. "I want to play a joke on Dad."

"Steph, honey." I put my arm around her. "It's okay. We're just kidding."

She pouts. "No, you aren't. You think it's weird."

"We think it's weird," I pronounce, "because it *is*. Besides, it's never actually going to happen."

Even though the tattoo idea is gross, I can sort of understand where Steph is coming from. Like so many of the kids who go here, her family life is less than enviable. Ethan is pretty much all she has,

even though her parents come around often enough. Like I said, Steph's dad is an attorney. He's well-known within the dorms for having outbursts of anger over the most trivial of issues. For instance, at the beginning of the year, he threw a fit when he found out that his daughter—his *princess*—was staying in a captive room with no fire escape outside the window. He threatened to sue everyone: the school, my dad, our dorm mother. Like most of his outbursts, it ended in a compromise. Now, under her bed in her room, Stephanie has one of those collapsible cloth ladders with metal hooks that can be attached to the window in case of a fire. I still remember my dad standing there, shaking his head, telling Stephanie, "Now make sure you use this to sneak out of your dorm every night, okay?"

He was kidding. But we do it all the time.

The four of us make our way into the school parking lot, where my dad's black Escalade is parked outside his office.

"Okay," Steph murmurs. We're all staring at my father, who is clearly visible sitting at his desk, head bent over a pile of paperwork. "He'll definitely see us if he looks outside. Somebody has to distract him."

I shrug. "I'll do it."

"But then he'll know it was us," Grace says.

"Grace," I say, "we're putting a plate on his car that says 'Dad-mobile.' He has one daughter. The four of us are the only people in the world who call him 'Dad.' He's going to know it was us anyway."

"Then what's the point?" she asks. "Do you think I can smoke a cigarette out here? Because I'm very nervous. Did anyone bring cigarettes?"

"Grace, be quiet. You can't smoke out here. Now, listen. Here's what we're going to do. I'll go inside and talk to him. You three stay out here and switch the plates." I pause. "Did anyone bring a screwdriver?"

Steph holds up a flathead.

31

I frown at her. "Where did you get that?"

She'll only give me a Cheshire smile. "I have my sources."

"Okay." I shrug. Her "source" is most likely Ethan. "Whatever. Good. I'll be right back."

It's always weird to be in the school at night, when it's empty. Aside from my dad and possibly Digger, there's nobody in the building.

His office door is open. I step inside and wait for him to notice me. Glancing toward the window, I can't help but roll my eyes a little bit. My roommates are all huddled around the back of the car. Grace is on her tiptoes, and she's audibly clapping in excitement. Franny is, of course, tugging her hair out. Steph is crouched down, doing all the work. The thought *How many boarding students does it take to vandalize the headmaster's car?* crosses my mind.

"Emily," my dad says, surprised. "What are you doing here?"

I step in front of the window. "Nothing, Daddy. Just, you know, wanted to say hi."

So there's that: none of my roommates have ever called my dad "Daddy." I suppose it's possible I'd be a little irritated if they did.

"You should be at your dorm." He pauses, smiles at me. Then he says, "Have a seat."

Are they finished? How long can it possibly take them? I imagine the three of them out there, falling all over each other in giggles. God, I hope they don't set off the alarm.

"That's okay," I say, glued to my spot in front of the window. "I just had a question."

"Okay. What's up?" He leans back in his chair, crosses his arms behind his head.

"Did you . . . um, did you let in a new student today?"

For a split second, I see a flash of something cloudy in his expression. But as quickly as it appears, it's gone. "Yes, I did," he says. "A very smart boy." He nods to himself. "He'll be a great asset here."

"Uh . . . Grace and Steph told me he has a tattoo."

My dad shrugs. I can tell he's only pretending to be unaware. "Does he?"

"Well, Steph said it's kind of hard to miss."

"His name is Del," my dad says. "And he's absolutely brilliant. Now, that's between you and me." And he winks.

"So I should make friends with him?"

There's that cloudiness again. Just for an instant. "Sure," my dad says. "Why not?" He narrows his eyes. "Why won't you sit down, Emily?"

They have to be done by now. I can *sense* that they're finished. At least, I can't hear Grace clapping anymore. "Oh, I have a bunch of precalc to study. It was nice talking to you, Daddy. Don't work too hard in here, okay?"

"What, are you leaving already?"

I'm at the door. "Yes."

He frowns. "That wasn't much of a visit. Come give me a hug."

So I do. My father holds me close for a second. I turn my head to look out the window, and I don't see my roommates anywhere. They're finished.

"Emily," he says, "about the new boy."

"What, Daddy?" I keep my tone light and innocent.

"It's just . . . nothing. I think you should focus on academics, that's all."

Like I said, I'm lousy in school.

"Well, you know how I love to study."

"Uh-huh. Okay, get outta here. I'll see you tomorrow."

"See you tomorrow." I kiss him on the cheek.

When I leave the building, I take a second to look at his car. I giggle out loud. The Dadmobile vanity plate looks ridiculous. I wonder how long he'll drive around before he notices it. I don't worry for a minute that he'll be mad; he just isn't like that. He'll be

33

flattered. He loves the nickname Dad; I think it makes him feel appreciated.

Every night after dinner there's a two-hour study hall in our rooms. We have to leave our doors open while the faculty strolls from dorm to dorm, offering help to whoever needs it, making sure that nobody's slacking off.

Emotional stuff, like my nightmare earlier in the day, Franny, and the whole exchange with Renee, always leaves me physically exhausted, which makes my reluctance to sleep that much worse. I can hardly keep my eyes open as I try to get through my last two pages of precalc homework. Franny sits at her desk, struggling to stay awake as well while she reads what seems like the same page of *Catcher in the Rye* for the whole two hours.

Finally, she tosses the book on the floor. "I give up," she says. "Steph loves this book. She'll tell me all about it." She yawns. "I'm going to go put on my jamiflams."

I pause in my homework. "Your what?"

Franny gives me a timid smile. "My jamiflams."

"What the hell are *jamiflams*?"

"The word I made up for pajamas."

I'm almost speechless. I just want to hug her, to cuddle, to let her know how much she's loved. "That," I say, tossing a pencil playfully in her direction, "is the cutest thing I've ever heard in my life."

Her eyes brighten. "You like it?"

It breaks my heart how little it takes to make Franny happy. "I love it."

There's always a weird feeling of restlessness on Sunday nights, at least for me. Even though this has been my life for as long as I can

remember, I always feel a kind of disappointment at the beginning of another week, which is sure to be almost exactly the same as the week before. I'm so tired tonight that all I want to do is fall into a deep, dreamless sleep, the kind that makes you twitch as you're drifting off. So I figure, what the hell—after Franny has changed into her jamiflams and quickly fallen asleep, I go ahead and take three of Dr. Miller's pills right before I climb into the top bunk.

"Emily. Baby, wake up."

It's like someone has yanked me out of my own body. Before I can shout or move, I feel a hand over my mouth. "Shhh. It's just me."

I blink in the darkness. My bones feel like Jell-O. I'm not wearing my contact lenses.

"I can't see," I say, my voice muffled by the hand still over my mouth.

"It's me." It's Stephanie. She's crying. "Here." She hands me her backup glasses; we wear almost the same prescription, and have been sharing since the seventh grade. As silly as it sounds now, it was one of the things that initially made us such close friends. There was a time when we seemed to have everything in common. Things feel different now; I'm almost surprised that she decided to wake *me* up and not Grace, since they've been spending most of their time together since school started.

Once the glasses are on my face, I realize that Steph is sitting cross-legged beside me in bed. She's fully dressed in a blue and white Stonybrook Academy sweat suit, her face red and streaked, her pretty hair tied into a quick messy ponytail. "Will you come to Winchester with me?"

I shake my head, still foggy with sleep. "Right now? It's the middle of the night."

"It's barely midnight."

I glance at my alarm clock, struggling to focus. It's 12:47 a.m.

"What for?"

"I have to go see Ethan, and I don't want to go alone."

"Steph, I am, like, so heavily medicated right now. Can't it wait until morning? What's so important? Ethan's probably sleeping."

She shakes her head. I can tell she's going to start crying again, that her momentary composure was only summoned in order to wake me up and bring me along. "I got an *e-mail*. From my dad."

"Yeah?"

"He and my mom are getting a divorce. He's in Saint-Tropez right now, and she's moving out of our house like *right this second*, and they decided to send us a freaking *e-mail* to tell us."

"Oh, Steph." I wrap my arms around her. "You're kidding. I'm so sorry."

Her voice is shaky. "You don't have any idea, Emily. Your parents aren't getting divorced. My mom and dad have been married for*ever*." She shakes her head, rubbing her runny nose against my pj's. My jamiflams. And I don't care. The whole thing still feels like a dream. "It's like I don't know anything that's real all of a sudden." She pulls away to look at me. "Come with me? Please?"

I hesitate. "Why do you need me to come?"

She looks at me like I'm stupid. "Because you're my best friend."

I straighten her glasses on my face; the whole world feels suspended halfway between sleep and waking, slightly out of focus.

"Okay," I say. "Just let me pee first."


Digger is late–night campus patrol. He's Digger-the-dining-hall-carving-station-attendant's twin brother. Depending on who you ask, they both graduated from Stonybrook like forty-five years ago, when it was still an all-boys' academy, and basically never

left. I'm not sure what their whole story is, but they don't seem like they were ever Joe Harvard types. My dad says they're harmless, and he seems to enjoy having them around for posterity. Beyond that, he's mum on their backgrounds.

The Diggers share an apartment on campus, in the middle-school boys' dorm. I'm not sure what their first names are, but it doesn't matter; you can always tell which one someone's referring to based on context. Like, "Digger sneezed on my beef au jus last night," or "Digger caught us smoking a joint behind the field house, so we gave him fifty bucks and a fifth of Wild Turkey not to turn us in." See? Obvious.

Without waking Grace, Steph opens her window and lets the rope ladder fall almost to the ground. She gives it a tug to make sure the hooks are firmly in place. Then we both climb out the window. Just like that. The whole process takes fewer than ten seconds.

As Stephanie and I hurry across campus, we spot Digger strolling near the tennis courts with a flashlight, a hand-rolled cigarette tucked behind his ear while another burns between his lips. He spots us right away, pointing the flashlight in our direction.

"Prince! Meckler! Kinda late for a stroll, dontcha think?" His voice is rough and unfriendly.

Stephanie is a blubbering mess. She and I are holding hands as we walk; I tug her along as I hurry over to Digger.

"Sir, we have to go over to Winchester to see Stephanie's brother. It's an emergency."

Digger is not easily impressed, intimidated, or coerced. He's the kind of guy who can smoke an unfiltered cigarette all the way down to its nub without once having to take it out of his mouth.

"Uh-huh." He shines the flashlight in my eyes. "Let's see those pupils."

I squint into the light. "They're not dilated."

"No, they aren't." He sighs, almost disappointed, taking a long

drag from his cigarette and exhaling out his nose. "You know what time it is?"

Stephanie is just standing beside me, clutching my hand so tightly that it's almost numb.

"I know it's late. I'm sorry—we'll be fast, I promise."

He considers. "If your father was to hear about this, and you had to explain this so-called *emergency,* what would he have to say about it?"

"Pleeease!" Stephanie says. Her tone is uneven and frantic. "I need to see my brother, sir!"

Digger peers at her, shines the flashlight briefly at her pupils. "All right. Make it quick. Don't let me run into you girls out here at four in the morning."


Winchester is a one-story dorm, about two hundred feet kitty-corner from our dorm, Ellis House. Because Stonybrook Academy is situated on a hill, even though we're miles from the beach, the air is moist enough to carry the smells of sand and salt. It's overwhelming, sensory-wise, holding on to Stephanie's hand as she trembles, the two of us rapidly approaching Winchester, damp gritty soil working its way into the edges of my sandals as we hurry along in the cool, still night.

Ethan must have known we were coming. His desk is just beneath his window, which is open, and I can tell right away that he's been crying. I help boost Stephanie into her brother's room. Ethan wipes his eyes and gives me a sweet, grateful smile. "Thanks, Em. You're the best, you know that?"

"I'm sorry about your parents."

He nods, gritting his teeth. "I'm sorry my dad's an *asshole.*"

"Ethan, don't say that." Stephanie's arms are around her brother's neck; for the first time, I notice he's wearing only a white

T-shirt and boxer shorts. Just as the jolt from the sight of him is dissolving, I realize that neither of them seems to have any plans to help *me* into the room.

"So I guess I'll just . . . I can wait out here? Or do you want me to go ahead back, Steph?"

She shakes her head. "Stay. Ethan, can you let her into the common room to wait?"

I meet him at the far end of the building, where there's a set of double doors locked from the inside. Since Ethan is a prefect, he has a key, so he can let me in. As we're standing alone in the dark, silent hallway, all of a sudden he puts his arms around my waist and folds me into a tight hug.

The dampness from his eyes and cheeks smears onto my face and neck. He holds me for what feels like a very long time. I hug him back, so aware of his whole body against mine that I can hardly breathe. This is *Ethan*; I've known him since we were twelve. He's never acted so affectionate before. To be honest, even though his good looks aren't exactly a matter of opinion—he's definitely hot—the whole scenario feels kind of . . . icky. I mean, Ethan is the brother I never had.

He pulls away like nothing happened. Maybe it didn't; maybe he's just so upset about his parents that he needed someone to hold on to. But then he takes my *hand*—I'm so startled that I almost yank it away without even thinking about it—and leads me to the common room, where the lights are off but the television is on low.

We stand together in the doorway. "I mean it, Emily," he repeats. "You really are the best."

Two sleeping pills would have been plenty—it occurs to me there's a possibility that I'm hallucinating, or totally misinterpreting him, or both. *Please God*, I think, *don't let him try to kiss me. Or do. It's entirely up to you.*

"Um. Thanks."

"Listen," he says shyly, "I know this is a weird time to be asking you something like this . . ."

*Oh, my God. Is he going to ask me out?* I can feel myself breaking into a sweat. He's like a brother in lots of ways—but he's *not* my brother. Any girl would be crazy not to go out with him.

"We're starting a band," he says. "Me and Max and Chris." He looks at the ground between us while he talks. "And we need a singer."

I'm not a good student. I'm not a good athlete. But if there's one thing I *can* do, it's sing. And if there's one thing I love to do, it's singing. Ethan knows this; he's in the chorus with me. Of course, he's good at practically *everything* musical. He's always playing drums in the music room during free periods and after school. Because of this, his forearms are toned like nobody's business. Whenever he wears his shirtsleeves rolled up in class, I can't help but stare at his muscles—none of the girls can.

I've sung in chorus plenty of times—I've even had solos, and I've been singing with my mom while she plays the piano for as long as I can remember. But being the singer in a band?

"I don't know," I say. I shake my head, staring hard at the carpet, suddenly uncomfortable. "That's a lot of—you know, *exposure*."

He reaches toward me. My hair is loose and spilling over my shoulders. Ethan takes a tendril between his fingers and tugs at it, ever so lightly. My entire body breaks out in an instant, cold sweat. "Come on," he says. When I look up at him, he's smiling at me, despite his puffy eyes and the obvious weight of the evening. "There has to be a wild redhead in there somewhere. You'd be fantastic." He pauses. "I don't know if I want to do it without you. Every time we've rehearsed so far, I've imagined your voice singing the lyrics."

I am dying from the attention. All I can think to say is, "Steph's probably waiting for you."

He nods. "You're right. I should go. Just . . . promise me you'll think about it, okay?"

"Okay. Sure."

And then he turns and walks away, shutting the door quietly behind me, and I hear his light footsteps as he hurries down the hall, back to his room and to Stephanie.

The TV is on the far end of the room, against the wall, opposite the sofa, and I walk toward it. In the dark, someone is watching an old episode of *Columbo*. I used to watch *Columbo* all the time with my dad; it was like our thing when I was a little girl. Every once in a while, we still manage to catch an episode together. For an instant I imagine my father at home, staying up late, watching the same channel all by himself, and I feel a pang of sweet, grateful love. I know I've got a good life. My parents will never get divorced; my dad will never run off to Saint-Tropez with his mistress. I'd never admit it to Steph, but I'm not at all surprised that her parents are splitting up. All they ever did when I was around was fight.

"You never meet his wife," I murmur.

All I can see is the back of a head and shoulders against the glow of the screen. It's too dark to tell who it is.

"What do you mean?"

I don't recognize the voice.

"Haven't you seen this before?" I ask. "He talks about his wife all the time. It's, like, part of the whole *Columbo* appeal. But you never see her. It's almost as if she isn't real."

He turns around to look at me. In between the smell of sand and salt and the heavy cape of night that is tugging me toward exhaustion, there's something else: Cigarette smoke, and an acrid smell that I can't quite identify. Eyes so blue I can see their color in the almost-dark. He stretches his arms above his head, and there it is: on the inside of his left wrist, a tattoo of a bright red apple with a bite taken out of it, a single green leaf hanging from the brown stem.

41

"I'm Del Sugar," he says. "Who are you?"

My breath catches in my throat. "You weren't at dinner."

He squints at me, confused. Behind him, Columbo is closing in on the killer. *"See, there's just one thing that doesn't make sense to me here. Just one thing I need you to explain to me, ma'am . . ."*

"I wasn't hungry."

The explanation seems so simple, so obvious. "Oh."

*"You stupid old man. You're right—I did poison his marmalade. Just like I poisoned the marmalade you're eating right now!"*

"Sorry to interrupt your time with—what's his name? Your boyfriend?"

"Ethan. And he's not my boyfriend." I shake my head. "You shouldn't be out here. Why are you still awake?"

His lips curl into a slow grin. "One in the morning and a girl in my dorm's telling *me* I shouldn't be out here? And just who are you?"

"Emily Meckler." I swallow. The room seems very bright, even though I know it's not. I'm embarrassed to be wearing Stephanie's old glasses. Everything still feels a little off-kilter, but more focused now, my gaze steady as Del and I stare at each other.

"Meckler," he says, sitting up a little bit straighter, interested. "Like Dr. Meckler?"

"My dad," I say.

"Mmm."

"Why are you starting school here now? Nobody ever starts late."

*"Ma'am, this isn't the marmalade that you made. You see, my wife likes to make marmalade, too. I switched her marmalade with yours just before you served it to me. So you see, ma'am, I won't be dying. Not today, anyway."*

"My parents," Del says. "They were my foster parents for three years. They finalized my adoption two days ago." His smile widens. "And then they sent me away."

42

# chapter four

There are more than a few rumors going around about Del Sugar. There's the rumor that he's some kind of genius, and that Stonybrook is the only school in the country with any hope of giving him a good education. There's the rumor that he was a juvenile delinquent when his parents adopted him, and that after only a few days of his being their *real* son, they were too scared of him to keep him at home. Someone—Beth Slapinski, who's in my civics class—heard that when he was at his old school, he dented someone's skull with a baseball bat just for talking to his girlfriend. Supposedly Del didn't kill the guy—he just hurt him badly enough to get kicked out.

I'm not sure how much I believe any of the rumors. If any of them were true, aside from the one about Del being a genius, my dad would have given me some inkling of it. Besides, my dad wouldn't let someone in if they'd done some of the things that Del is supposed to be responsible for.

But it's true that he's gorgeous, with his mussed blond hair and tall, thin build . . . and that *tattoo*. Where does a seventeen-year-old get a *tattoo*?

All the girls want him. My roommates, my friends—even me.

How can we not? He always seems bored and disinterested. He doesn't talk very much. But there's no question that he's smart as can be: he's in math and chemistry with Stephanie, and she says he barely stays awake in class, but all of his test scores are 100 percent. With, like, zero effort.

"I got to be his partner today," she tells me as we're walking back from school together.

"Really? Did he pick you?"

"Well . . . no. We were assigned."

"Oh. Did he talk to you?"

"Kind of. We talked about chemistry, mostly. Emily, he's *brilliant*. He barely had to do the experiment, and he figured out most of the calculations in his head. And he told me that the four of us" (she means our quad) "should sit with him at dinner tonight." Stephanie is almost shaking with excitement. She hops up and down on the balls of her toes in a gesture that's reminiscent of Grace. "Emily, I think I'm gonna go for him. I think I like him." When I don't say anything, she adds, "I'm pretty sure he likes me, too."

"Really?" I feel a twinge of something I don't quite recognize at first—then I realize it's annoyance. "Are you sure he wasn't just being nice?"

She shakes her head. "There was more to it than that. He seemed interested in everything I had to say." She pretends to shiver. "He's so smart, I can't stand it. It's amazing."


*"And then they sent me away?"* Renee raises a single eyebrow. "He's, like, a *mystery*. Plus he's sexy." But then she shrugs. "Lots of guys are sexy, though. Big deal."

I don't know what I'm doing in here, I really don't. It's just

before dinnertime. Franny is asleep, taking her usual after-school nap. Grace is at cross-country practice. Renee and I are part of only a handful of students who don't play a fall sport. It was actually my dad's idea; he prefers that I stay focused on studying, even though it never seems to do me any good. As a joke, my roommates call me a bookworm. But I'm naturally skinny, and lord knows Renee always looks ready to strut down a runway . . . so what would be the point in exercising? Better to just enjoy being young, I figure. Besides, it's not like there's any sport that I'm particularly good at. All I have is singing, and I can do that all by myself, anytime I need to get away. I just close my eyes, open my mouth . . . and forget about the rest of the world.

I'm still thinking about Ethan's offer to sing in his band. I have to admit, there's a part of me that's genuinely intrigued by the idea. It's unlike anything I've ever done before, and would be an exciting change from the day-to-day routine that I've gotten so used to over the years. Besides, the thought of spending more time with Ethan isn't exactly unappealing.

But when I told Stephanie about it, she only rolled her eyes. "Ethan and that stupid band," she said. "Emily, you can't. He's got too much going on as it is, between school and baseball and being a prefect—not to mention all of the crap that's going on with our parents. You can't drag him into a *band*."

"But *he* asked *me*," I said. "I'm not dragging him into anything. If I don't do it, he'll just find someone else, won't he?"

"I don't know," she said, "but you shouldn't encourage him." And she smirked at me. "Besides, you're too shy to do something like that. You'd die onstage."

After that, she didn't want to talk about it anymore. Maybe she's right; I *am* shy. Maybe I'd just end up making a fool of myself. Still, I can't stop thinking about Ethan's words a few nights earlier:

*I don't know if I want to do it without you.* Why *not* without me? What does he see in me that I can't see in myself?

Right now, though, I'm in Renee's room, talking about Del and not much else. Over the past week, Renee and I have had brief conversations here and there. I can't help it; since our first real talk, I've been fascinated by her. And it turns out she's easy to talk to. At least, most of the time. Right now, Hillary is lying on her own bed—she doesn't play a sport, either—propped up on one arm, glaring at both of us. The duct tape still runs down the center of the room. Renee's half is still a mess. I don't remember being in her room much when Madeline was here, but she must have kept things nicer; Madeline was a neat freak.

Throughout our conversation, I've been tempted to suggest that we go to my room and leave poor Hillary, who's obviously annoyed by us, alone. But it *is* kind of thrilling to know how much we're irritating her, to see that Renee obviously doesn't care. Besides, even though she's pretending to be agitated, it's obvious that Hillary is just as curious about Del as everyone else.

Renee shrugs. "Well, he's clearly got some secrets, but who doesn't? I'm not impressed."

Hillary makes a disgusted noise.

"I'm *not*," she says. "There are plenty of geniuses here, and there are plenty of kids whose lives are more screwed up than Del Sugar's, I'm certain of it. Besides, his parents sent him away after they adopted him—but he lived with them for three years before then. So they must *love* him and everything. I mean, they adopted him, and then they sent him to boarding school. So what? Lots of kids go to boarding school." She shakes her head to emphasize the point. "Practically everyone I *know* goes to boarding school." And she starts taking a mental count on her fingers.

I pause, thinking about it. "I guess you're right. I mean . . . everyone *I* know goes to boarding school."

Hillary snorts again. "You *live* at a boarding school, Emily. You grew up here. Of *course* everyone you know goes to boarding school. God, naive much?"

Renee gives Hillary a stony look, which is enough to give me the confidence to ignore her remarks. "So you don't think I should bother sitting with him?" I ask, a tad disappointed. I want Renee to like me so badly. I'm not sure why. But if she thinks Del is no big deal, then I suppose he's not.

"No," she says. She grins. "Sit with me."

So I do. That night, I see Stephanie trying to make eager conversation with Del throughout the whole meal. The school intern, Mr. Henry, is supervising their table halfheartedly (he's only twenty-two and just out of Harvard) while Grace and Franny and Stephanie giggle and fuss over Del. Oddly enough, despite the earlier enthusiasm that Steph said he showed when inviting her to dinner, he seems almost bored.

But after dinner, Steph catches me walking back to the dorm and squeals, "He's going to come over!"

"What?" I look around for him. "Now?"

"No. He just said *sometime*. He was asking when we were all around, and he said he wanted to stop by and visit us sometime *soon*. Emily, I really think he likes me. Oh my God. I could die."

I'm happy for her; really, I am. But something just doesn't feel . . . right. Steph is beautiful and popular. And don't get me wrong—she's my best friend. But she has an attitude to her that not everyone likes; a lot of people, people who don't know her like I do, are more afraid of her than anything else. She likes to get what she wants, when she wants it, and she doesn't like it *at all* when things don't go her way. And I can't help but feel like, just from our very brief conversation, I kind of *know* Del. He didn't

strike me as the type of guy who would go after someone so . . . well, someone like Stephanie. He seems like the kind of guy who would see right through her pushiness, and maybe even find it unattractive. Call it a hunch; I don't know how I know. I just can't picture the two of them together.

The following morning, Grace is at a cross-country meet; Franny and Stephanie sleep through breakfast, so I go up alone. I'm walking back to the dorm when I feel a cool hand on my shoulder. It's Del. He reaches out and touches me—just like *that*, like it's no big deal at all.

"It's the *Columbo* expert," he says. He's supposed to wear long sleeves all the time to hide his tattoo, but as far as I can tell, he's completely disregarded the rule. I can see his veins beneath the flesh of the apple. I can see the pain, so bright red and deep that I can almost feel it myself.

I try to pretend that I'm not interested in talking to him, for Stephanie's sake. But he has these blue eyes that look like a thousand ice crystals, a crooked smile, and slightly imperfect teeth—he's gorgeous in a fully human, vulnerable way, and there's something just slightly needy about him.

Besides, everyone is still so curious about his history. Nobody knows who his real parents are, or where he came from; nobody has the nerve to just *ask* him. Not even me.

"Del," I say. Then, trying to be . . . I don't know, aloof, maybe even a little rude, I ask, "What's that short for? Delbert?"

He winces, almost imperceptibly, for just a split second, before the coolness returns to his expression. "No. It's just Del."

"Your mom gave you that name?"

"I told you, I'm adopted." It's not exactly an answer.

It's still unbelievably warm, so I'm walking back from breakfast

in Stonybrook Academy athletic shorts (borrowed from Grace) and a T-shirt I bought in town that reads: STONYBROOK! 500 RICH PEOPLE CAN'T BE WRONG! My dad rolls his eyes every time I wear it, and has begged me to get rid of it more than once. He's real touchy about the perception of elitism at Stonybrook—even though it's so blatantly elitist.

Del's gaze lingers at my chest, longer than it takes to read the writing. Then he looks me in the eye. "Do you have any brothers or sisters, Emily?"

*Say my name again.* In that moment, I realize it's all I want in the world.

I shake my head. "No. Do you?"

He nods. "I have a sister. She's older, but we're less than a year apart. Her name is Melody."

"Oh? And where's Melody?"

We're almost to his dorm. "I don't know," he says. "I got adopted. I'm not certain, but I think she's still in a foster home somewhere. She'll be there until she's eighteen, and then . . . who knows if I'll ever find her again?" His tone is bitter. He licks his lips, which appear soft and full and *please say my name again. Just once.*

"Do you want to go for a walk or something?" he asks.

"What? You mean right now?"

"Why not right now?"

"Um . . . lots of reasons. Where would we go? We can't leave campus."

"I don't know. We can just talk. Take a little walk around. There are places."

I consider. It isn't like I have a boyfriend or anything. And it isn't like he and Stephanie are *dating.* Maybe he wants to talk about her. Or maybe he just wants to talk. *It's only a walk,* I think. That's harmless enough. "Okay," I say. "But not right now."

"What's the matter? You have somewhere else to be?"

We stop at his dorm. We're standing in front of one of the windows to the common room. Looking inside, I can see that Ethan has his drums set up. Max Franklin, who plays guitar, is with him. When Ethan notices me looking at them, he raises his hand in a "come here" gesture.

"What does he want?" Del asks.

I'm suddenly embarrassed. Just the thought of singing for them, of being the center of attention, is enough to make me feel mortified. "Nothing," I say. "He's goofing around."

Ethan tosses a drumstick at the window. I flinch as it hits the glass.

I stare at the sidewalk. Last year, they replaced a few squares of concrete in front of Winchester. While the cement was still wet, almost everybody who walked by took the opportunity to write their initials in it. There's an "E.P." for Ethan Prince, "S.M." for Sam Marshall, "W.H." for Winston Howard, and—in a corner by itself—"M.F. LOVES H.S." for "Max Franklin loves Hillary Swisher." There's an "A.S." (Amanda Stream), "S.P." (Stephanie Prince), and "M.M.P." (Madeline Moon-Park). There are a bunch of other initials, too, from kids in different grades.

Del follows my gaze. "Where are yours?" he asks.

"They're not there."

"Oh yeah? Why not?"

Ethan throws his other drumstick in our direction. "Emily!" he calls. "Get in here and sing!"

"I didn't want to get in trouble," I say to Del.

"You thought you'd get into trouble for writing your initials?"

"Emily!" Ethan shouts again. "Get in here and sing!"

"Yes." I can feel blood rushing to my face.

"It doesn't look like anyone else was afraid."

"Well, I was."

"..."

"..."

Then he says, "It seems like they really want you to go in there and sing."

"I'm not going." I look up at Ethan, who is staring expectantly at me through the window. I shake my head.

"Why not?" he shouts. He sticks out his bottom lip in a pout.

"Someone ought to shut them up," Del says. "They woke me up at nine thirty with that noise."

I look at him. "It's not 'noise.' They're good."

"Then why don't you want to sing for them?"

"Because . . . I'm shy."

When Del smiles at me, the corners of his eyes crinkle like tissue paper. His skin is so smooth that it almost seems translucent. "You're pretty, too," he says.

The air feels hotter all of a sudden. Del reaches out with his tattooed arm and tucks a strand of loose hair behind my ear. "What are you doing right now? Why can't we go somewhere and talk?"

"I told you, I can't. I'm supposed to study with my roommate." And it's true; Franny is going to help me with precalc.

"All right. What time, then?"

Inside, Ethan and Max begin to play "In My Life" by The Beatles. Ethan is singing. He's got a fantastic voice; I don't know why they even want me.

I stare at the sidewalk again, focusing on the "M.M.P." for Madeline Moon-Park. Beside her initials, she'd drawn a crescent moon and three tiny stars. She might be gone, but a part of her is here forever, in stone. "Four o'clock," I tell him.

I can *hear* him smiling. "Okay. I'll come over and get you."

"No," I say quickly. I don't want Steph to see me with him. "I'll come here."

He nods. He begins to back away, toward the double doors to Winchester. "All right, Emily. I'll be waiting."

I need to tell someone what's happening, and I obviously can't tell any of my roommates, so I stop in Renee's room on my way back from breakfast to tell *her* what's going on.

She's sitting cross-legged on the floor in front of her mirror, working her wet hair into two long braids. "He likes you," she tells me. "Ooh la la."

"Stephanie thinks he likes her," I say. I'm sitting at Renee's desk. Her notes for English lit are scattered all over the surface. She has sloppy handwriting. Big surprise.

"He obviously does *not* like Stephanie," Renee says.

I frown. "But she's beautiful."

"So? She has the body of a game show hostess and the personality of a Komodo dragon." Renee finishes her braids and takes a long moment to stare at her reflection. Then she turns around to look at me. "This is very exciting, Emily. You should be happy. Don't worry about Stephanie."

When I don't respond, she adds, "I'm a little bit jealous, you know. Del is the only boy around here who's actually interesting."

From her place on the bed, Hillary rolls her eyes and speaks up. "Renee. Didn't you go out with Mark Foster last summer?"

"That's right, you did!" I say. Mark Foster is a child star. Over the summer, I saw dozens of photos of him and Renee, hand in hand as they exited clubs together late at night.

Renee shrugs. "Mark Foster is a boring snob. This is a *real* person with a history and a personality. Do you know how dull people in show business are? They're all completely self-absorbed."

Hillary yawns. "Self-absorbed, I can see. Dull, I'm not so sure about."

"Don't you have someplace to *be*?" They take what feels like a full minute just to glare at each other. But beneath the surface of their expressions, I can sense the slightest hint of a smile in both of them.

"Can I just start calling you Madeline?" Renee asks. Her smile grows a bit wider. She breathes a wistful sigh. "Could you just, like, act exactly the same and maybe dye your hair black?"

Even Hillary loved Madeline. "We should find out where she went, Renee," she says. "I'm sure we could track her down on Google."

"You think I haven't tried that?" Renee, standing beside me, tugs me out of my chair and toward her bed. "I've looked. There's nothing." To me, she says, "Sit down, Emily. Let me braid your hair."

"Well, there has to be some way to find a phone number for her, at least," Hillary says. "She's probably at another school, right?"

"*Obviously* she's at another school," I say. "Where else would she be? Come on, let's think about it. I want to help."

"Keep looking," Hillary tells Renee. "You'll find something. And, Emily, you weren't even great friends with her. Aside from getting some private information from your dad, what help can you possibly be?"

I frown at Hillary. But when I think about it, I realize that she's right. I didn't know Madeline all that well. Since I've been going to school here, I've hung out almost exclusively with Steph, Franny, and Grace. I wish I'd taken the time to get to know Madeline better. Now that she's gone, I'll never have the chance.

There's one thing I remember, though. "You know what's weird?" I ask. I try to keep my head steady as Renee tugs at my hair with a brush.

Hillary sits up. She goes to her own mirror on her closet door and begins to dab foundation over a faint hickey on her neck. "What?"

"I never met her parents. In all the time she was going here, never *once* did I see Madeline's parents. Did either of you? Renee, you were her roommate—did you ever meet her mom or dad?"

Renee is quiet, thinking. "Umm . . . no," she says, "I don't think I ever did."

"Well, that's kind of strange." Hillary peers into the mirror, squinting as she blends the foundation. "I mean, lots of parents aren't around much—but to *never* have seen them? Weird."

I feel goose bumps on the back of my neck as Renee winds my hair into two long braids. "That's enough about Madeline," she says. "We shouldn't talk about her like this."

"Fine. But you spoil everything fun, you know?" Hillary is at the door. "I'm going to see Max. I'll be back later."

"Take your time," Renee says.

"Put my hairbrush back where it belongs," Hillary tells her.

I glance down at the bed, where the brush is sitting beside me. "Hillary" is written in permanent marker on the handle.

"Why are you using her brush?" I ask, once Renee and I are alone.

"No reason. I just don't have one of my own." Renee stands up to look at me. "You look great." She smiles. "You look ready for your date."

I feel my face growing warm. "It's not a date. We're just going for a walk."

"Okay. Right." She winks. "Come see me when you get back. Then you can tell me if it wasn't a date."


When I get to Winchester, Del isn't in the common room; nobody is. Ethan's drums are still set up, and for a moment I stand there looking at them, part of me wishing I had the nerve to sing with him.

"Emily."

It's Max. Hillary is standing beside him, her arm around his waist. "Are you looking for Del?" he asks.

"Yes."

"He's behind the building. He told me to send you back."

"Oh. Okay. Thank you."

Max gives me a suspicious grin. "Whatcha doing, Em?"

Hillary stands on her tiptoes and whispers something into his ear. He nods, listening. Then he says, with a knowing smirk, "Ohhh . . . I see how it is."

"I'm not doing anything!" I almost shriek the words. "Hillary, what did you tell him?"

"What?" She looks at me innocently. "I didn't tell him anything."

"You'd better be a good girl, Emily," Max says, tugging Hillary toward the door. "We wouldn't want you doing anything to disappoint Daddy."

When I find Del, he's leaning up against the brick wall of his dorm, smoking a cigarette. I fan the air as I approach him, wrinkling my nose at the smell.

"I wish you wouldn't smoke," I say. "It's disgusting."

To my surprise, he says, "Oh. Okay." And he flicks the lit cigarette butt into the woods. He smiles. "Better?"

I'm impressed. Even my roommates won't listen when I ask them not to smoke.

"I like your hair," Del says, stepping closer to me. He leans forward and touches one of the braids lightly. "Neither of your parents has red hair, do they?"

"No."

He looks at my face, into my eyes. "Where did it come from?"

"I don't know." It's warm enough that Del is wearing a short-sleeved white T-shirt. I stare at his tattoo.

"It's a mystery, then?"

I've never thought of it that way. "I guess."

"I see." He nods toward the path at the edge of the woods. "Well? Are you ready?"

After a few moments of walking along the path, we meet up with a stone wall that surrounds campus. On the other side of the wall, there's a stream. Without saying anything, Del takes me by the hand and helps me as we both climb over the rocks.

Being so close to the water gives me chills. It isn't only the water in my dreams that scares me; it's running water, still water, all water. Even if there's no breeze, even if I'm standing in a hot shower in my own house, it chills part of me right down to my bones. I hate it. It terrifies me like nothing else—nothing except fire.

"Do you want to sit down?" Del asks.

I give the stream a hesitant look. It's not just being near the water that makes me uncomfortable; it's being alone with Del, who I barely know, and who I shouldn't even be out here with. "I thought we were going for a walk."

"We did." He follows my gaze. "What's the matter? You don't like water?"

"Not really."

"It's just a stream, Emily." He tugs me gently to the ground. "Relax. I won't bite."

We sit quietly for a few minutes, both of us staring at the water. Del leans back on his elbows and gazes at the clear sky. "I like it here, in Connecticut," he says. "It's nice being near the ocean."

"Where does your family live?"

"Outside Boston." He bites his lip. "If I tell you something, do you promise you won't laugh?"

I nod. "Yes. I promise."

"I had never been to a beach until a few years ago."

"Really?" Even though I don't like water, I've still been to the beach a million times with my family and my friends. Who hasn't?

"Really," he says. "Nobody ever took me when I was in foster homes."

"Wow. That's . . . too bad."

He swallows. "That's not all. I didn't even learn to swim until I was fifteen. Nobody ever thought to teach me, not until my parents—I mean, the people who adopted me—found out I'd never had lessons." He squints at the stream. "My adoptive dad took me to a swimming pool one Saturday and taught me how. You should have seen me in the water with all those kids. There were six-year-olds swimming circles around me." He continues to stare at the sky. "I looked ridiculous. It was pretty awful."

The breeze is chilly. I pull my knees against my chest, trying not to shiver. My braids are so long that I can feel them resting halfway down my back. For a second, I remember the rumor that's going around about him taking a baseball bat to someone at his last school. I can't imagine Del hurting anyone.

"So . . . you're adopted," I say.

"Yeah."

"What are your parents like? I mean, your adoptive parents?"

"My father works for the government. You know, top secret kind of stuff." Del seems proud of the fact. "And his wife—my mom—she's a dermatologist."

"Why did they send you here right away?"

He shrugs. "It's not that interesting. I lived with them for something close to three years, and I went to Howard Academy the whole time. Boarding school's nothing new."

"But how did you even get in here? We never take new students like this."

He smiles. The expression goes right to my gut and makes me feel like I've been punched in the best kind of way. For just a moment, the coolness of the stream vanishes, and I'm warm all over. *Say my name say my name say my name.* "You ought to know, Emily. Big checks can do big things."

The explanation seems simple enough. I nod. "Right. I guess they can."

"And what about you? You've always gone to school here?"

"Yes. My dad is the headmaster, so I started in seventh grade. It's like a family." I swallow. "You'll like it here."

He stares at me. "I already do."

I have never even kissed a boy. Del is a good six inches taller than me, so as he leans in, he seems much older. I have no doubt he's more experienced than I am. I feel almost dizzy as he gets closer, a sense of suffocation surrounding me. He smells like cigarette smoke and kerosene and sweat.

"Del? Can I ask you something?"

He bites the edge of his thumbnail. "Sure."

"Why did you leave your last school?"

He shakes his head ever so slightly. "It's not important."

I hesitate. I wonder if he knows about all the rumors going around. "Well, then, what was it? Did you get kicked out?"

"No." He tilts his head downward. That *smell*—it's both delicious and gross. But his mouth is so beautiful, his lips full and teeth slightly crooked, so I can tell he's never had braces. "Can I tell you something?"

I don't know what I'm doing out here with him. I feel like a little kid. "Sure."

"I like you, Emily."

I feel numb. "Del," I inform him, "you like Stephanie."

"Do I, now?" He grins.

"Yes. Yes, you do."

"Stephanie's a pretty girl." He considers. "She's a beautiful girl."

"Right," I say. "She's popular, too. And rich."

"Is that so?"

"Yes."

"Good for Stephanie." He's so close to me now that our fore-heads are touching. "But I like you."

I pull away. He reaches out and holds on to my arm. "You don't know me at all," I say. My voice is breathy. "And I don't know anything about you."

"You know about my family. You know I didn't learn to swim until I was fifteen."

"That's not anything. Tell me something else." I pause. "Where'd you get your tattoo?"

He shakes his head. "Not important."

"You're seventeen. You shouldn't have one of those yet."

"Emily, shhh." He tugs on my arm. "Come here. I want to kiss you."

For a second, I freeze. He doesn't like Stephanie. He likes me. We're alone in the woods. He's holding on to me. There is nowhere else to go.

He glances down at the tattoo. "If I tell you where I got it, will you kiss me?"

"No. We should go back."

But he ignores me. "A few years ago, my sister and I were in the same foster home. It was the last time I saw her. Her name is Melody."

"You told me her name already."

"It wasn't a good place. Sometimes people . . . they take in kids just for the money, you know?"

I giggle. "Kind of like here?"

"No," he says, serious. "Not like here. This place is differ-ent." He licks his lips. "Anyway, my sister hurt herself. She felt

like . . . I don't know, like damaged goods, I guess. So we had this neighbor who owned a tattoo parlor, and we convinced him to give her a tattoo on her wrist. We convinced him to give one to both of us."

It occurs to me that what he's describing is exactly what Stephanie wants to get with Ethan—matching tattoos. Funny, though—the way Del's telling the story makes it sound interesting and intimate, almost beautiful. Not gross.

"She was hurting herself?" I ask. "What do you mean? Like, she cut her wrists?"

Del nods. "Something like that."

I can't even believe what he's saying. "And you were *fourteen* when you got the tattoo?"

"Yes. I've been in foster homes my whole life. My parents now are really good people, though. I got lucky." He looks at the apple. "My adoptive mom wants to help me get this removed. But I'll never let them take it."

"Why not?"

He inches his face closer to mine. "My sister. I don't know when I'll see her again. I don't know where she is. The tattoos are the only thing we have that keeps us connected, you know?"

I nod, but I don't know. I just know that, as scared as I am, I don't want to move; I could stay here all afternoon with his breath on my face. It's like a slow asphyxiation that feels better than anything I've ever known

"Why an apple? Why the bite?" I ask, my voice lowered to a whisper. *I'm so sorry, Steph.*

He slides both of his hands to the back of my neck. "Because of sin," he says. Then he kisses me. His mouth feels almost hot. I hear the stream, the sound of water rushing past me, but I don't feel cold anymore. I don't feel scared anymore, either. Del nudges

me back against the ground until he's resting above me, his hands moving from my neck to my hair to my body.

I feel safe. I feel warm and protected, unafraid of the water that's so nearby. I feel as if, all these years, I've just been waiting for him to show up.

Del pulls away for a moment. "Emily," he asks, "what's your middle name?"

I smile. "Alice."

"Emily Alice Meckler." He traces my lips with his fingertip. "Tell me something else about yourself."

"I like to sing."

"Oh yeah? Are you good at it?"

"Yes." I nod. "Now you tell me something. What's your middle name?"

He kisses me again, for a long time. I almost think he's forgotten about the question. Then he pulls back and says, "I don't know my middle name."

"What do you mean?" Our lips are touching as we speak.

"I mean I don't know. I don't even know if I have one." There is a part of him that is so unbelievably sad.

I want to stay here with him all afternoon, to make him feel safe and happy. I've never felt this way with anyone until now.

"I shouldn't be out here with you," I say.

He laughs. "Too late."

"People will talk about us." I think of Max and Hillary earlier in Winchester. "They already are."

"Oh yeah? What will they say?" And he takes his fingertip and brushes it over my eyelids so that they fall closed.

"They'll say we're going to get into trouble." I can feel his face close to mine, his breath against my cheek. "Are we?"

"Yes," he tells me. "That's the plan."

# chapter five

About a week after that first afternoon next to the stream, I wake up in the middle of the night. At first I think I'm at home, in my room, and that my mother is trying to wake me up from a night terror. But I'm not; I'm in my dorm room, and before I realize what's happening Franny smacks me across the face. I take a deep breath and realize that I wasn't breathing.

This happens sometimes; I lose my breath. It's just a few seconds' pause now and then that I have to struggle to get past. Officially it's sleep apnea, which can be deadly in extreme cases, so it's horrifying when I wake up trying to gasp, air everywhere and not a drop to breathe.

Even though the smack is justified, I can't help myself from shoving her away, hard, as I suck in a deep lungful of air. For someone so tiny, she can *hit*.

"God, Franny, what are you doing?"

She blinks. "Waking you up. You seemed like you were having trouble breathing."

I rub my cheek. "Thanks. What time is it?"

She doesn't answer. Her typically dull eyes flash with excitement. "I thought someone was breaking in. Look!"

I glance at the clock. It's past one in the morning; there's no sound from Stephanie and Grace's room. Then my gaze drifts to the floor, to the moonlight spreading across it. The light bathes the hardwood floor in a glow, revealing shards of broken glass from the window. Beside it, red and shiny, is an apple.

"What the . . ."

Franny rubs her hands together in excitement. "It's for you." Then, lowering her voice, she whispers, "It's *Del*."

She doesn't have to tell me; only Del would throw an apple. But Franny doesn't know that.

"Did you see him?" I ask.

She nods. "He's right outside."

"Shit," I say, feeling myself start to panic. "It didn't wake up Steph?"

Franny shakes her head. Her face is scrunched into a tiny, excited grin. "Emily . . . do you want to tell me what's going on?"

"Nothing," I say. "We're friends, that's all. We spent a lot of time talking the other day. Maybe he can't sleep."

Franny isn't buying any of it. She might be a lot of things, but she isn't stupid. "Ohhh," she says, still keeping her voice at a whisper. "You bad friend. Bad *girl*. Stephanie is gonna be *pissed* at you."

I haven't talked to Del since last weekend. I don't know what to say to him; I'm embarrassed by what we did, by how close I let him get to me. The entire afternoon was so out of character for me, I can't imagine how we could possibly move forward from here. And there's Stephanie to think of, too. I feel terrible for having sneaked around with Del behind her back; I don't know how I'll possibly tell her what happened. My only solution is to pretend that it didn't happen at all. It's not going so well; even though I haven't talked to Del, I can't stop thinking about him. I can feel

him looking at me at mealtimes, and every time we pass each other in the hallway. I know I can't avoid him forever.

But even though she has her suspicions about what might be going on, Franny doesn't know about what happened by the stream last weekend, or that I'm eventually going to *have* to tell Stephanie that Del isn't interested in her; all she knows is that the new, hot boy has just broken our window with an apple and some excellent aim.

The only person who knows what happened over the weekend, besides Del and me, is Renee. I don't know why I confided in her. Maybe it's because Stephanie has been in an ongoing session with Dr. Miller for the past four nights, ever since she came home from the weekend at her parents' house, and I can't bear the idea of hurting her right now. Or maybe it's because, unlike the other girls, Renee doesn't seem at all overwhelmed or intimidated by Del Sugar. She's just as curious as everyone else, sure, but she's been around enough famous people to know that, deep down, he's just like any other boy.

Except I feel like he's not.

Franny looks at me. In a silent, calculated motion, she reaches toward her face and plucks a single eyebrow from above her left eye. *Gross.* "The doors downstairs are locked," she says. "There's only one way you're getting outside, unless you want to wake up a prefect."

We both glance toward Steph and Grace's closed door. "I know," I say. I bite my lip hard.

"I'll shut the light off in here," she offers, "and you can crawl in like a ninja."

It's not totally dark in Steph and Grace's room; Stephanie has a Sleeping Beauty night-light that she's owned forever, and it's glowing in the corner of the room, directly beside her bed. It was a birthday present from her parents when she was, like, eight years old. Ethan, I happen to know, has a matching one, except that it's Prince

Charming. They are both extremely attached to their respective night-lights, which I find kind of weird and sad and lovely all at once. I can just imagine Steph showing up at college with hers, trying to explain why she doesn't want to go to sleep without it.

I creep across their floor on my belly. I crawl to Stephanie's bed and start feeling around for the rope ladder. So far, she and Grace haven't stirred.

Until now. Just as my hand closes on the ladder, Grace sits up in bed. I can't see her, but I can hear her weight shifting on the mattress. When I look up, unable to contain a guilty expression, she's leaning over the top bunk, staring at me upside down. "Emily," she whispers. "You scared the hell out of me. What are you doing?"

"I'm—uh—" I tug the ladder out from under the bed, still crawling on my belly, and press a finger to my lips. "Shhh. Don't wake up Steph, okay?"

Grace's eyes go wide. "You!" she says, her voice so loud that I cringe. "You're going to meet Del Sugar, aren't you? You're going to fall in love with him. Oh my God, is he outside now?" She's wide-awake, sitting all the way up in bed.

"Shhh!" Franny hisses from our bedroom. "Emily is being a ninja. We need quiet!"

"I just want the ladder," I say, refusing to elaborate.

"What for? Sneaking out? Ohhhh, Emily, you're so bad! What are you doing? You're going out with Del, I *know* it." She pauses. "Sometimes I think I might have psychic abilities, Emily."

"Okay, well, we can talk about that later." I'm almost out of their room. I tug the door shut, stand up, and go to our other, unbroken window. As I'm tossing the rope ladder out, Franny shakes her head at me.

I pause. "What?"

"Emily Meckler, I didn't know you had it in you." She tugs at another eyebrow. "Should I wait up?"

I hesitate. I want to say no, but I know I'll want to talk to *some-one* about what's happening. Besides, I don't want Franny to be stuck cleaning up the broken glass all by herself.

"Yes," I tell her. "I won't be long."

And then I hoist myself over the edge of the window and climb down. The whole thing—the apple, the ladder, the secrecy of everything—feels like a fairy tale. I can't believe it's really happening. Not to someone like me, not with someone like Del. I can barely do long division, and he's a genius. Why is he interested? What could we possibly have in common?

Once I see him, I can't even force myself to be angry that he broke my window, and that I'm going to have a hell of a time explaining what happened. But I do my best to pretend.

"Are you aware that you broke my window?" I ask, trying to glare at him. "Do you know how much trouble I'm going to be in?"

"You can blame it on me." He smiles. "I don't care."

"Del . . . ," and just as suddenly as I've managed to muster it, my confidence is lost. I stare at the stone patio beneath us. We are illuminated by a bright moonlight, the rest of campus so quiet that I can hear the wind moving downhill through the branches on the trees. I feel my heart beating faster, blood rushing behind my ears as Del takes a step closer and puts his arms around me.

"You'll be in big trouble," I tell him. "I'm serious."

"I was talking about you with Ethan Prince," he continues, as though the broken window is nothing at all to be concerned about.

"What did you tell him?" I ask, curious. Why were Del and Ethan talking about me?

"He was telling me all about what a wonderful singer you are," Del says. "He said you have a voice like an angel, and he doesn't understand why you won't join his band." And he leans in closer to me, kisses me on the forehead. "I told him you were too

shy, like you said earlier. But he said he'd known you for years, and that once you worked up the courage, you'd be fine."

"He said that?" I don't care anymore, though. I close my eyes as Del kisses my cheek, and then my lips.

"Mmm-hmm. He said you're in the chorus and you sing in front of other people just fine."

"That's different," I murmur. "Lots of people are in the chorus." I open my eyes to watch him curl a piece of my hair around his finger.

"Do you ever sing by yourself?" he asks. His pupils are dilated in the almost-darkness.

"Yes. Sometimes I sing when I'm alone, and I feel like I want to . . . I don't know, to disappear." I'm so nervous, it takes real effort to swallow. "When I was a little girl, I used to sing myself to sleep at night in my crib. At least, that's what my parents tell me. I don't remember anything like that."

"Hmmm." Del tugs at my hair wrapped around his finger. "You get more interesting every day."

I shake my head. "I'm not interesting. I'm boring."

"You are interesting. You're beautiful, too."

"I'm *not*. I have a pretty voice, that's all. Having a pretty voice is . . . it's nothing."

Del lets his fingers slide all the way into my hair as he pulls me closer, stepping toward me until our bodies are pressed together. "If you only knew how *not boring* you are, Emily. You don't see what I see." He hesitates. Then he says, "Well, it's good that you aren't going to be in the band."

"Oh yeah? Why's that?"

"Because," he says simply, "I don't think it would be right for my girlfriend to spend so much time with a bunch of other guys. All those rehearsals together . . . I'd be jealous." He smiles. "I'm the jealous kind, you know."

*My girlfriend.* I've never had a boyfriend. I don't know how to be somebody's girlfriend. Before I have a chance to gather my thoughts, to say *anything* to him, Del asks, "Can you sing me something?"

I shake my head. "No. I told you, I'd be too embarrassed."

"Come on." He sniffles. I've noticed that he's had the sniffles since he got here tonight.

"Are you okay? Do you have a cold?"

"Don't change the subject. I want to hear your voice."

"What else did Ethan tell you about me?"

Del looks me in the eye, shrugs. He wasn't kidding; he almost seems jealous already. I can't believe he's just *presuming* that I'll be his girlfriend. But I'm not arguing. "Why does it matter?" he asks.

"Because you were talking about me behind my back."

Del kisses the tip of my nose. "He said you were a sweetheart. Sweetest girl a guy could hope to know." He sniffles again. "Sing me something. Please?" His gaze is so sincere, his eyes so big and beautiful, I can't bring myself to tell him no.

"What do you want me to sing?"

He shrugs. "Anything."

"Okay . . . ," and I start with the first thing that comes to mind, the most innocuous song I can think of: a lullaby.

*Daisy, Daisy, give me your answer, do.*
*I'm half crazy all for the love of you.*
*It won't be a stylish marriage,*
*I can't afford a carriage.*
*But you'll look sweet upon the seat*
*Of a bicycle built for two.*

I close my eyes and go somewhere else while I'm singing, someplace where I'm safe, unafraid, and unembarrassed. It's the only time I feel truly free.

But Del yanks me out of the moment. Before I'm finished singing, he kisses me hard, stepping backward until we're both against the outside wall of my dorm, the two of us intertwined and sweating in the warm night. As he's kissing me, I don't care about the window, or how late it is, or anything at all. All I want is to be with him.

He pulls away suddenly. For the first time since I've met him, he seems shy, almost embarrassed. He keeps his arms around me but stares at the ground for a minute.

"Hey," I say. "What's wrong?"

He looks up at me. "I have one good memory of my mother. At least I think it's my mother. You know what—I'm sure it was."

"How do you know?"

He blinks. His pupils grow larger. "Because I just know. And it's the memory of her singing that song to me." He shakes his head. "How could you know that?"

I shrug. "I didn't. I just sang the first thing I could think of."

He laces his fingers through mine. "We have a connection, Emily."

"Del?"

"Hmm?"

"When did you go into your first foster home?"

He pulls away. He rubs his tattoo. "I was three. My sister was four. They put us in the same place for about a year, and after that it was hit or miss. My whole life was like that until Doug and Sharon Marshall came along."

"Those are your adoptive parents?"

He nods. "Yes. But you know . . . they're too good for me. I don't know why they even wanted me."

I don't think I've ever heard anything so sad. Even being sent away to boarding school in seventh grade seems far better than going from temporary home to temporary home. Better than not knowing where your own sister is.

69

"What happened to your real parents? Why were you taken away?"

Del shakes his head. "I'm not telling you that." He's suddenly, obviously uncomfortable. "I should go. I'm sorry I broke your window. I'll take all the blame, Emily." He pauses. "How did you know that song, anyway? Did your mother sing it to you?"

I think about it for a second. "I don't know. I guess she must have." I know the song because it's a popular lullaby, but I can't remember my mom ever singing it to me. I don't remember much of anything from when I was young.

"Well, look at what we got here. If it isn't the headmaster's little girl with the new bad boy on campus. What would Daddy think of all this, you suppose?"

Digger shines his flashlight right in our faces. Then he shines it past me, against the dorm wall, illuminating the rope ladder. He doesn't say anything about it, just looks at us with what almost seems like admiration. I can tell he's pleased with his discovery. "You know what time it is, kiddos?"

Del and I quickly pull apart, shaking our heads. Del shades his eyes as Digger shines the light in his face.

"I'll tell you what time. Time for all the good girls and boys to be in bed, that's for damn sure."

It's, like, his favorite line in the world. He's probably been saying it for years to students who are out after bedtime.

Del puts his hands up. "We're going, man. It's not her fault. I came over here and woke her up."

"Uh-huh. You two know you got an audience?" He points his flashlight at Stephanie and Grace's bedroom window, which is open all the way. Grace, Stephanie, Franny, and Renee are all crowded in the frame, staring down at us. When Digger's light hits them, they freeze for a moment. Then, one by one, as though we don't know they've been watching us, they lower slowly out of sight.

Once they're all gone, a lone arm—I think it's Stephanie's—reaches up to close the window. A few seconds later, the light goes out.

Digger's flashlight doesn't shine on my broken window, and he doesn't say anything about it. But I know he must have noticed.

I work my way up the ladder with unsteady hands, terrified that it will snap and send me falling onto the stone patio below. When I finally climb inside the window, I look to my right and see my roommates, along with Renee, sitting in Grace and Stephanie's room, waiting for me.

Steph is the first to speak. She's in a foul mood already because of her parents—not that I blame her. But she really unloads on me, tears welling in her eyes, and I feel so guilty. I am a terrible best friend. What kind of girl steals the boy her best friend likes? A bad girl, that's who. A bad friend.

"First of all, Emily, I don't know how you're going to explain that broken window." She glares at me. On my way in, I'd noticed that someone—undoubtedly Steph, who is the neatest of the four of us—had already swept up the glass. And she's right, there really is no good explanation.

"Emily," Renee says, "we heard you singing to him. What were you *doing*?"

I stare at her. I don't even know how she got in here; Franny must have woken her up, since she knows Renee and I have been spending more time together lately.

"Yes, our little songstress. Illuminate us, will you? Why were you singing?" Steph snaps. She won't even look at me now.

"He wanted me to sing something," I say, hoping it will be enough of an explanation, hoping I don't have to elaborate: *And somehow I ended up choosing the only lullaby that he remembers his mother singing to him before she lost custody of her children.*

It's weird; I know that. But it's also sad and touching and just so . . . fascinating. There are so many unanswered questions surrounding Del, and I have so many unanswered ones of my own. Somehow, even though we barely know each other, I feel like the two of us could find answers together.

My friends are not convinced. "What did you do with him?" Stephanie demands, wiping her eyes.

"Steph, nothing." I shake my head, maybe a little too insistently. "All we did was kiss. It was a mistake."

"He's got *issues*," Franny says. "Emily, he's from a foster home. Those kids have experiences we don't even know about. My first stepfather was a family court judge, and I used to hear all about how screwed up foster kids were. He's been around, Em. He's going to . . . *expect things*." She stares at her hands. "But I guess they all do, huh?"

"But he's so *hot*," Grace chimes in. I can always count on her to be the voice of reason. "So if he wants Emily, I say go for it."

"He broke our window! With a freaking apple! What are we going to tell people?" Stephanie puts a hand to her forehead in frustration. It looks like she's about to start crying again. "This is the worst week of my life."

"Steph, I'm sorry. . . . Look, I'll take the blame for the window—"

"I don't think you should do that," Renee interrupts.

"Oh, really?" Steph snaps. "Who should we say did it, then? The bogeyman? I think we should just be honest." She crosses her arms and shoots a glare at Renee. "What are you doing in here, anyway?"

Renee stays calm and cool. She ignores Stephanie. "Say you woke up and found it that way. Say it was vandalism."

The four of us pause, considering. It's actually a good idea. Every once in a while, kids from the local public school will come

onto campus and mess something up. It wouldn't be completely unbelievable.

"We'll have to lie to *Dad*," Stephanie points out.

Renee smirks. "Like she hasn't lied to her parents plenty of times before."

Renee is wrong. I've almost *never* lied to my parents. But this situation is different. I'd do anything to avoid getting Del in trouble. "Okay," I say, "that's what I'll do." I look around at my roommates, at Renee. "It's late. I'll go see my dad in the morning. Right now, we should all go to bed."


Franny falls asleep right away; the girl requires something like ten hours a night just to be functional. It hasn't been more than ten minutes before I can hear her breathing deeply above me. I've always wondered what she dreams about.

There's a light, almost imperceptible knock on my door. When I open it, Renee is leaning in my doorway, wearing her loosely knotted bathrobe and nothing else.

"We should talk," she says.

"Right now? We should *sleep*."

"Like you're anywhere near sleep." She tugs me by my elbow into the hallway. We slide down against the wall and sit cross-legged in the dark.

She puts her head on my shoulder. For a moment, I'm surprised by the easy act of affection. Then I'm surprised by how natural it feels. "You really like him?" she asks.

Being close to her is comforting, almost totally relaxing. "I really do, Renee. I'm sorry about Stephanie, but I can't help how he feels."

"What do you know about him?"

I shake my head, thinking about the question. *Not much . . . but*

*it's enough.* "I know that he's had a tough life. And I know that he likes me."

"Lots of boys like you."

"Oh, they do not."

"Yes, they *do*. You just don't realize it." She sighs. "But Del isn't 'lots of boys,' is he?"

I shake my head again. "Nope."

"I just want you to be careful, Emily. He was a foster kid. I'm sure he's seen and done a lot that you can't even imagine."

"I know that. I can't help it."

She doesn't say anything. She just reaches over to hold my hand, and we sit that way in the dark, alone, for several moments.

The closeness between us almost feels wrong—like it's something I should be sharing with Stephanie, and not Renee. I hate to admit it, but it's been a while since I've felt completely comfortable around Stephanie. As much as my easy comfort with Renee calms me, I hate that things are changing, and there's nothing I can do about any of it. I feel like I have no choice but to hold on to what makes me feel good, and try to hold on to the things that *used* to make me feel good. Life, all of a sudden, has gotten so confusing, so unpredictable. It's like I don't even recognize myself.

Renee breaks the silence. "You aren't just any other girl," she says. "You know that, don't you?"

"What do you mean?"

There is a long pause. "I can't explain it. I just know. You have that incredible voice. And you're a sweet girl. You don't give yourself enough credit."

"Well . . . thanks, I guess."

She squeezes my hand. "I mean it. Be careful." And then she stands up, leaving me to sit alone as she disappears into her room. I stare at the door until the light beneath it goes out and the whole world around me seems to become still.

# chapter six

Dr. Miller's office is about as transparently "I'm down with teens" as a high school shrink's office can get. There's the mandatory leather sofa and big wooden desk, plus a wall with so many diplomas that it's almost funny—I've never known anyone who went to Harvard, Yale, Princeton, *and* Brown except for her—but then there are all her knickknacks and books: she has the entire Harry Potter series on prominent display (in hardback, of course), all of the Gossip Girl books, and—I'm not kidding—running subscriptions to both *Seventeen* and *Teen Vogue* magazines.

I'm sure there's some kind of strategy going on here. I mean, a person doesn't practically collect degrees from the Ivies without learning *something*. My best guess is that she's trying to keep her thumb on the pulse of what teenagers are into, while trying to find relevant connections between that and whatever problems we might have. For instance, on the same shelf as Harry Potter, there's a bunch of books on homesickness and grieving the loss of a loved one. Whatever. Despite all her so-called efforts, it seems like Dr. Miller's favorite panacea is to hand out prescriptions.

She's a well-dressed woman in her fifties, but she's too thin and has wisps of gray hair in her blond bob, which makes her look older than she really is; she's widely known on campus as the Crypt Keeper. Some kids really do find her helpful—or at least they find her prescriptions helpful. I know Stephanie has been sleeping soundly lately, thanks to the same sleeping pills I'm supposed to be taking.

This afternoon, I'm in her office with my parents, who sit on either side of me. I'm agitated, and this is the last place I want to be. Ever since the incident with the broken window (whose explanation I don't think my father believed for a *second*), Stephanie has barely been speaking to me.

And there's Del. The more I get to know him, the more I realize he might be the smartest person I've ever met. Right after he took his placement tests, they put him in all AP classes. I've never even seen the inside of an AP textbook. My grades so far this year have been mostly Cs and a few Bs. I can always count on an A in chorus . . . but it's *chorus*.

Del doesn't seem to care about my academic problems. More than once, he's offered to do my homework for me.

"You're part of the problem," I told him one day after lunch as we were standing at my locker together.

"How?" He gave me an innocent stare.

"Because you're always distracting me."

"Is that what I am? A distraction?"

We've been together for a few weeks, but people still stare when they see us talking. Aside from being with me, Del keeps mostly to himself. He has a tendency to disappear sometimes for entire afternoons or evenings; even I don't know where he goes, and he won't tell me.

I know what people are thinking: *what's so special about her?* What I'll never tell them is that I don't *know* what's so special about me. Del sees something that I don't, or can't.

On most nights, after my roommates have fallen asleep, I

climb down the rope ladder and sneak across campus to his dorm. He waits for me outside. He always brings this old blanket that he told me he's owned ever since he can remember, to keep us warm in the cool night air. "I took it from house to house," he said, watching as I felt the worn fabric, which is threadbare in a few places, between my thumb and index finger.

"What else did you take?"

"Nothing."

"How many times have you moved?"

He closed his eyes. "From the time I was a kid until I moved in with the Marshalls, I lived in sixteen different foster homes."

"And you took this blanket with you every time?"

"Yes."

We were on the ground, beside the stream. "But you're getting it covered in dirt," I told him.

He was leaning over me, his cigarette breath warm against my face. He still smokes all the time, just not around me.

"It's not covered in dirt," he said. "It's covered in *you*."

I don't know if my parents have any clue what's going on. If they do, they haven't said anything yet. Besides, we don't talk about things like boys when we meet with Dr. Miller. We talk about nightmares.

Dr. Miller, my parents, and I have been having basically the same session for the past year or so. In short, we're not making any progress aside from what she always says at the end of every session: "So, Emily. It's very important that you get the rest you need in order to develop into an intelligent adult. I'm going to increase your dosage, and we'll see how that works." Then she winks. "Okeydokey?"

Usually I just pretend to go along with whatever she wants to

do. But since I've been seeing Del, I've felt more . . . I don't know, more *liberated*. I don't *want* her to increase my dosage. I don't want to have to take the pills. All I want is for the nightmares to stop.

So I tell her this, my parents listening. I can feel both of them stiffen at my sides as I speak, more than a hint of annoyance in my voice. They both know that most of the kids treat Dr. Miller as kind of a joke, but I guess she is highly qualified.

She leans forward in her chair, fingertips pressed together, listening. She actually seems excited that I'm challenging her. "So you haven't been taking your pills on a regular basis?"

I hesitate for only a moment. "No. I only take them when I'm desperate."

Her eyes are wide with interest. "Desperate for *what*?"

"For *rest*. *Real* rest—for sleep without dreams."

"Okay. But everyone dreams, Emily."

I sit up straight, shaking my head. "Not like me. You know that."

"You mean sleep without nightmares."

I don't say anything. I put my head on my mom's shoulder. Her body is still stiff. On my other side, I can tell that my father is frustrated by our lack of progress. He's barely said three words the whole hour. I get the feeling he's as tired of this as I am.

"Emily, I know I've asked you this before, but do the nightmares ever change?"

"Not really. They're always about fire or water. Sometimes I'm *in* a fire, kind of trapped, like I can't breathe. Other times it's nothing but a lot of smoke everywhere. Sometimes I'm in a big body of water, and I can't find the surface, or else there's this deluge, like I'm standing under a waterfall. But they all make me feel the same way."

"And what way is that?"

I swallow. It's hard to say out loud. "Like I'm going to die."

"You aren't going to die, though. They're only dreams. Dr. and

78

Mrs. Meckler, I know we've been over this before, but is there anything at all from Emily's childhood that might be prompting these memories?"

Over my head, my parents glance at each other. We've been through this a million times; I don't know why Dr. Miller bothers asking. My parents wouldn't just *lie* to me.

"No," my mom says. "Nothing I can think of."

My dad is still quiet.

Dr. Miller taps her fingertips together again. She takes a good fifteen seconds to consider the situation. Finally, she says, "Okay, Emily. Here's what I'm going to do. I'm going to increase your medication, and I want you to promise me that you're actually going to *take it*. I want you to take it every night for two weeks. And during that time, I'd like you to keep a detailed dream journal. Every time you have nightmares, write down exactly what happens. Maybe"—she winks—"if you do what I say, we'll be able to get to the bottom of this and really start dealing with the root issues."

The *root issues*? I hadn't even considered that there might be root issues. I've never been in a fire. I've never almost drowned. What *root issues* could there possibly be?

For the first time since I've been seeing her, I decide to do exactly what Dr. Miller wants. I'll take the pills every night for two weeks. At this point, I'll do anything to get the nightmares to stop.

But something tells me they're not going anywhere. I'll take the pills, I'll keep the journal, and then she'll see that they're only night terrors. People get them sometimes, and I happen to get them a lot. Maybe they'll never go away. Maybe I'll learn to live with them. I might not have a choice.

We're leaving Dr. Miller's office when my dad puts his hand on my shoulder and says, "Emily. Talk to me in the hall."

School is over. We stand in the quiet hallway, our voices echoing. "I want you to come home before dinner," my dad tells me.

I bite my lip. I'd been planning on stopping by Winchester to see if Del was around.

"I don't know," I say. "I kind of have other plans."

"Plans to do what?"

I start to feel uneasy. I almost never go to my parents' house during the week. "I have plans, that's all. Why? What do you want to talk about?"

My father stares past me, down the hallway. "Come home. Now."


While my mom goes upstairs to change her clothes, my dad sits me down in his home office. I don't know why we can't sit in the kitchen or the living room like we usually do. In the past couple of weeks, my dad has been more reserved than usual. Maybe it's because of the broken window. Maybe it's something else. I honestly don't know.

Unlike in Dr. Miller's office, I feel a lot more comfortable relaxing in my dad's office. I settle on his leather sofa (identical to the one in his office at school, the one in Dr. Miller's office, *and* the one in the office of our college admission director, Dr. Sendell) and prop myself up on my side while he takes a seat behind his desk.

He opens a white file folder and quietly looks it over. Then he gazes at me with a combination of affection and concern. I've seen the look a million times.

"What is it, Daddy?"

"What is it?" He takes a deep breath. He seems weary, older all of a sudden, and I feel a flutter of anxiety in my stomach.

Then he says exactly what I've been hoping not to hear: "I'll tell you what it is, sweetie. Del Sugar."

His look is grave, but I can't suppress a smile. I remember the first conversation we ever had about Del, the night of the Dad-mobile incident—which my father hasn't mentioned yet, although

the plate is no longer on his car. I remember his quick, cloudy expression of hesitation when I'd asked if I should befriend Del.

"Okaaay," I say, pretending to be clueless. "What about him?"

"You're dating him. Is that right?"

I'm not sure why I don't tell him the truth. Maybe because I know it won't make him happy.

I try to keep my tone light, but it's hard. Like I said, I almost never lie to my parents. "No," I say. "Stephanie likes him."

He rubs his temples, taking another deep breath. "Emily, don't play dumb. I am not in the mood for it. I have seen you two on campus together. The Diggers have told me they've seen you taking walks off campus. Holding hands. Kissing." My father stretches his arms behind his head. "I need to know the truth, Emily. Now."

I hesitate. "Okay. We're friends." I nod, like I'm trying to convince myself that it's the truth. "We're good friends."

I can tell my response doesn't please my father by the way he leans back in his chair, goes *"aghhhhhhhh,"* and then stares at me with wide, tired eyes, and says, "Emily. This doesn't make me happy. At all."

All of a sudden, I realize what he's looking at in the folder that's sitting in front of him: it's Del's whole history, or at least whatever his parents decided to disclose. Seeing the folder makes me think of something else.

"You have a folder like that for everyone," I say.

My dad nods.

"Even ex-students?"

He taps his fingers impatiently on the table. "Emily, what are you getting at?"

"Can you tell me what happened to Madeline Moon-Park? She just disappeared off the face of the *planet*, and everyone wants to know—"

81

"Let me stop you right there." He closes the folder and slides it closer to his body, as though I'm going to leap across the room and grab it. "Whatever I do or do not know about Madeline is confidential, honey. You know that."

"So you know what happened? You know where she went?"

"I didn't say that. And you're trying to change the subject. I brought you in here to tell you that I don't want you seeing Del anymore."

I tilt my head. I squint at my father. "I told you, we're friends. What's wrong with that?"

"From what I understand, it's a pretty close friendship." He gives me this heartbreaking look. "And it's going to stop."

The words come out before I even realize what I'm saying. "No, it's not."

"And why is that?" His tone becomes mildly sarcastic, just enough to irritate me. "Do you *love* him? This boy you know nothing about? You've known him for how long? Two months?"

"What makes you say I know nothing about him? You didn't even know for sure I was seeing him until what—ten seconds ago? What is it, Dad? Is it his tattoo? Is it the fact that he was a foster child? Oh wait, let me guess. It's that his father isn't in Congress, or on the board of directors of one of the companies you're a shareholder in, isn't it?"

My dad is stunned. I've never spoken to him like this in my *life*. "No, Emily. That's not it."

"Then what is it?" Even I'm a little surprised by my attitude.

My father blinks a few times, like he's trying to calm himself down. He opens the folder, stares at it, closes it, opens it again. "Emily," he says quietly, "you do not know this boy the way you think you do."

"Why don't you tell me, then? Why did you let him in if he wasn't *Stonybrook Material*?" My tone is beyond sarcastic.

"Del's adoptive father, Doug Marshall, is a close friend of mine."

"I've never heard you talk about him."

"Would you listen to me? We were college roommates at Penn. The Marshalls are good people. They love their son." He sighs. "What I'm about to tell you is confidential."

"Oh, please. Tell me."

"Del was taken from his mother's home when he was just a toddler. He ran away from a number of foster homes before the Marshalls found him. He was abused, Emily. His sister was abused. Every time he ran away, the act was twofold: to find his sister, who he hasn't had contact with in years, and to escape a terrible situation."

I shake my head. "I already knew. Del *told me* about all of this."

My dad studies me. "He didn't tell you everything."

"How do you know that?"

"Did he tell you what happened at his last boarding school?"

I only hesitate for a second. "Yes," I lie.

"Oh, he did? He told you that the Marshalls pulled him out because, in the first week of school, his roommate—who also happened to be his best friend—almost beat another student to death with a baseball bat for allegedly raping a girl?"

I shake my head. "What?"

"Del's roommate was his best friend," my father says. "His name was . . . I don't remember, Keith or Kevin or something like that. Kevin's sister was on a date with another boy, and she accused him of raping her. So Kevin snuck into the boy's room in the middle of the night with a metal bat and put the boy in a coma."

Del has always been gentle. I swallow. "So? What does that prove? You don't know if Del had anything to do with it."

"Emily, they were seen leaving the dorm together that night, right after it happened. Who's to say they didn't both come up with

the idea? Del was lucky not to get kicked out, or I couldn't have done his father the favor of admitting him here." My dad takes a deep breath. "Del is incredibly intelligent. He might be a nice boy, I don't know. And I don't know what the two of you have been up to with this *special* friendship of yours. But I am certain that he is not the boy for you. Emily, he is *damaged*. It might not be his fault, but it's true."

Before I can say a word, my dad continues, his voice growing louder with every syllable. "And another thing. Let's talk about that broken window in your room."

I give him my most innocent stare. I can't believe the way I'm lying to my own father. "What about it? I told you, we woke up and found it that way."

"I find that very interesting, Emily. Because I was having a conversation with Digger shortly after it happened, and I don't think you're telling me the whole truth."

"Which Digger?" I bat my eyelashes.

"You know *damn* well which Digger. The same Digger who saw you outside your dorm that night with Del. What happened? Did he throw something at your window to wake you up? I am telling you, Emily, you're done with him. Case closed."

He sits back in his chair, taking a moment to let it all sink in. While we're sitting there in silence, he takes the folder, places it back in the filing cabinet beside his desk, and locks the cabinet door with a tiny key on his keychain.

I know he expects me to be shocked, and I suppose I am. But I can tell that he also expects me to be disturbed by what he's told me, upset with Del, and ready to turn my back on him like any good girl would.

But all I want to do right now is find Del. I want to tell him I don't care what happened at his last school; I know that he couldn't have been involved. All I care about is *now*.

"It's almost dinnertime," my dad says. "You should go get dressed. I want you to sit with your mother and me tonight."

I nod. "Okay."

"And I don't want you seeing Del Sugar anymore. You understand?"

I clear my throat. For a few seconds, I don't say anything.

"Emily? You understand, don't you?"

It's easier not to fight. "I guess so."

"Good. Come here."

I cross the room and sit in his lap, like I've done countless times before. He pulls me into a hug. "Emily," he says, his arms wrapped around my waist, "if you knew how much I love you—"

"I *do* know."

"No, you don't." He looks into my eyes. "Children never know. You won't understand until you have babies of your own someday."

"Dad, okay . . . I have to go."

He holds on to me, studying my expression. "That seemed too easy."

*It sure did.* "Don't think that," I say. "I'll tell Del I can't see him anymore. It's okay. I understand."

My dad nods. I can tell he's not buying it 100 percent. Maybe not at all. But I don't care; all I want to do is get out of here.


I don't even have to knock on Del's window; he's perched on the edge, leaning his head out to smoke.

"Hi," I say.

He tosses the cigarette away when he sees me. "Hi, yourself. What took you so long?"

"I had to talk to my dad."

Del shakes his head. "You are a daddy's girl."

I ignore the comment. "I couldn't wait to see you."

"Oh, you couldn't?" He grins. "I'm flattered. Want to come in?"

"I can't." I really do have to get ready. "Just . . . look, I can't talk much at dinner. My dad wants me to sit at his table. But I wanted to make sure you were coming by tonight."

He studies my expression. "Emily? Is anything wrong?"

"Are you coming tonight?"

He nods. "Yes. Sure, I am."

"Then everything's fine." I stand on my tiptoes, leaning forward to give him a kiss before I begin to back away. "Everything's perfect."

# chapter seven

During Friday morning's school announcements, we learn that Mr. Henry, the intern, has come down with double pneumonia. Our announcements are personal like that. My dad's secretary, Paula, does them over the loudspeaker in her office. After she tells everyone about his pneumonia, she adds that it would be nice if we made him a card.

For some reason, Franny gets it in her head that we should make him soup. From *scratch*. She doesn't actually ask the rest of the quad if we're interested in helping; instead, she goes to the store on her own early Saturday morning and returns with three grocery bags full of food.

Stephanie, Grace, and I are sitting on my bedroom floor, studying vocab words for English class.

Stephanie doesn't look up from her cards. "Whatcha gonna do with all that food, Franny? You sure as hell aren't going to eat it yourself."

When Franny tells us about the soup, we all stare at her for a few seconds. Then we start laughing.

"What?" Franny asks. "What the hell's so funny?"

"Franny," Grace says, "I've never even seen you boil water. Have you ever cooked *anything*?"

Her bottom lip trembles a smidge. "I thought it would be a nice thing to do for him. He has double pneumonia, you guys."

"I know," Stephanie says. "We made him a card in my Latin class."

"You did?" I ask, frowning at her. "In Latin?"

"Yes," she says. "It said Get Well Soon. In Latin."

"He's my study hall proctor," Franny continues, raising her voice. "He's always nice to me. I like him." *Tugtugtug.*

"Franny," I tell her, "we can't make that in the kitchenette. There isn't enough space." It's true; all we have downstairs is a tiny electric stove, a minifridge, and a microwave.

"I know that, Emily." *Tug.* "We're not using the kitchenette. We're using your parents' house."

My mouth falls open. "How are we going to do that?"

Franny is pleased with herself. "I talked to your mom about it at breakfast." She shifts her gaze to Stephanie. "And Latin is a dead language, you know. It's completely useless."

Steph flicks a vocab card at her. "Not if I'm going to be a doctor, it isn't."

"Ha!" Grace blurts. "There's no way you'll get into medical school. You're going to be an aerobics instructor."

Franny covers her mouth as she giggles.

"You're awful. I can't stand any of you," Stephanie announces. She frowns. "I could be a doctor if I wanted to."

"Sure you could," Grace says. "And Emily could be an astronaut."

I don't even pretend to be offended.

Grace and Stephanie keep arguing all the way to my parents' house. My mom is waiting for us.

"This is so sweet of you, girls," she says. My mom isn't wearing any makeup yet, but she still looks pretty.

She gave Franny a list at breakfast with everything we'd need to make chicken noodle soup. Before we begin, my mom makes us strawberry milk shakes. The four of us sit at the kitchen table, drinking through bendy straws, while my mom helps us get started.

First, she puts the chicken in a pot of water on the stove. Then she starts chopping vegetables in the food processor. We're still watching.

"What are you girls doing this weekend?" she asks.

The four of us exchange a silent look. There's a party at Amanda Stream's beach house tonight, but we can't tell my mom about that.

Before the pause becomes too long, Franny says, "Probably going to the mall."

At exactly the same moment, Steph says, "We're going to stay in and study." They look at each other. Steph kicks Franny under the table.

My mom pretends to ignore them. To me, she says, "What about you, Emily? Any plans for this weekend?"

She says it innocently enough, but I can tell she's feeling me out, trying to see if I'm hiding something from her, which I definitely am. There's no doubt I'm going to spend a lot of my free time this weekend with Del.

I haven't seen him since yesterday. He wasn't at breakfast, and he wasn't at his dorm afterward; he's pulled another one of his disappearing acts. Every time I ask him where he goes, he either ignores me or changes the subject.

We hang out in my parents' kitchen until the early afternoon. Once the soup is finished, I realize that my mom has done all of the work herself. She has been so kind, so genuine and helpful

and wonderful. Even though I'm sharing her with my friends, I feel so grateful that she belongs to me.

My roommates seem oblivious to the fact that we are in no way responsible for the finished product; it's like they think they can take credit because they were in the same room as the soup.

"Should we take it over to him now?" Stephanie asks.

"I should go running before the—I mean, before we go shopping," Grace tells everyone. She fidgets as she leans against the counter. Grace gets anxious if she doesn't run every single day.

"I can take the soup to Paul," Franny says.

We all look at her.

"Did you just call him *Paul*?" I ask.

*Tugtug.* Even my mom is staring at Franny, waiting for an answer.

"Um. Yes," Franny tells us. "He told everyone in our study hall to call him Paul."

Stephanie shakes her head. She makes a face. "That's weird, Franny. He's a teacher."

"It's not that weird. He's only twenty-two."

"Yeah. He's twenty-two and we're sixteen." Grace is already stretching her hamstrings.

"Don't call me weird, Stephanie."

"Then don't *act* weird."

"Ladies. Calm down." My mom is smiling. She winks at me. "Why don't you all take it to him? I'm sure he'll be flattered."

But once we leave my parents' house, Grace starts trotting away. "See you later," she calls, waving at us over her shoulder. She'll be gone most of the afternoon.

Franny, who is holding a big Tupperware container with the soup, looks at me and Stephanie. "Really, I'm fine," she tells us. "You two go ahead. I'll be back soon." I can tell she's dying

to pull her hair out, except she doesn't have a free hand to reach with.

When we get back to the dorm, Steph and I sit on my bedroom floor to try and do homework together, but we keep getting distracted.

"You're going to the party tonight, right?" she asks.

"Yes." I squint at my open precalc book, unable to comprehend much of anything that I'm looking at. I should have taken geometry instead.

Amanda Stream's parents have a beach house about five miles away at Groton Long Point. The place is massive; it even has its own three-par golf course. Her parents spend about two weeks a year there; her mother is this prominent playwright who apparently—at least according to Renee, who heard it from Bruce—has major Emotional Issues, and her father is a psychiatrist who caters to the whole swanky New York set. (That's Renee's word, not mine—leave it to her to say "swanky" without it seeming the least bit cheesy.)

Anyway, apparently Amanda's mother is so anxiety-ridden and almost constantly tortured by her Art that they barely ever leave the city, which actually turns out to be a great thing for all of us here at Stonybrook, because everyone knows the security code to the beach house (4-4-1-1) and Amanda doesn't mind—at least not too much—if you come and go as you please, and she has parties there herself most weekends, and in general it's one of those sad situations that ends up working out great for the kids in the short term, but which will undoubtedly leave poor Amanda damaged for life long-term. I can picture her on a shrink's sofa someday, complaining about her absent parents and how retrospectively *miserable* her adolescence was.

But my point is, everybody goes to these parties. Even Renee. Even Ethan, who is usually such a complete Boy Scout. And even Del, who almost never socializes with anybody except me.

"Of course I'm going," I say to Steph. "So what?"

Stephanie's anger toward me has cooled over the past couple of weeks. She has other things to worry about: her parents are in the middle of a custody fight for her and Ethan, and her father doesn't want to pay alimony. Her mom already has a new boyfriend. Steph has lost at least ten pounds since the beginning of the year. I don't blame her for being so edgy; her family is in pieces.

"So, you should talk to Del, Emily. Someplace where there are plenty of people around." She pauses. "Not in his room. Not in the woods."

I stare at her. "How do you know about that?"

"Oh, come on." She tosses her stack of vocab cards aside. I close my precalc book.

"Everybody knows what you've been doing, Emily. And everybody thinks it's a bad idea. Your father doesn't want you to see Del. Why not? He has to know something you don't."

For an instant, as Stephanie's talking, I catch a glimpse of just how much she looks like Ethan when it comes to her subtle facial features: the curve of her small, perfect nose; the prominence of her cheekbones; the way her earlobes are small and attached, which she once informed me was a sign of superior breeding. "Even Renee doesn't like him," she says, "and you *know* it's a bad idea if Renee doesn't approve."

I shake my head. "How do you know everyone thinks it's a bad idea?"

"Because we've been talking about it. I know Del is all hot and mysterious and brilliant. But there's something so *off* about him. Something isn't right. What kind of person is involved in beating someone up with a baseball bat?" I'm not sure how, exactly,

but by now everyone has heard one version or another of what happened at Del's last school. I certainly haven't been the one telling them. "Think about it, Emily," she continues. "How well do you actually know him?"

"I know him better than anybody," I insist. "He tells me everything."

"Really?" she says coolly. "Where is he right now? Where does he go when he disappears?"

I don't know what to tell her. I don't say anything.

"That's what I thought." She stands up, crosses the room, and sits down at Franny's desk. She begins to brush her long blond hair, examining it for split ends.

"Listen," I say, "I don't know where he goes, but I'm sure he's not doing anything wrong. Maybe he wants to be alone."

"He can't be alone in his room?"

I ignore her. "My dad doesn't even know for sure that Del was involved with what happened at his old school. Nobody knows for sure what happened."

"Del knows," she says.

"It was a long time ago. It doesn't matter now."

She scowls at me. "Don't be stupid."

"I'm not being stupid. I trust him."

"Well, if there's one thing I can tell you," she says bitterly, "it's that you don't know him the way you think you know him. He's barely been here for three months. I thought I knew my father, and look what he did. You shouldn't trust him, Emily. You're being naive."

I narrow my eyes at her. "I shouldn't trust your father? Who are we talking about?"

"Shut up. You know I mean Del." She tosses the brush onto Franny's bed and stands up. "Just do me a favor. Do *all* of us a favor. Please?"

The space between us is awkward. I want her to leave. "What do you want?"

"Ask him about his old school. Find out more about him before you get into trouble."

"Stephanie, he isn't going to get me in any trouble."

"Promise me you'll talk to him."

I nod. "Okay. I will." I want to believe that Stephanie is actually concerned about me. In the back of my mind, though, I remember how all the girls reacted when Del first got here. Until he started paying attention to me and me alone, *everyone* wanted his attention. The more likely scenario, I think, is that Stephanie is jealous.

That night at Amanda's house, it takes me forever to find Del. He's alone in one of the bedrooms, lying on his back in bed, gazing at the ceiling.

We're in Amanda's older brother's room. Her brother, Ty, is in college now—at Bard? Brown? Someplace like that. Anyway, the room is at the corner of the house. It has a balcony with a killer view of the ocean, a vaulted ceiling with four big skylights above the bed, and two telescopes positioned to check out both the sky and whatever's going on down the shore. The room is far away from the rest of the house, far away from the party downstairs.

"Come here, Em," Del says, still staring at the ceiling. How does he even know it's me?

*Talk to him . . . someplace where there are plenty of people around.*

I sit beside him on the bed. "What are you doing up here?"

He reaches out to hold my hand. "Looking at the sky. Thinking."

"About what?" From down the hall, I hear the lilting of voices carrying toward us. I don't feel the least bit unsafe with him. Even if we were alone in the house, I realize, I would feel completely at ease.

94

"About how I got here," he says.

"What do you mean?"

"I mean that I'm in this beautiful house with all of these beautiful people . . . I have everything I could want. I have you. I have parents who love me."

*But they sent him away. He said so himself.*

His gaze is penetrating and intense. His blue eyes are big and watery. I start to feel a little uneasy. Where was he this morning? As far as I know, he didn't come back until late in the afternoon.

"Del," I say, frowning, "everyone's parents love them."

"No, they don't." He shakes his head. "You're so naive, Emily."

I am getting *so tired* of people calling me naive. "You think there are people who have kids just because?"

"Kids aren't always intentional. And even if they are, people change their minds. Or else they find out they aren't up to it, after it's too late. People do awful things all the time. You don't have any idea."

"You're right. I don't."

"Your parents are practically perfect, aren't they? Is that what you think, Emily?"

I nod, remembering the way my mom looked as she made soup this morning. She was so happy. "They're pretty great."

"Right," he says. There's a hint of sarcasm in his tone. "You are one lucky girl."

". . ."

". . ."

"Del . . . can I ask you something?"

"Sure."

"Where did you go this morning?"

He stares up at the ceiling. He sniffles. "Nowhere. Sometimes I go for long walks."

The answer doesn't ring true. "You go for walks," I repeat.

"Yes."

"Can I ask you something else?"

He nods.

"What happened at your old school? Why did you leave? And I don't mean that your parents pulled you out. I mean specifically—*why* did they pull you out?"

He's still holding my hand. I can feel his grip tighten a twinge. "Who told you about that?"

"My dad. He thinks you might be dangerous."

Del grins. "Oh, he does? Dangerous how?"

"I don't know. He doesn't trust you. He told me that you were involved in an . . . an *incident*. With a baseball bat."

"That's such bullshit. That isn't what happened."

"Then tell me what happened."

Del reaches toward the floor, where there's a half-empty beer bottle that I hadn't noticed before. He picks it up and takes a long swig. "Okay, Emily," he says, "you want to know what happened at my old school?"

His face and neck are sweaty. His breathing is heavy. If I didn't know him better, I might be afraid of him.

"Yes," I say. "I want to know what happened."

He takes another swig from his drink. "This girl—my roommate's sister—she got raped."

I cringe at the word "raped." "Okay."

"My roommate decided to do something about it." Del pauses. "And I didn't stop him. I guess it makes me *involved* in a way."

"But you didn't get expelled."

He spreads his arms wide. "I didn't do anything wrong!"

"What happened to the boy? The one who . . ."

"The rapist?" He smirks. "He spent some time in the hospital. Then his daddy took care of things, and instead of getting

arrested like he should have, it turned into a he-said-she-said, and my roommate was the one who got in all the trouble. So now this little girl—this *fourteen*-year-old—is at school with her rapist, and she doesn't even have her big brother anymore. Real fair, right?"

I'm quiet for a while. Finally I say, "There are other ways to deal with things."

"Not always. No, Emily." He's getting more and more excited. "Some people have things coming to them, you know? Some people are rotten inside. This guy was one of those people."

It should bother me—shouldn't it? It should make me afraid. But instead I feel the opposite way. Del didn't actually *do* anything . . . he just stood by and let it happen.

There is so much about him that I don't know. But I know he was abused. I know his sister was abused. Coming from a background like that, how else would he know to react?

He slides a hand behind my neck and pulls me toward him until our foreheads are touching. "Hey," he whispers. "Don't be scared, Emily. I would never hurt you."

"I know," I say. And I do know; I believe him like I believe my own name.

He kisses me on the lips. The smell on him almost makes me want to gag: it's kerosene, sweat, beer, and cigarettes. "What do you want to do?" he asks.

"I want to go find my friends," I tell him. "And I want you to come with me." I pull back a little bit. "People want to get to know you. You need to give them a chance to see that you're . . ."

He grins. "Normal? I'm not."

I close my eyes. For a moment the room is totally silent except for the sound of our breathing. "I know that, Del."

"You want me to pretend?" he asks. "For you?"

I nod. "For me."

He kisses me again. "Okay. Anything for you."

Downstairs, almost everyone is gathered in the great room, where there's a huge fire burning in the fireplace and beer bottles scattered on all the tabletops and empty surfaces. Even the lid to the baby grand is covered with them.

People pretend not to notice, but everyone looks at us when they think we're not paying attention. Del leads me by the hand to the sofa, where Steph, Grace, and Franny are sitting with Renee and Ethan. All of them are drunk and talking about Madeline Moon-Park.

Madeline is probably the only subject that could engage my roommates and Ethan in such an animated conversation with Renee. Madeline has become something like an urban legend since her failure to return this year. There are no seventh graders at this party, but they all know her as the coolest, most aloof person in Stonybrook's history, which is a little bit of an exaggeration, but not by much.

She was one of those kids that show up in a shuttle from the airport on the first day of seventh grade. Like I've said before, her parents didn't visit. Nobody has ever even *seen* them. Madeline almost never went home for the holidays. She was an only child. She was fiercely smart, fluent in Korean, and never talked about where she came from. And then she was gone. We can't find anything on Google. My father won't tell me what happened to her. It's like she's vanished.

Del and I sit down with everyone else. He's still holding my hand. More looks are exchanged among my friends. Their gazes move past me to stare at him, his T-shirt revealing the infamous tattoo. He and I pretend not to notice.

"Anyway," Renee continues—she's the only one who's not staring at us, and she seems oblivious to the fact that everyone else is—"I've exhausted all of my resources. The Internet, Emily's dad, the Diggers—nobody will tell me where she is or what happened to her. All my e-mails come back as undeliverable. Her cell phone is disconnected." Renee presses a finger to her lips in thought. "We were best friends," she says. "I don't know why she would leave without telling me anything."

"Maybe she's dead," Grace says.

Renee is startled by the suggestion. We all are. "She's not dead. Don't even say that." And she wraps her arms around her body, like she's trying to give herself a hug.

"Well, then, what happened to her? How does somebody just slip off the face of the earth?" Grace asks.

"If she died," Ethan says, "there would be no good reason for the faculty to hide it from us." He takes a moment to look around the room at everyone. I notice that he intentionally avoids meeting my gaze. "Something terrible must have happened to her," he continues.

"What makes you think that?" Stephanie asks.

"Because," he says, "if it weren't terrible, she'd have no reason to hide."

And out of nowhere, it seems, Del speaks up. "I bet I could find out what happened to her."

My roommates gape at him. Ethan raises his eyebrows. For the first time since we've sat down, Renee gives her full attention to Del.

"Oh, really?" she asks. Her tone is sarcastic and doubtful. "And how would you do that? You've never even met her."

I've never heard Renee talk down to *anyone* before. But she was protective of Madeline; she seems agitated by the idea of Del meddling in the situation.

"I'm resourceful," Del says, grinning at her so that all of his teeth are exposed. "Come on. Don't you at least want to know where she is?"

Renee nods slowly. "Sure. But I don't want to violate her privacy."

"How is that violating anything?"

"Well, how would you find out?" She hugs herself more tightly. "Some kind of . . . espionage or something, right? You'd have to stick your nose somewhere where it didn't belong, wouldn't you?"

"Espionage?" Steph says, frowning. "Renee. He's not James Bond." Then she turns to Del. "Can you really find out?"

He looks the crowd over. He gives them a smug smile. "Give me two weeks."

# chapter eight

It's a couple of weeks after the party, and I'm back at my dorm after class. I gaze out the window at my parents' house, trying to figure out how I'm going to continue keeping Del a secret from them when pretty much everybody else knows we're a couple. Somebody's standing on the periphery of my parents' property, smoking a cigarette. I can't make out who it is—my contacts are out, and I'm wearing an old pair of glasses with a slightly weak prescription—but it's undoubtedly someone who doesn't under-stand the consequences if the headmaster *himself* catches you smoking. It's one thing to stink and blame it on the cleaning ladies; it's entirely another to be caught red-handed by someone other than Digger.

As I'm staring out the window, somebody comes up behind me and wraps their arms around me. I don't need to turn around to know that it's Stephanie.

Her touch gives me a weary sense of comfort. I like having her here because I know her *so* well; at the same time, there's a small part of me wishing that she was somebody else—maybe Renee, or even Del. I hate feeling this way about Stephanie. She and I have been best friends for four years. We've shared more hugs than I can count. Trying not to think about all the distance that seems to have grown between us almost overnight, I cover her hands with mine. She rests her head on my shoulder to peer out the window.

"How are you, sweetie?" I ask.

"I'm okay." She sighs. "That's not true. I'm a mess."

She's talking about her parents' divorce. Even though I saw it coming, I kind of can't believe they're actually going through with it, after so many years together.

"I know," I tell her, squeezing her skinny arm. "It'll be okay, though."

She tightens her grip on me. "I don't know what I'd do without you and Ethan."

"Steph, I want to apologize. I feel like I've been so wrapped up with Del that I haven't even been around lately. You know you can talk to me about anything, right? It's really happening? The divorce?"

"Yes. And yes, you've been too wrapped up in Del."

I know I shouldn't keep talking about him. It's insensitive. But Stephanie is my best friend, and I want her to know what's going on. "My dad will flip if he finds out we're still together."

She hesitates.

"What?"

"He might not be so wrong, Emily."

"I know what you think. I know what everyone thinks, Steph. But I can't tell you what it's like when we're alone together. You don't know him the way I do."

"How well do you really know him? Did you talk to him about what happened at his last school?"

"Yes," I say.

"And? What did he tell you?"

"It isn't what you think. Believe me, there's no reason for me to be afraid of him. I trust him."

"Emily." Her tone shifts to shock. "Oh my God. Do you see that person smoking?"

It's gotten darker quickly; by now, I can barely make out the silhouette in the evening. There is only the glowing red tip of the cigarette moving in the night, almost like it's trying to send a message.

"I do see someone. Right by my parents' house."

"Emily . . . my God, is that your *mother*?"

Stephanie and I both lean closer, our bodies still together, to squint out the window.

"I can't tell who it is," I say. "My vision isn't good enough. These glasses are old."

She takes off her own glasses. "Here. Switch with me."

I put her glasses on and squint harder at the figure in the dark. It looks like a woman. "But my mom doesn't smoke, Steph."

"I know. But there's something about the way she's moving." She presses her nose to the glass. Her mouth creates a circle of fog. "It looks like your mother."

"But my mom doesn't smoke," I repeat.

And before we can debate the issue any further, the light from the cigarette goes out, and we can barely make out the body walking away. All we can tell is that it's walking toward my parents' house. Most of the lights are out in the downstairs, so I can't tell if the person goes inside. I can't see anything at all.

I turn around to look at Stephanie. Her glasses make everything up close a little blurry. "Well, that was weird."

She nods. "It sure was."

We switch glasses again. We are both quiet. The situation seems impossible. We're talking about my *mother*. I would know if she were a smoker.

*Fire. Smoke everywhere. My mother's body stiffening beside me when I mentioned my dreams in Dr. Miller's office earlier.*

I shake my head. "There's no way it was her. Come on, we're going to be late for dinner if we don't hurry."

As we're getting dressed, Grace returns from cross-country practice, and Franny comes back from wherever she's been. Lately she's been disappearing a lot. I've been meaning to ask her what's going on.

They're in the middle of a heated discussion; at least it seems that way at first. But once Steph and I start listening, we realize what they're arguing about: ice-cream flavors. They've been talking about what ice-cream flavor people's personalities would be.

"I told her she'd be shaved ice. No flavor," Grace says. "And now she's *all* pissed off—"

"Shaved ice is not a flavor!" Franny insists.

"Exactly!" Grace says. "You would be flavorless!"

Franny has tears in her eyes. "That's so mean, Grace. Honestly, you're such a bitch sometimes."

"I'm just telling the truth!" Grace rolls her eyes. She's covered in sweat from practice, her hair pulled into a messy ponytail. She looks alive and beautiful and vivacious. "Okay. If you had to be a flavor, you'd be air. Is that better?"

"No!" Franny picks up a history book and hurls it across the room at Grace. "And I don't think any of your choices were accurate, by the way." She sniffles in my direction. "Emily, she said you'd be Neapolitan."

"Neapolitan?" I frown. "But that's so boring."

"No, it isn't," Grace says, excited. "I've been doing a lot of thinking about this. Two hours of thinking." Because she's a distance runner, Grace tends to find herself in these meditative states of bliss. It's not unusual for her to come back from practice wanting to discuss two hours' worth of meandering thoughts with us. "Emily, on the surface you might seem kind of dull, right?"

104

"Thank you," I say drily, holding my middle finger in the air beneath her nose.

"Let me *finish*," Grace says. "Jeez. Okay, so you might *seem* innocuous and innocent and dull and naive—"

"I already said thank you—"

"—but you're not. You actually have multiple layers to you, and if people would just look past the surface, they'd see that you're rather complex." She begins to tug the ponytail from her hair. Beads of sweat are still gathered on her tan forehead. "For instance, there's your relationship with Del." She frowns. "He must see something fascinating in you, right?"

Before I can say anything, she continues. "And there's your voice. And your red hair. And your nightmares." She narrows her eyes, nodding in satisfaction, wiping the sweat from her forehead. "There's more to you than meets the eye. Definitely Neapolitan."

"But I don't like Neapolitan," I tell her.

She shrugs. She stretches her arms over her head. "Not my problem."

"At least you're not *shaved ice*," Franny says. *Tug. Tugtugtugtugtug.* She starts to change into her uniform for dinner.

"Hey, what day is it?" Steph asks. "Franny? Could you help me?"

We all stare at Franny's underwear. My mouth falls open. "Franny," I say, "what's the matter with you?" Her bra says TUESDAY!—which it is. But her underpants say WEDNESDAY! Something's definitely going on with her.

"Shut up," Franny says. "All of you." She starts to pull on her clothes. "And I wouldn't be so chipper if I were you, Steph. Ask Grace what flavor *you'd* be."

"It was a toss-up," Grace tells her, "between Rocky Road and praline."

I snort. "Why was it a toss-up?"

"Well, at first I was thinking Rocky Road because of all the drama with her family. But then that got me thinking about how she's a twin, and I almost went with chocolate and vanilla swirl. But that didn't feel right, either." Grace's tone starts to become more fevered. "At this point, guys, I was on, like, mile three of a six-mile run, lots of hills, and I was really in the zone. You know? So I finally decided praline, definitely praline for Steph."

"And why am I praline?" Steph wrinkles her nose. "I hate pralines."

"Because," Grace says, almost shrieking now, "your relationship with your brother is so *icky*, and pralines are the ultimate ick factor when it comes to ice cream!"

Franny just shakes her head, rubbing her eyes. "I like praline, Steph."

The three of us—Franny, Steph, and I—decide telepathically to give Grace the silent treatment all the way up to dinner. It doesn't stop her from yapping away the whole time about other people's flavors. Renee? Peanut butter and chocolate, because she's so *rich*—both literally and figuratively, Grace explains. Renee is walking up with us, and doesn't seem a bit fazed by the description. She shrugs and says nothing.

Del's flavor? Grace isn't sure, but she's positive he'd be something with chunks. And Madeline Moon-Park? According to Grace, Madeline is the only person who she couldn't think of a flavor for.

"Shows how much you know," Renee says.

"What?" I ask, suddenly interested in the conversation again—although I've got to admit, I'm hurt and confused by the whole "Neapolitan" label. "What do you mean, 'shows how much you know'?"

Renee gives me a smooth smile. "Madeline," she pronounces, "would be pumpkin pie."

"Why?" I ask.

"Because," she says, shivering a little bit inside her blazer, "autumn was her favorite season. She used to say it made her feel so alive to have everything around her dying. *And* she loved pumpkin pie." She pauses. "Any word yet from Del about getting her contact info?"

I shake my head. "He says he's working on it. We'll see."

At dinner, Del sits across the room from me at Dr. Sella's table. She's the Italian teacher, and her house is right next to my parents'. When I'm pretty sure they aren't looking, Del and I exchange small grins. At one point he mouths, *tonight*, and I feel a tingle of electricity run down my spine. *Tonight tonight tonight.*

As I'm hugging my parents good-bye after dinner, I remember the scene from earlier outside their house. I hold on to my mother, trying to sniff her hair, her clothing.

It was her. She's changed her clothes and put on perfume, but there's that unmistakable gross smell still clinging to her hair. My mother *smoking*? She barely even drinks. Does my father know? He can't possibly.

What else don't I know? Smoke, fire, water . . . her body stiffening. She's lied to me—at least, it's a lie of omission, a secret big enough that she's kept it from me for God knows how long.

My mom pulls away from the hug. "I love you, Emily." She smiles, reaching out to touch my hair. She's chewing on a mint.

"I love you, too, Mom. Hey—you know what?"

"What?"

"I'm going to take those pills and keep that journal, like Dr. Miller wants me to. I think it will help."

Her smile wavers a little bit. "Good. I think that's a good plan, sweetie."

"See you later, then."

"Of course."

It's another warm night. When I get to Winchester, Del is inside his room with the window open. As usual, he tosses his cigarette into the woods when he sees me coming.

"You're late," he says. It's past eleven.

"I know. I'm sorry." I wait for him as he climbs out the window. He's holding the red blanket beneath his right arm. We walk into the woods together, until we're at the very edge of campus, to what has become Our Place beside the stream.

We sit together in the night, the evening lit by the bright moon above us.

"It's so warm," I say.

"You're right. It's almost hot." Del yawns. Then he pulls his T-shirt over his head and tosses it aside in a ball. He leans back on his elbows, staring at the sky.

I've seen him without a shirt on before, but the sight always startles me. Del has a flat stomach with visible muscles that curve at his hips. He's still wearing his dress pants from dinner, but he's taken off his belt so the pants are loose around his waist. I can't stop looking at him.

"Well?" He yawns again. His stomach muscles flex. "What do you want to do?"

The question alone is enough to make my blood rush to my cheeks. My face gets hot.

"Emily? You're so quiet."

He blinks at me, the edges of his eyes wrinkling in a smile.

"I'm thinking," I say.

"About what?"

"Nothing." I'm too embarrassed to tell him. "You're right. It *is* hot out here."

"Take off your sweatshirt, then." I'm wearing jeans and a tank top covered up with a Stonybrook Academy sweatshirt. "Here," Del says, leaning forward to help me. When he pulls the sweatshirt over my head, my hair falls against my face.

Del tosses my sweatshirt aside. He looks me over. "You're so pretty," he says. Then he nudges me back against the ground until I'm leaning on my elbows. He brings his face close to mine.

"Sing something."

He loves to hear me sing. Usually, when we're outside, I love singing for him. It puts me in an entirely different place, a place so relaxing and calm and far away from all of the chaos of school and nightmares and everyone's disapproval of Del.

But I feel so shy right now for some reason; maybe it's because he's half-naked. The idea of singing seems mortifying. "I don't want to." When I shake my head, the tips of our noses brush together. "Somebody could hear us," I say. It's never stopped me before. "We have to be quiet."

"Then sing quietly."

"What do you want to hear?"

"I don't care. Your voice."

I can't think of anything. "I don't know," I tell him. I start humming the scale that we always warm up with in chorus. It's a boring exercise. It seems very Neapolitan.

I stop singing to tell him about the conversation my friends and I had earlier with Grace.

"You," he says, tugging on my red hair, "are anything but Neapolitan."

"Oh yeah? What am I?" I lean back farther on the blanket and

stare at the sky, which is bright with stars. "There isn't a flavor that goes with 'stupid.'"

"Emily, stop it. You aren't stupid."

"I don't know what you're doing with me," I tell him. "Our GPAs are totally incompatible."

"GPAs mean nothing," he says. "I'm not even going to college."

Somehow, the revelation doesn't surprise me. What *does* surprise me is how little I'm bothered by it.

"No college?" I ask, tracing the outline of his tattoo with my index finger. "Won't your parents be disappointed?"

He's quiet for a while. Finally, he says, "I have other plans."

"Oh yeah? Like what?"

He hesitates. "We can talk about them later."

I want to ask, *Do they include me?* But I'm afraid of what the answer will be.

"You aren't singing," he says.

"I don't want to sing."

The whole time we've been talking, he's been lying above me, against me, his face close to mine. Now he leans on his side and rests a hand against my stomach. I stare at him. His blue eyes are wide and glassy.

"I want to tell you something," he says.

"What?"

"You know I love you. Don't you?"

I nod. "Yes," I whisper.

"You love me, too?" As we start kissing, I realize he's crying. We both are.

"Yes."

Del is my first kiss. He's my first boyfriend, and my first love. It feels right that he would be my first *everything*.

"We can stop," he says. "Nothing else has to happen."

I wipe my eyes. I can't stop staring at him. "I'm not going back," I tell him. "Not now."

He's still crying. "Okay." He nods. "Are you sure?"

All I can see is Del. All I can hear is his breath. "Yes," I say, "I'm sure."

It's after two in the morning. The wind is whistling through the trees as we lie wrapped in the blanket together. I imagine even the Diggers must be asleep by now.

"I should go back," I tell him. My eyes are closed. "I need to go to sleep."

Then he does the strangest thing.

"Open your eyes," he says. "Can you see me?"

I nod. "Yes."

He says, "I want you to trust me, okay? Hold still. Keep your eyes open." And he takes his index finger and slides my contact lenses—one eye, then the other—off to the side of my eyeballs, so that everything is blurry.

"Can you see me now?"

"No."

"I can see you, Emily." He kisses me again. "I can see parts of you that you don't even see yourself."

I blink my contacts back into place. "What do you mean?"

"I mean what I said." He yawns. "You're right. We should go. I wouldn't want Daddy to find out what we've been up to."

"He'd kill us," I murmur.

Del smiles. "It's more exciting that way, don't you think?"

I kiss him again, for a long time, before saying, "It sure is."

\* \* \*

When I finally get back to my dorm, at almost three in the morning, I'm so tired that my whole body aches. I grab a quick shower and get into bed. It's only after I've taken one of Dr. Miller's pills, only once I'm drifting off, that it occurs to me there might be consequences to what we've done.

But we love each other. And we were careful enough. I'm sure of it.

The pills work quickly. It seems like only a minute or two before I can feel myself falling asleep. The nightmares start immediately. They don't stop until morning.

part two

# chapter nine

"It's rain," I tell Dr. Miller. It's been almost a full month, and my dream journal is filled with notes. I've been keeping it beside my bed, along with a pen, and have gotten used to writing down everything I can remember as soon as I wake up. "I don't think it's *drowning* that I'm afraid of. I think it has something to do with rain."

She's so thrilled, she actually claps her hands. "Oh, Emily. We're making progress, aren't we?"

I nod, smiling. My parents aren't with me this time; they're at a board meeting. It's so much easier to talk with Dr. Miller when they aren't here—even though, no matter what, talking with Dr. Miller is *not* my favorite thing.

"Are there any memories from your childhood that you can think of having to do with rain?"

"It's more than rain," I add, flipping through the notebook. "I wrote it down right here: *violent rain, so hard that I can't breathe in it. Like standing in the shower, right under the spray, or being outside in a storm.*

She shakes her head, thinking. "You know, it could be something as simple as a harmless memory. Maybe you were traumatized by being in a car wash when you were a baby, Emily. The car wash used to *terrify* my kids."

This is the kind of crap from Dr. Miller that makes it hard for me to get along with her. I've been taking her pills and keeping a notebook for a month, and her suggestion is that I'm like this because of a *car wash*? "No," I say, biting my lip. I can't help but feel disappointed by her lack of insight. "That isn't it. This is vivid. I feel like I'm drowning." She's so off that it's giving me a headache.

"That's the nature of night terrors. They seem very real."

"It *is* real," I insist. "You aren't paying attention. I remember being in car washes when I was a kid. I wasn't afraid of them. Trust me, it was no car wash." I sit back hard on her sofa, sighing, glaring at her. "You're a big help, Dr. Miller. You ought to have your own television show."

She doesn't seem offended. Her demeanor is still friendly, irritating as hell. "Emily, I've never seen you so hostile before. Is something else going on?"

"No." I cross my arms. "I'm just tired of coming here and not getting anywhere." I sniffle. "And I think I'm getting sick."

She nods. "Well, it's almost flu season. As far as not getting anywhere, though—it's understandable that you would feel frustrated. What about the fire? Any progress in that area?"

I shake my head but don't say anything. All of a sudden, I've had enough of her. All I want to do is get out of here.

Dr. Miller rests her chin in her fists, elbows propped on her desk, and gives me a long look. "Okay, Emily. This is what I'm going to do. I'm going to increase your dosage a bit, and I want you to continue with the dream journal."

"Really? That's shocking. That's a surprising plan, I have to tell you. I never would have expected something like that from you."

She squints at me. "Are you sure there isn't something else you want to talk about?"

"*Yes*. I'm sure."

"Okay, then." She hands me a new prescription. "I'll see you in two weeks. In the meantime, my door is always open." She pauses. "Well, you know, metaphorically."

As I'm leaving her office, Stephanie jumps out of the way. She's been listening, I know, ear pressed to the door.

"Were you listening?" I snap.

"I didn't even know it was you at first. I have an appointment in ten minutes."

"Have fun. I can already tell you what she's going to say."

In spite of herself—Stephanie hasn't done much smiling since her father moved his mistress in a full eighteen hours after her mother was out of the house—Steph giggles. "What's she going to say, Em?"

I lower my voice to a deep, professional tone. I don't care that Dr. Miller can probably hear me from the other side of the door, which I've pulled shut. "Stephanie, what I'd like to do is increase the dosage of your medication a bit, and see you back here in two weeks."

Steph's grin fades just a little. "You're almost right. I've been seeing her twice a week."

"Oh."

"You don't know because you've been spending so much time with Del. And Renee." There's a hint of bitterness to her voice.

"Steph, Renee is great. So is Del." I lace my fingers through hers and we swing our arms back and forth as we stand in the hall together. "But you're my best friend." I smile at her. "We complete the quad."

She doesn't seem so sure. "Renee is just so . . . I don't know, Em, she's in the *tabloids*. And the whole thing with Bruce Graham is so weird."

"It's not that weird," I say. "She isn't close with her mom. It's different, that's all."

"Huh," Steph says. "You really like 'different,' don't you?"

I frown. "What does that mean?"

She ignores the question. "I have to go," she says. "I don't want to be late."

I give her a quick peck on the cheek. "Hey. You can talk to me anytime, you know. I love you."

"All right," she says, over her shoulder. "How about tonight, after lights out?"

I hesitate. I know she's testing me, assuming I'll be sneaking out to meet Del, like most nights.

When I don't say anything, Stephanie just shakes her head, walking into Dr. Miller's office without knocking. "That's what I thought."


I feel sicker and sicker as I make my way back to the dorm. My headache gets worse, and I start to feel nauseous. I have to rush into the bathroom as soon as I get inside. I throw up with *force*. Renee is in the stall next to me.

"Hey," she lilts, coming out of her stall, tapping on my door. "Got some morning sickness in there?"

I gag into the toilet. "You're funny."

And then I pause, thinking. It's just long enough that Renee says, "Emily—"

"No," I say. "There's no chance."

But she can hear the doubt in my voice.

"Come to my room," she says.

118

Hillary, as usual, is not around. Renee goes to Hillary's desk, opens the bottom drawer, and rifles around until she comes up with a pregnancy test.

"She's on these birth control pills where she only gets her period once every three months," Renee explains, tapping the box against her open palm. "So she's constantly paranoid that she's pregnant. I don't know why the moron doesn't just switch to regular pills."

"Won't she know it's missing? Won't she think—"

"If she says anything, I'll tell her I took it," Renee says. "I'll pay her back. It's not a big deal."

"I can't be pregnant," I tell her, trying to reassure myself at the same time.

"You slept with Del. I mean, you're sleeping with him. Right?"

I nod.

"Are you taking the pill? What are you using?"

I'm embarrassed to admit how irresponsible I've been, especially to someone like Renee, who I feel sure would never be so careless.

When I don't say anything, Renee raises one eyebrow. "Emily. You're going to take this into the bathroom and pee on it. Right now."

So that's what I do. My hands are shaking. My whole body is nauseous as I sit on one of the toilets in the girls' room. I've never taken a pregnancy test before; Renee, however, seems to be quite experienced with them. "It's digital," she tells me, "so there's no room for error. It will say 'pregnant,' or 'not pregnant.' It's designed to detect the hormone your body makes when it's pregnant. It can't pick up something that isn't there."

She stands guard outside the door to the bathroom while I pee. I'm shaking so badly that it's hard to imagine I've even peed enough on the stick to get a response.

Turns out, it was plenty. I stare at the results for a good thirty seconds. Then I throw up.

"Emily," Renee whispers, coming into the bathroom, locking the dead bolt behind her. "What the hell's going on?"

I open the stall door. I hand her the test.

She peers at the screen. "Oh shit."

"Oh shit is right."

"Emily . . . you're pregnant."

"I am."

"I can't believe this." She seems almost more shocked than I am. "You're the headmaster's *daughter*. Oh—oh, don't cry. Listen, you have to do something. You have to . . . um . . ." Her voice trails off. For the first time since I've known her, Renee seems completely at a loss. She takes a step backward, leans against the wall, then slides slowly to the floor and sits cross-legged, gazing at the test. "I guess you should tell someone."

"I'm telling you." I still can't believe any of this is real.

"Not me." She shakes her head. "What can I do? I can't do anything. You have to tell Del."

The thought alone makes me go cold. I shake my head. "No. No, no, no. I can't tell Del. I can't tell anyone. That would make it real." I reach out to grip her arm. "Oh my God . . . my parents . . ."

"Are you meeting Del tonight?" she asks.

I stare dumbly at the test. "We have other plans."

"What do you mean, you have *other plans*? What can be more important than this?"

When I sigh, my breath comes out shaky. I wipe tears from my eyes, my vision blurry. "We're breaking into my parents' house to steal Madeline's file. Remember, Del promised he'd find out what happened to her?"

"He said it would take two weeks," Renee says. "That was months ago."

I nod. "He's been distracted."

Someone is knocking at the bathroom door. It's Amanda Stream.

"Helloooo. I have to take a shower. Unlock the door already."

Renee slips the test up the sleeve of her shirt, not caring that she's getting my pee all over her arm. "My room," she says. "Now."


Once the door to Renee's room is locked, she sits on her bed for a moment, quiet, thinking hard. Finally she says, "Emily, what do you mean you're breaking into your parents' house?"

"I told you, we're going to steal Madeline's file. It will probably say what happened, and where she is now."

Renee shakes her head. "That's a bad idea. Why can't Del do it by himself? Why drag you into it?"

"Because it's my parents' house. If he's alone, it's breaking and entering, not to mention burglary. But if it's me and him . . . well, I guess it's just entering."

Renee studies me.

"What?" I ask. "What is it?"

"It's . . . okay. Emily, it's just that I cannot *believe* you were so irresponsible. What did you think would happen? You took health class. You're not stupid. How could you just *not use anything*?"

I stare at a coffee stain on her carpet. "I didn't say we *never* used anything. We did, sometimes."

"Sometimes isn't enough."

"I was going to get on the pill. We were careful most of the time."

" . . ."

" . . ."

"I don't think that's much of an excuse."

I look at her. "What?"

"You heard me. You both should have known better. And I'm not just talking about pregnancy. I'm talking about diseases. You don't know anything about who else Del has been with, do you? Did you even ask him?"

"No." I don't want to think about the other girls he's been with. But I know Renee is right; Del could have given me anything. "We didn't exactly talk about it."

"Uh-huh. Maybe you should have."

"I can't believe you're lecturing me right now! You sound like somebody's *mother*."

"Maybe I do. I don't care." She puts a hand to her forehead. "Oh my God. We're in an after-school special. Emily, what the hell are you going to do?"

"I don't know." I take a deep breath. "Would you stop? You're practically yelling at me. I feel stupid, okay? I feel naive and irresponsible and—and I don't know what I'm going to do." My nose is running all over the place. I use the sleeve of my uniform to wipe it. My hands are shaking. I feel like throwing up again. "Can you just be my friend? Please?"

"Oh, sweetie." She sighs. Her anger appears to fade. "You are in a *load* of trouble. Listen to me. You cannot break into your parents' house tonight. If Del loves you so much, why would he ask you to put yourself in a position like that?"

"I volunteered to come with him," I say. But it's a lie. Del is the one who convinced me this was the easiest way to get to Madeline's information.

"What time are you meeting him?" Renee asks.

"Eleven."

She shakes her head. "That's so late. You'll have to sneak out."

"We have to wait until my parents are in bed."

"Emily, you have got to tell him that you're pregnant."

I put my head down. "I don't know."

"What don't you know?"

I wipe my nose again. "I don't know anything. I'm in so much trouble, Renee."

She lets out another deep breath. "Okay. You need to sort this out. Go find Del right now, before dinner. Tell him you aren't coming with him later tonight. We don't need to know what happened to Madeline, not right now. You've got bigger problems. Talk to him. He's in just as much trouble as you are. I mean, it's his baby, too."

I nod dumbly. "Talk to him," I repeat.

"Yes," she says.

I stand up. I can't think or see straight. I feel dizzy and sick and dirty. I use the duct tape along the floor in Renee's room to guide me toward the door.

"Good luck," she says. "I'll wait up for you."


But, of course, I don't listen to Renee. Instead, I convince myself that things can't get any worse; unplanned teenage pregnancy trumps breaking and entering any day.

Once the clock hits eleven that night, I sneak out of the dorm as quietly as possible. I'm wearing a heavy coat over my pj's. It's almost Thanksgiving, and the warm spell is long over. Outside there's a light snow beginning to fall, covering the campus in a pretty blanket of white. I love Stonybrook Academy because it's my home, but I'll always love Connecticut for its weather, its refusal to be meek.

Del meets me on the patio outside my dorm.

"I told you to dress in black," he says. He's wearing a black sweat suit and black ski mask. He's obviously more experienced at things like this than I am; beneath my gray coat, my pajamas are pink.

We've been planning this for weeks. Over the weekend, I

intentionally left my copy of *For Whom the Bell Tolls* in my bedroom at home. During study hall, when my dad was making rounds at the dorms, I went back to get it. But I also got something else: the key to the filing cabinets in his home office. I gave it to Del, who snuck off campus right away to have a copy made. Then, before study hall was over, I went back to my parents' house and returned the original.

Without speaking, we sneak across campus, avoiding Digger's usual routes. We let ourselves into my parents' house using my key. The whole process feels surreal. Aside from the nausea, I can hardly feel my body. Every time I look at Del, he seems different somehow. Maybe Renee was right. Maybe it was wrong of him to involve me in something like this. I don't care, though. Things can't possibly get any worse.

Once we're inside, we slip off our shoes and carry them in our hands. The house is over two hundred years old, all creaky woodwork and tiny crevasses. Normally, this is why I love it, but tonight I can feel my heart beating hard in my chest, terrified that our steps might make a sound.

But the house is dark, all the lights out. Once we're in my dad's office, Del peels off his mask, and we take a few moments to rest in the space beneath my father's desk, catching our breath.

"We made it," he whispers, grinning at me.

I nod. "It should only take a second. Then we can go, right?"

"Right." I'm amazed by how nervous he *isn't*. It seems like this is just any old thing to him; does he even realize how much trouble we could get into? Stonybrook is loose when it comes to its rules, but breaking into the headmaster's house is different. I'm not sure how that wouldn't justify immediate expulsion for anyone but me.

I wait under my dad's desk while Del, key in hand, goes to the filing cabinets at the opposite side of the room. I listen as he works,

finding the right drawer almost immediately, slipping in the key, and—holding a penlight between his teeth—searching calmly through the files until he finds what we're looking for. Then I hear him shut the drawer, relock it, and move to another cabinet.

"What are you doing?" I whisper.

"Taking some other files," he hisses. "If it's just Madeline's, your dad is going to know right away who was responsible." He pauses. "I don't want to get you in trouble."

The thought almost makes me laugh. Almost.

I listen as he rifles through some more files. Is he looking for something in particular? It seems to take forever. Finally, he slips back beneath the desk. His breath is calm and even. He gives me a big, satisfied smile.

"I got it," he whispers. "It's thick—there's gotta be something in here—"

"Shhh!" I hold a finger to my lips.

There's someone on the stairs.

"What time is it?" I whisper.

"It has to be close to midnight," he whispers back. "Didn't you tell me your parents are in bed before ten?"

Taking the files from him without a glance, my whole body shaking, I slip the folders up my shirt, securing them beneath my bra. We're going to get caught. I'm pregnant, and we're going to get caught, and Del is going to get kicked out. Renee was right. I should have backed out of this.

I can tell from the footsteps that it's my mother, which is a relief, even though I have no idea what she's doing up at this hour. Maybe she's getting a glass of water. At least it's not my dad. Oh God. I can't imagine how my father would react if he found us here. There would be yelling, that's for sure.

"What's she—"

"Shh." I cock my head, listening. I hear my mother bundling

up in the hallway. I picture her putting on her coat and boots, her suede hat with the earflaps and sheepskin lining that she's had since I was a kid. Then she patters into the kitchen, rustles around for a few moments, until we hear the sliding glass door open. It leads to a stone porch that wraps all the way around the back of the house.

Is it really possible? It can't be. But then we see her outside, standing all by herself in the still night. She's smoking again, secretly. She probably waited until my dad was fast asleep, and she's probably so bundled up that he'll never smell it on her in the morning. I can't believe my mother is hiding something so huge from me—from *everyone*.

I whisper all of this to Del, explaining how bizarre it is for my mother to be behaving this way, expecting him to be just as shocked as I am. Instead, he gets on his hands and knees, crawls slightly out from beneath the desk, and cranes his neck to get a better look out my father's sliding glass doors, which lead to the same porch.

"You're right," he says. "She *is* smoking. God, she must be freezing out there."

"I can't believe this. How does somebody keep a secret like that for so long? She must have been doing this for years, don't you think? People don't just start smoking when they're middle-aged."

Del only shrugs. "Everyone has secrets, Emily. So your mom smokes. Big deal."

I don't say anything. I feel overwhelmed by everything that's going on.

He blinks at me, his eyes flashing in the darkness. "Emily? You look upset."

*I'm pregnant. I'm sure of it. I took a test. We've been stupid.*
*You're pregnant?*

126

*Yes.*

*Okay. I'll take care of you. There's nothing to worry about.*

I start to cry, trying not to make too much noise. From the kitchen, I hear the sliding glass door open, my mother hurrying to put her things back. I'm not worried that she'll sense something's amiss in the house and come in here; she's got her own secret to take care of right now.

"Emily. What's the matter?"

I shake my head. "We have to get out of here."

"Well, yeah." He pauses. "Are you sure there isn't something else? Hey, calm down."

He puts his arms around me. I could tell him right now. I could tell him the truth, and he would understand, and he would help me. Why don't I? Why can't I?

"Emily, you're shaking. We're leaving now, all right? Everything will be okay."

I shake my head. "Don't say that."

He frowns. "Why not?"

"Because it's not okay. Nothing is going to be okay. Let's go, all right? Let's get out of here."

He nods slowly. "All right. Sure." And with his arms still around me, he reaches down to squeeze my hand. "Hey—don't cry. Nobody saw us. Everything will be all right." He gives me another big grin. "We did it."

"We sure did," I whisper.


When we get back to my dorm, we stand outside and I pull the files out from beneath my bra. The top one is Madeline's. I don't even look at the others.

I'm still shaking like crazy. "Do something with these," I say, shoving the others at him. "Destroy them or something, okay?"

He nods, taking them from me without question. Before he leaves, he turns around to ask, "Emily? You're acting weird. Is there something you want to talk about?"

"No," I say. "I'm fine. I'm good." I pause. "Good night, Del."


Once I'm back inside, Renee and I sit in the hallway together and stare at the closed file.

"I can't believe we did it," I whisper. "We *broke and entered*. We stole from my *father*."

"I can't believe anything about tonight," she murmurs, putting her arm around me as I rest my head against her body. "I can't believe you went with him. I told you not to go! Did you tell him?"

"No."

She is quiet. Finally, with doubt in her voice, she says, "Everything will work out."

*No, it won't.* "I don't want to talk about it."

"Okay. I'm sorry."

"So." I swallow. "Should we open it?"

Renee licks her lips. It's almost as though the anticipation is more exciting than what might be inside, even though I know we're both dying to find out.

"Tomorrow," she says. "Let's wait until then."

"Are you kidding?"

"No. I'll keep it with me so you can't get in any more trouble. I'll keep it hidden really well. Don't worry. Your dad won't even notice it's gone."

"Okay." I hand her the folder. "For your safekeeping until tomorrow."

"Study hall? Fifth period?"

"All right. Meet me in the library. You won't look at it before then?"

"No. Of course I won't." There's no way I'd trust anyone else with something this big, but somehow I know Renee won't touch it. We've been through so much together already. I know she'll wait for me.

We both stand up and give each other a long hug. She holds the folder close to her chest. The tab on it reads, "Moon-Park, Madeline."

"See you tomorrow," she whispers.

"See you tomorrow."

"Sleep tight."

But we both know there isn't going to be much sleep tonight. Not for Renee, and not for me. How can I possibly sleep when everything is about to change, and I have no idea what's going to happen? There is no control anymore. There's another life here in the hall with us, one that only she and I know about. I know we will both lie awake all night, thinking about it, about the files Del and I have stolen, about how it will be so much colder soon, and there's nothing we can do to take back any of it.

# chapter ten

As it turns out, there isn't anything interesting in Madeline's file. The entire process of breaking into my parents' house was for nothing.

"We'll keep trying," Renee tells me, as we're sitting in the back of the library together, both of us staring in disappointment at the open folder. All it contains is a simple demographic sheet, a copy of Madeline's transcripts, and a receipt showing that her tuition was paid in full for the previous year. Considering the risk we took by breaking into my parents' house, the payoff is awfully disappointing. If anything, some more information about what happened to her would have been a welcome distraction from the misery of reality.

The night before everyone leaves for winter break, there's a big holiday party at my parents' house. It happens every year. We're all supposed to get dressed up, and we sing Christmas carols, and everyone eats appetizers and finger sandwiches from trays the cafeteria staff and the Diggers carry around throughout the evening.

It's a very idyllic, Christmas-in-Connecticut kind of thing, and I used to love it.

But not this year. This year, the dynamic is awkward at best. I have known that I'm pregnant for almost a month. Aside from Renee, nobody else knows. I'm still getting used to the idea myself, waking up from my nightmares every morning to the brief possibility that it has all been part of a bad dream. But it hasn't; instead, my entire *life* has become a bad dream.

It's my last night to see Del before he leaves for break, and even though I know he's at the party, I can't talk to him because my father always seems to be around, watching me, keeping an eye out to make sure Del isn't bothering me. If he only knew.

So while everyone else is mingling, I head upstairs to my bedroom to get away from things. It's my house, after all; I should be able to go wherever I want.

I haven't been in my room more than thirty seconds when there's a light tap on the door. I hold completely still, willing whoever it is to go away. *Anyone*, I think to myself, *but Stephanie . . . or Del . . . or my parents.* But then the door opens and Renee walks in, and I feel a strange sense of relief that it's her. Renee is the only person I feel truly comfortable around right now.

"Did you follow me up here?" I ask, lying down on my bed, staring at the ceiling.

"Wow," she says, ignoring the question, "this is like stepping into a time warp."

She's right. My bedroom hasn't changed since I was a little girl. The carpet is a light pink shag whose color matches the billowy curtains that are held back with ornate hooks, revealing the snowstorm outside. We're supposed to have at least six inches on the ground by morning.

On one wall of my room, there's a desk and dresser with hutches

that still hold all of my favorite childhood books: the Boxcar Children series, the American Girl books, and even some old Nancy Drews. The walls of my room are decorated with shelves holding my old doll collections; above my bed, there are hand-painted letters on the wall (courtesy of my mother) that spell out EMILY.

And then there's my bed itself. It's a twin mattress, complete with a pink-and-purple-striped bed skirt, a thick pink comforter, and a canopy. At sixteen, I almost don't fit in it anymore.

It's funny—my parents' whole house has been given the once-over by a personal decorator. Every other room has the latest furniture and accessories, to the point where the place looks like something out of a magazine. Every room, that is, except mine. Mine looks like it belongs to a ten-year-old. And I've never heard my parents discussing any plans to change it, almost like they still think I'm a little girl. It's not like I've ever asked them, though. Since seventh grade, I've always felt that my *real* room was my dorm room. But now that I'm thinking about it, the whole setup seems a little bit creepy.

Renee seems to feel the same way. She takes a long look around, shudders, but doesn't say anything more. She sits down beside me on the bed. She's wearing a red velvet Christmas dress that looks like it came from the Goodwill. Her hair is messy—it almost doesn't look *brushed*—and I notice that her fingernails are bare and raw looking, like she's been chewing on her cuticles.

Somehow she still looks beautiful. "These parties are great, Emily," she says. "They're so innocent, you know? I love eating those little Christmas cookies and singing 'Rudolph the Red-Nosed Reindeer' and pretending that we're all just kids with no problems." She pauses. "Just for one night. Everyone deserves that, don't they?" Before I can answer, she nudges me and says, "*You* deserve it. Besides, everyone wants to hear you sing."

Since I was a kid, way before I was even a student at

Stonybrook, I've been expected to sing a song at the Christmas party. It's always something light and easy, like "Here Comes Santa Claus" or "Jingle Bells." Even though I'm shy about singing in public, singing at the party has always felt comfortable and intimate, like I'm singing for my family. This year, though, it's the last thing I want to do. It's impossible for me to pretend that everything is normal. All I want is to hide.

"I don't want to sing," I tell her. "I want this night to be over. I want everyone to go home."

"People are wondering where you are." Renee pulls a hand through her hair, tugging at a knot. "It will look weird if you stay up here."

I pretend not to hear her. I don't want to go anywhere. "You're leaving for New York tomorrow?" I ask.

"Uh-huh." She continues to tug.

"Will you see your mom?"

"Probably not. But it's okay."

There is a long silence. I realize that I'm trying not to cry. It's not that I feel sorry for Renee—she certainly doesn't seem upset by her situation—or even sorry for myself. It's that everything is changing so quickly, and there's nothing I can do about it. If someone had told me at the beginning of the school year, just four months ago, that I'd be sitting in my bedroom with Renee the night before winter break, trying to escape the holiday party, I wouldn't have believed it for a second. Four months ago, life was so manageable and easy, so *predictable*. Then everything changed so suddenly. I am going to have a baby. I can't even say the words out loud.

"Things are not okay," I tell her. "My life is falling apart. I don't know who my friends are anymore, I don't know who I can trust. I don't know how Del is going to react when I tell him. And I can't stand Stephanie half the time."

133

Renee giggles. "That's shocking. She's so likable."

I can't help but smile. "She has good qualities."

"Like what?" Renee seems genuinely curious.

"She's beautiful."

"That's not a personality trait."

"We've been best friends since seventh grade."

"Things change. People grow apart."

"I know that. But I don't *want* everything to change."

Renee studies me. "I'm sorry," she says.

"You don't need to be sorry. It wasn't your fault."

"I know. I'm still sorry." She pauses. "I just came up to get you, you know. We have to go back downstairs. Your presence is being demanded."

I close my eyes, feeling sick to my stomach. "I don't want to go."

"Too bad," she says. She takes me by the hand and gently tugs me off the bed. "Come on, sweetie. You don't have a choice."

When I reach the foot of the stairs, I practically run into Ethan. He's wearing a pair of plush reindeer antlers on his head, and a big grin.

"Emily!" he says, a shade too enthusiastic. "There you are!"

"Here I am," I say, forcing myself to smile.

He looks around the room, his eyes wide and glassy. "Isn't this a freaking *fantastic* party?"

I catch a whiff of something on his breath. It smells like liquor.

"Ethan?" I squint at him. "Is something wrong?"

"What could possibly be wrong?" he asks. "Tomorrow morning I'm leaving for Colorado, where I will officially spend my first Christmas as a child of divorce. Just me, my mom, and Stephanie. My father isn't even going to see his kids. He's got a *new* family." His cheeks are flushed. "Hey," he says brightly, "you never gave

me an answer about our band. Are you going to sing for us?" Before I can answer, he continues. "Because we've been practicing without you. Kelly Reulens has been singing for us."

"She has?" I get an achy sense of jealousy. Kelly Reulens is a soprano. She's a senior. "Why didn't you tell me?"

He hiccups. "Because I'm not supposed to talk to you."

"What?"

"Yeah, I'm not allowed. Del told me to stay away from you." He pauses. "Maybe I shouldn't be telling you this." He brings his voice to a loud whisper. "Let's keep that information between the two of us, okay?" And he gives me an exaggerated wink. His eye-lashes are long and thick. His face gleams with sweat. *He is*, I think, *the sweetest person I know.*

And even though it's obvious that he's really drunk, Ethan is still boyish and kind of adorable and absolutely exuding charm. He'll probably be incredibly embarrassed later on, but there's really no need.

He nods his head, grinning at the sound of the bells jingling on his antlers. A stray piece of hair slips across his forehead and into his eyes. Without thinking about it, I reach to brush it away.

Ethan flinches as my hand touches his face. I pull quickly away. What am I *doing*? Del, I realize, could be *anywhere*. He's probably watching me right now.

I look past Ethan to see Stephanie—who's wearing an identical set of reindeer antlers—staring us down. Her pouty lips are pursed in agitation. She's practically glaring at me, and I'm not sure why. Lately, it seems as if she's much happier being miserable.

"Ethan," I say, trying to keep my tone light, even as I'm feeling nauseous and sweaty, "I'm sorry I can't be in your band. You can talk to me, though. Don't listen to Del." I lower my voice. "What's the matter with you, anyway? Why are you so drunk? You hardly ever drink like this."

"Why shouldn't I drink?" he asks. "Everybody else does it."

I don't have an answer for him, but Ethan's never been the type to bend to peer pressure before. And I'd certainly prefer it if he were sober right now. What is going on? Why is the entire world crumbling? Things are definitely going askew if Ethan Prince is drunk at the headmaster's house.

"Why won't you be in my band?" he demands, his voice a shade too loud. "You think I'm boring, don't you?"

"Ethan, no, it isn't that." I feel like I have to get him out of here, and *fast*, before someone else—someone like my father—notices him.

"Why isn't it enough for someone to be a nice guy?" he asks. He gives me a curious look. "Why doesn't that get me anywhere?"

His antlers have slipped from his head a little bit, and are resting at an awkward angle. He looks sad.

The whole room seems to slip away as I take in what he's saying, the way he's looking at me. My body goes a little numb as I really look at him, into his big eyes, as he stares at me. *Oh, Ethan.*

"I really am sorry I can't be in your band," I tell him. "But it's impossible right now." I pause. "Everything is very complicated."

He lifts a hand to scratch his head. The antlers slip a little farther. He looks disheveled, defeated, much more like a little kid than I've ever noticed before. I want to hug him, but I know I shouldn't.

"I want you to know," he says, "that I'm not as boring as you think."

"I know that," I say, breaking out in a cold sweat as I look around the room. "I know you aren't." From the corner of my eye, I can see Stephanie approaching. "You need to get out of here," I tell him.

"Why?" He frowns.

Before I can answer, Steph is standing beside us. "What's going on?" she asks.

I step away from Ethan. "He's drunk," I whisper. "You should take him back to Winchester."

She nods. Her antlers, which also have tiny bells attached to their ends, jingle in agreement. "Okay." She takes him by the arm. "Come on."

As they're leaving, she turns to look at me. "Thanks, Emily."

And then they're gone. If I don't go back to the dorm tonight, I realize, I won't see her until after the New Year. She didn't even say good-bye.


Del seems to have disappeared, and the party drags on as I try to stay by myself as much as possible, while simultaneously keeping an eye out for him. But he doesn't show, not until well after midnight, once the party is over and I've been forced to sing "Rudolph the Red-Nosed Reindeer" to a room full of people who have no idea what a mess my life is.

It's still snowing outside, a few inches accumulated since the beginning of the evening, and I'm watching as the flakes drift toward the ground in the moonlight, when a snowball hits my window.

Immediately, I know it's him. I hurry downstairs to let him in. My parents have been in bed for over an hour, but I'm still nervous they'll wake up.

"Where have you been?" I ask, pulling him inside. "Hurry up, before someone sees you."

He's not wearing a coat. His head is covered in snowflakes; his cheeks are bright red. He looks so alive and gorgeous that I can hardly stand it.

We sneak upstairs to my room. I lock the door, and we sit cross-legged on top of the covers on my tiny bed, our knees touching.

Del reaches out to touch my hair. He's always doing that. "How was your night?" he asks.

"It was fine. Where were you?"

"I was around." There's a pause. Then he says, "Ethan Prince is back at my dorm, sick as hell. He's passed out on the bathroom floor."

"Oh, really?"

Del nods. "Uh-huh. I saw you talking to him tonight."

The idea that he was sneaking around, watching me, is slightly annoying. "What does that matter? We were only talking."

"He'd steal you in a second if he could." I see the slightest flicker of insecurity in Del's expression. "Could he?" he asks.

I almost laugh. After all, I'm *pregnant*. But Del doesn't know that.

Instead I ask, "Did you tell him he couldn't talk to me?"

He gives me an innocent look. "I don't remember saying that."

He's lying, which annoys me even more. "Ethan remembers."

"Maybe I did. It's possible."

"Who are you to say who I can and can't talk to?" My voice is light, but only because I'm nervous. I don't want to get into a fight. But I find myself imagining Ethan over in Winchester, on the bathroom floor, sick and lonely. He doesn't deserve to feel that way.

He stares at me. "I'm your boyfriend, Emily."

It's so quiet in my room, I can almost hear the snow falling onto the ground outside. The whole world seems muffled.

"Emily," Del asks, "what's the matter?"

I could tell him now. The words are on the tip of my tongue.

But then I realize he's not going to know how to help me.

Maybe he'll only make things worse. I need to figure out a solution first, on my own.

Tears are stinging the corners of my eyes, though; I have to tell him *something*. "I had my precalc final today," I say.

"Oh, right. How did it go?"

I shake my head. "Not good. I'm pretty sure I failed."

"Emily," he says, "but it's so easy. Didn't you study?"

"Yes! I studied and studied." I'm openly crying now, wiping tears from my eyes. "But when I look at the test, it's like I've never even seen the material before."

"I'll help you," he says. "Don't worry."

I sniffle. "I can barely do basic algebra. I don't know how I'm supposed to make it through precalc, let alone calculus next year."

"So you take statistics instead. It's no big deal." He frowns. "Why are you freaking out?"

"I'm not freaking out."

"Yes, you are. Emily, are you sure there isn't anything else going on?" He blinks. "Did Ethan say something to you? Did he do anything?"

"Would you stop talking about Ethan? I don't want to fight with you."

"Then stop fighting."

"..."

"..."

"Listen, precalc will be fine. Don't worry."

"Uh-uh." I stare at my comforter. "I'm too stupid. I can't do it."

"You *can*. I'm telling you, it's easy." He pauses, like he's thinking about something. "Math is just a matter of manipulation. There's nothing to it."

I sniffle. "What do you mean?"

"I mean, it's just a matter of manipulating the variables. Once

you figure out how to do that"—he spreads his hands, giving me a bright smile—"everything else is easy."

His words, for some reason, make me break out in a sweat.

"What did you say?"

"I said it's just a matter of manipulation."

"Uh-huh." He thinks everything is so easy. He always finds a way to manipulate things to get exactly what he wants.

An awkwardness begins to spread in the space between us. We stare at each other.

He glances at the clock on my nightstand. "I hate to say this, but I should go soon. I have to pack. My parents will be here in the morning."

"Okay." I feel almost relieved that he's leaving. I just want to be alone.

I give him a kiss. "You should go, then." I force a smile, even though I'm sick to my stomach, and the kerosene smell that's always clinging to Del is making it more intense. "I'll see you next year."

Since I'm pregnant, I obviously can't take Dr. Miller's pills any-more. As a result, the nightmares come fast and intense, making sleep almost impossible. With campus all but deserted, my nights are spent alone. More than once, way after she's supposedly gone to sleep, I see my mother through my window, sneaking outside to smoke. Each time it happens, I consider confronting her. But what would be the point? I've got secrets bigger than hers.

Our house phone rings a few days before Christmas. I recognize the area code as a Colorado exchange. Stephanie.

I pick up the phone and say, "What's up, sweetie?"

There's a long pause.

"Emily? Is that you?"

It's Ethan.

I can feel the blood rising to my cheeks. "Ethan. Yes, it's me. Is everything okay? Why are you—"

"Why am I calling you? I wanted to apologize."

"For what?" I ask, pretending to be oblivious.

"For the Christmas party. You know I was drunk. Steph is so pissed about it, she's barely been talking to me. She said I made a total fool of myself."

"Oh, it wasn't that bad."

I can hear the tension in his voice. I imagine him at home in Colorado, with his mom and Steph, spending their first Christmas without their dad. I feel sorry for him—and for Stephanie—and so selfish, in a way, for how distant I've been toward all my friends. Unlike them, at least I can say I've got my family.

"So I bet you're missing Del," he says.

"Yes," I admit. "I am." I imagine how furious Del would be if he knew I was talking to Ethan. And I can't quite explain it, but somehow the fact makes me feel almost satisfied. Why should Del get to tell me who I can and can't talk to? Beyond that, I'm excited to be talking to Ethan. He might have gotten drunk and acted stupid, but he's still *Ethan Prince*.

"Your dad still doesn't want you two together?"

"Nope."

"That must be hard." He swallows. "I mean, to not be able to really be with the one person you want more than anyone else."

I don't know what to say to him. I've *never* had a telephone conversation with Ethan before. He's been so strange in the past few months; is it really possible that he likes me? It seems that way. Not that it matters—it isn't like anything could ever come of it now. Ethan might not know it yet, but I am *trouble*.

"So . . . ," I say, trying to move the conversation along, "is Steph there? Can I talk to her?"

"Oh," he says, his tone almost surprised, "no. She's not here."

"She isn't?" The awkwardness takes a leap. "Um. Does she know that you're calling me?"

"Well, no. Should she?"

"..."

"..."

"Ethan . . . look, I should probably go. Don't worry about the Christmas party, okay?"

"Thanks, Emily. There's just one other thing."

*Oh, God.* "What is it?"

"I missed hearing you sing. After I left, what song did you sing?" I can *hear* him smiling. "I remember last year you sang 'The Twelve Days of Christmas.' It was great. And the year before that, you sang 'Jingle Bells.'"

I can't believe he remembers all of this. "Thank you," I tell him. "This year, I sang 'Rudolph the Red-Nosed Reindeer.'"

"Emily?"

"Yes?"

There's another long pause. "I just wanted to say merry Christmas. That's all."

"Oh. Well, merry Christmas to you, too."

We hang up. I stand in the hallway for a few long moments, staring at the phone, thinking, *what was* that *all about*? But then I realize that I'm smiling.

When I go back up to my room, there's an e-mail waiting for me from Del.

Emily,

How's your lonely life on campus so far? I miss you terribly. My parents are going out of their way to make our first Christmas as a "real" family a superspecial one. I was trying to figure out what

to get you as a present, and then it occurred to me. Attached is everything you need to ace precalc for the rest of the year. Don't ask me how I got it; if I told you, then I'd have to kill you . . .

I'll be in touch sooner than later. Merry Christmas.

All my love.

I open the attachment. I put a hand to my mouth. It's a huge PDF document, and from what I can tell it's every quiz and test for precalc for the rest of the year. With all the answers filled in.

I'd like to believe that it's the pregnancy making me feel a little sick to my stomach as I stare at the document on my computer screen. But it's not.

I am the headmaster's daughter. I might not be a great student, and I might be seeing Del behind my father's back—and, of course, there's the whole illegitimate baby thing—but I am sixteen years old and I've never cheated on a test in my life. I know it sounds absurd, but if I *did* cheat, and I got caught, I couldn't stand how it would humiliate my dad. I have already let him down so much, and he doesn't even know it.

How could Del think I would ever use those answers? What is the matter with him? I delete the file. Then I lie on my bed, the door to my room locked, and stare up at my canopy. Without thinking about it, I start to sing quietly.

*Dashing through the snow . . .*

I remember that night at the party, although it seems like it was much more than two years ago. I remember the way my friends and I all wore Santa hats and the way my father tugged me under the mistletoe to plant a kiss on my cheek. I remember drinking nonalcoholic eggnog with Steph, Franny, and Grace until our stomachs hurt so much that we could barely move.

There is my life before Del, and there is my life with Del. The thought begs the question: what will life be like after Del? Eventually, something has to give. Something will break. Someone will learn my secret.

For now, I take comfort in the fact that my door is locked, that campus is deserted, and that my parents are both downstairs, with no idea of what's truly going on in my life.

I open my eyes and look around at my room, which has not changed for as long as I can remember. I try to ignore the fact that my legs have grown almost too long for the bed.

From downstairs, my mother begins to play the piano. I can hear her just well enough to make out the song: it's "Junk," by Paul McCartney.

I join in with my voice. It's the strangest feeling, there in my bedroom: she probably can't hear me, and I can barely hear her, but for the moment we are in harmony. Just for the moment.

# chapter eleven

On the Sunday before school starts after winter break, I go back to my dorm after breakfast to wait for my roommates. Since they're taking the school van from the airport together, they all arrive on campus at the same time.

They sound like elephants on the stairs. I've been lying in bed, holding my belly with one hand, sweating in the dry heat of our room, waiting. I didn't want to be at home with my parents, but now I don't want to be here with my friends. There's nowhere to go.

"We're baaaack!" Grace bursts through the door. "Emily! You're here!"

I force myself to smile. "Hi, sweetie. How was your Christmas?"

"Super." Grace tugs off her hat and fluffs her hair. "How was yours?"

"It was good." It was torture. I'd spent most of my time hiding in my room. My parents think I'm still upset with them about not being allowed to see Del.

Franny hurries in next. "Whatever you do," she says to me, "don't ask Stephanie how her vacation was."

I'm out of bed. Grace gives me a hug. "Are you okay, Em?" she asks. "You look pale."

"I'm fine. I only seem pale because you're so tan." Her cheeks are red and windburned. She looks healthy. She's probably been skiing a lot.

"Did you miss Del?" Just as Franny asks the question, Stephanie strolls into the room. She doesn't look healthy like Grace. She doesn't even look well rested. She goes straight to her room, drops her luggage on the floor, opens the window, and lights a cigarette.

"Hey." More than ever now, I don't want to be around smoke. "Please don't do that in here."

"It's my room," she says. "I can do what I want."

"It's our quad," I say, "and I'm asking you to stop."

She takes one last drag from the cigarette before tossing it out the window. "There," she says, glowering. "Happy?"

"You just walked in a minute ago. Are you seriously in a bad mood already?" I pause. "Would you rather be at home?"

Her hair is in a messy pile on her head. She pulls it free, and it spills over her shoulders and down her back. Even when she's angry, her eyes puffy, her skin dry, Steph is beautiful. "I would rather be at home with my family," she pronounces, "but that's impossible." She closes her eyes for a moment. Then she asks, "How about you, Emily? Did you have a perfect Christmas with your perfect parents?"

I could laugh. I want to cry.

I am terrified for school to start again. As soon as everyone is back from break, I feel overwhelmed by this kind of paralysis, an inability to act or fully understand, to tell anyone but Renee. At first, I'm anticipating that my body will go through everything a person sees in the movies and on television: morning sickness, odd food cravings, mood swings, weight gain. But instead, after a month of nausea, all I'm left with is the constant feeling that

something isn't quite right in my body, the reminder that something is growing inside me. I couldn't be more scared. I still have no idea how I'm going to tell Del.

On the weekends, when we can sneak away for appointments, Renee drives me to the free clinic in New Haven, where I hear a heartbeat and see a tiny blur on a black-and-white screen that appears hopelessly outdated. It doesn't look like a baby; it seems impossible that the wriggling, breathing form I see onscreen is inside me. When the ultrasound tech asks if I want to know the gender, I just shake my head. At almost every appointment, tears run quietly down my face. Renee has gotten over her initial anger, and now she is not judgmental or pressuring or anything that you might expect a person to be. She just stays beside me, holds my hand, and waits for things to sink in.

By mid-January, I am at the end of my first trimester and have not gained any weight; in fact, I've lost three pounds.

"It's not unusual," the doctor at the clinic tells me. Her name is Dr. Hwang. She's a soft-spoken, younger-looking Asian woman. I like her. She's been nice to me since my first visit, when I confessed that I didn't know what I wanted to do, that I hadn't told the father or my parents, and that the only other person who knew was Renee, sitting beside me in the room, looking blankly ahead, almost as though she felt she had no right to be there. But I wanted her with me; I don't think I could have gone by myself.

At the end of the month, Dr. Hwang brings me into her office for what she calls "a gentle talk." I know what's coming.

"Emily," she says, my medical file sitting open on her desk, "it's time for you to start thinking about a few things."

I only nod. I can feel the tears coming again.

"When you first came in, you made it clear you were opposed to termination."

The idea had been unthinkable. It's funny; before now, I've

always figured I'm pro-choice. But once it happened to me, I realized that I'm only sixteen. Sixteen trumps pro-anything. Sixteen means a decision this large is too much for one girl to grasp. So all I could figure to do at the time was refuse the option, and move on.

Dr. Hwang gives me a book called *Stacy's Story*, which is really more of a thick, staple-bound pamphlet about a girl like me who gets herself knocked up by a nice boy at school after their condom breaks. I can't say how many times I've gone over the first night I slept with Del, and the way I blindly believed that nothing could go wrong. And even as things between us have started to feel unsteady and uncertain, ever since the night before Christmas break, I've continued to meet him at night. I continue to love him as I withhold the knowledge of what we've created, and try to ignore the sneaking suspicion that he may not be all I hope he is. We're stupid, I know; we've done the dumbest thing two teenagers in love can do. The longer my pregnancy progresses, the more afraid I am to tell him what's happening. I don't know how he's going to respond. And my parents—my God, I haven't even *considered* telling my parents.

In *Stacy's Story*, she tells her boyfriend, Mike, as soon as she finds out she's pregnant. At first, Mike (a football player with a heart of gold) is scared, and tries to convince her not to keep the baby. But then he "comes to his senses" and assures her that he'll support her in any decision she makes. And when Stacy tells her parents, even though they're angry and disappointed at first, they eventually forgive her. At the end of the story, Stacy's baby is adopted by a young, infertile couple who couldn't be happier to receive their little bundle of joy, and life goes on for Stacy with regular therapy and oral contraception. I might be over my morning sickness, but the story alone is enough to make me want to puke. I can't help but wonder if there's a different pamphlet for teenagers who choose another option.

Renee does me the favor of throwing *Stacy's Story* out the window of her car as we're driving down Route 1 on our way back to campus.

"Yuck," she says, watching it flutter in the wind as we drive away. "You know who Mike reminds me of? That guy—you know—Stephanie's brother. What's his name? Evan?"

I'm *floored* that she could have been going to Stonybrook since the seventh grade without knowing exactly who Ethan Prince is.

"Ethan," I correct her. "You know he's Stephanie's twin brother. Renee. Seriously. How could you not know him?"

She shrugs. "He's so . . . so *wholesome*. So apple pie."

The description annoys me. She doesn't even know his name. I think back to the phone call he made to me over Christmas break, to the way he remembered all the songs I'd sung at previous holiday parties. "He's really nice," I tell her. "He's actually, like, the nicest guy I know."

She raises a single eyebrow, looks at me from the corner of her eye. "Oh yeah? Since when do you care about someone being a nice guy?"

The question stings. "I care about things like that."

"Uh-huh." She glances at my belly. "Sure you do."

" . . ."

" . . ."

"You know, Emily," she says, changing the subject, "it's possible you could go the rest of the school year without anyone even knowing that you're pregnant."

I take a deep breath. I'm relieved that we're talking about my pregnancy instead of Ethan or Del. It bothers me that we're talking about Ethan at all. I'm with Del. I love Del. Even though I've been hiding the truth from him for months.

I can't say I haven't thought about trying to hide the baby somehow. The idea seems crazy on the surface, but is it really? My

stomach is still pretty flat. I certainly don't look pregnant yet. By the time school lets out, I'll be a little over six months along. I've seen pictures of women at six months in the clinic; if I keep my weight down and wear loose shirts, the deception seems doable.

"What about the summer?" I ask. "Eventually, my parents are going to notice. And there's always . . . you know. The baby."

"I was thinking about that," Renee says. "School lets out the first week in May. Why don't you come and stay with me in the city this summer?"

"With you? In New York?"

She nods.

"I thought you were taking summer classes at Yale."

"I was going to. But I can wait until next year."

I stare at her. "Won't I be a drag? Besides, I'll be visibly pregnant. Won't your mom—"

"I don't live with my mom in the summers," she says. "I live with Bruce."

"Even so. What's he going to say about you bringing home your new knocked-up friend?"

She hesitates. "It'll be fine."

"You already told him, didn't you?"

When Renee doesn't say anything, I know the answer. The fact seems surreal: I imagine Bruce Graham sitting in a tux on a leather sofa, drinking a dry martini, surrounded by his Academy Award and Emmy statuettes, pondering the ramifications of sheltering a pregnant teenager for the summer.

"Emily. You're not going to keep this baby, are you?"

I shake my head. "I don't think so, no."

"You're gonna do things Stacy-style?"

I can't help but giggle. "I guess so. And then I'll live happily

ever after, and come back to school in the fall and support Del at the games when he makes first-string quarterback, and everything will be—"

"Perfect," Renee finishes.

It's ridiculous. I doubt Del has ever held a football in his life.

Renee puts on her signal to turn into campus. "So you'll come?"

"I have to ask my parents."

She nods. "Your dad isn't crazy about me."

I bite my lip. "Bruce Graham is really okay with this?"

She nods again, smiling. "You can just call him Bruce, Emily. And he's fine. It's drama. He loves a good drama."

"Is he making a donation to Stonybrook this year?"

Renee shoots me a look. But we both know what I'm thinking.

"I'm sure he could make one, if your parents have a problem with you staying in the city."

"And then what?"

"We'll find a doctor. We'll find a family. You have the baby in July, go on a crash diet, and nobody knows the difference when we go back to school in the fall."

"Do you really think it could work?"

She pulls her car into her parking space outside our dorm. "I think it will. I think it has to, Emily."

"What makes you say that?"

She doesn't miss a beat. "Because otherwise you're in huge trouble. Don't get me wrong, but Del is no Mike. He's not even close to an *Evan*."

"You mean Ethan."

"Right. And you're no Stacy. And your dad—well, let's just say he might not be intent on a happy ending."

\* \* \*

Renee and I part ways before I go into my dorm; she's off to watch one of her mom's movies with the still-awestruck and homesick seventh graders. When I reach my room, I find all three of my roommates waiting for me. None of them looks pleased.

"You've been out with Renee again, haven't you?" Stephanie demands. Her bad mood has not faded since she returned from winter break. She hasn't been willing to talk about it, but I've been spending plenty of time with Ethan at chorus practice, since we're both soloists. We even have a duet together. I haven't told Del yet.

Ethan has this incredible tenor voice that gives me chills every time I hear him sing. And the song itself is beautiful. The whole situation—after-school practices, looking into each other's eyes while we sing—could almost be romantic. You know, if I wasn't carrying Del Sugar's love child.

Anyway, according to Ethan, it was a pretty grim holiday. He and Steph stayed with their mom in her new condo, and everybody cried pretty much the whole time. On Christmas Eve, a courier showed up with a boatload of presents for Ethan and Stephanie from their dad, and they all cried harder before deciding to return the presents, unopened, to their old house—where their father is now staying with his new mistress and her three-year-old daughter. Yuck.

So I don't blame Stephanie for being angry or resentful. I can't imagine for one second how she must be feeling. That's just the thing, though—I'm supposed to be her best friend. I'm supposed to be there for her regardless, even if all I do is listen. That's what Renee has been doing for me, and I haven't even asked for it.

"I'm sorry," I say, locking our door behind me, trying to think of what to tell them. If I admit I was with Renee, they'll want to know what we were up to. "I was with Del."

Despite whatever concerns they might have about him, both

Franny and Grace find the whole secret-love situation with Del to be terribly romantic.

"Ohhhh," Grace says, nodding in understanding. "Where did you go?" Before I can answer, true to form, Grace rushes on. "You went to a motel. Didn't you? Oh my God, they went to a *motel*, guys."

I narrow my eyes at her. It occurs to me that it's beyond hypocritical for me to even pretend offense. "We went to the movies."

Stephanie blinks at me. "You did? What movie?"

"Um, at the Mystic Theater, they're running *It's a Wonderful Life* until the end of the month." I happen to know this is true.

Grace is getting ready to take a shower. "Well, we miss you. I know you're in *love* and everything, but we are the Quad."

"I think it's romantic," Franny says.

"Yeah, it's real romantic. Weren't you two about to take showers before dinner?" Stephanie is looking at me oddly. What does she know? She can't know anything. How could she?

But once Grace and Franny are gone, Stephanie beckons me into her room, shutting the door behind us. "Okay," she says, "spill. Where were you *really*?"

All I can think to do is try my best to uphold the lie. "I told you, I was with Del."

She nods. "Right. At the movies in Mystic?"

"That's right. At the movies in Mystic," I repeat, almost willing it to be true.

"You're lying to me, Emily. I was at Winchester with Ethan all afternoon. Del was there, too. In fact, I'm supposed to give you a message."

"Stephanie—"

"Just shut up. I'm supposed to tell you not to come over tonight,

because your father wants to talk to Del after dinner." She shakes her head. "Are you going to tell me where you really were? God, I feel like . . . I feel so pathetic." She stares at the floor. For a few long moments, we don't speak. There is a small part of me that *almost* wants to tell her the truth. I want to believe that she would understand the same way Renee does. But she wouldn't. I know Steph better than anyone does. At least, I used to know her better than anyone, before everything got so out of control. If I told her everything—especially the *biggest* thing—I can't even imagine how she'd react. I simply don't know her well enough anymore to take that chance.

Instead, I say the first thing that comes to mind. "Renee's mom is a mess, you know."

Stephanie, always interested in some good gossip, raises an eyebrow, looking at me. "Really?"

"She's on her third husband—"

"That's right! To that cameraman whose marriage she broke up. I know."

"Well," I continue, totally making it up as I go, "it's not going well. Apparently her mother has a drug problem."

Stephanie rolls her eyes. "Everybody knows that, Emily. She's been in rehab, like, six times."

"I know, but it's destroying her marriage. I guess her husband left a few weeks ago and went back to his ex-wife, and now Renee thinks her mom might be using again. Look, I'm sorry I've been so secretive. But I promised Renee I wouldn't tell anyone."

Stephanie gives me a hug. She gives great hugs; she always has. When she was in seventh grade and homesick all the time, we shared plenty. I would listen while she cried and talked about her family, and how much she wanted to be home with them. Ethan was here for her, too, but Stephanie and I were inseparable. I don't know what's happened to us.

"If anyone can understand what she's going through, it's me," Stephanie says. "I mean, my family is falling apart."

I nod. "I know. I should have told you sooner."

"It's okay." She hugs me more tightly. "You're a good friend, you know that? It's good of you to be there for her."

"I should be here for you more. I'm sorry I've been so distracted. It's been a crazy year."

She pulls away. She gives me a sad look. "It sure has."

Steph calms down after I tell her the lie about Renee. I feel terrible: life has become one lie on top of the next on top of a secret so huge I can barely comprehend it, a secret that's literally *growing larger* inside me every day.

We get dressed for dinner and walk up together with Grace and Franny. The four of us link arms along the way. As we're passing Winchester, Ethan comes up behind us, puts his arm around me (I'm on the end), and says, "Well, what do you know, lovelies. I'm a thorn among roses."

Franny beams. "Awww. Look at us. We've even got our prince!"


Del isn't at dinner; neither are my parents. Of course I'm nervous that my dad has somehow found out that we're still seeing each other. But I'm not too worried; even if Del admits that we've been together, if anything, he will get an angry lecture and a pile of work details.

As we're walking back from dinner, the four of us arm in arm again, Stephanie breaks away and begins to walk more slowly. Once she's a good ten paces behind us, she calls to me to slow down.

"You know what's funny?" she asks.

"Hmmm?"

"That it hasn't been in the tabloids."

I feel my whole body go cold beneath my winter coat.

"What do you mean?" I ask, keeping my tone casual.

"Well, you said that Renee's mom was using again. You said that her husband had left and gone back to his family."

I squint at the sunset. I can't look at her. "That's right."

"It's just that you'd think it'd be in the tabloids. You'd think other people would know about it."

She's totally right; it would be everywhere if Renee's mom's marriage were crumbling again. But there haven't even been rumors of a breakup.

"I guess they're doing a good job of keeping it quiet," I tell her. "It's kind of amazing, isn't it?" When she doesn't answer, I say, "Stephanie, I'm telling you the truth."

She appears to relax a bit. "Okay. I'm sorry. Listen, I want you to tell Renee that she can talk to me anytime about this. I kind of know what she's going through, at least a little bit."

"Okay. I'll tell her."

"Good." She smiles. "You sure there's nothing else?"

I give her my best reassuring grin. "Positive."

# chapter twelve

"Your father is furious with me," Del says. But I can tell he's not worried. Already, a slow grin spreads across his face as he leans over me in his bed and brushes the hair from my eyes.

"Del! You didn't tell him we're still together, did you?"

"He knows, Emily. It's like he has a *spy* or something. He just told me that you and I weren't fooling anyone."

*That's what he thinks.*

"He's going to try and have me kicked out," Del says. "He promised me he'd find a way."

I can think of more than a few reasons why that would be a plausible end to Del's tenure at Stonybrook. But instead of saying that, I take a deep breath and stare at his ceiling, trying to be brave. I've been thinking long and hard about this. I'm going to Renee's for the summer; everything is in place. There's only one thing left to do. I've been working up the courage all week; I have to tell him sooner or later. I might as well get it over with.

"Del," I say, swallowing hard. "I have to tell you something."

His grin vanishes. "What? You're not going to break up with me, are you? I didn't mean to offend your dad, but come on,

Emily—he's completely out of touch. We love each other. He should know that he can't go around telling you who to—"

"I'm pregnant." I whisper the words.

He stares at me silently for a long time. Finally, he asks, "What did you just say?"

I don't want to repeat myself; it's too hard to say out loud. "We were stupid. We should have been more careful."

"Emily. Oh, holy shit. Okay, Emily. Calm down. It's okay. Are you sure?"

I nod. "Almost four months sure."

He puts a hand on my still-flat stomach. "But you don't look any different. You don't seem any different."

"It's not like in the movies. It takes a long time to start showing."

"Oh."

" . . . "

" . . . "

"Are you angry?" I whisper.

"Emily, no! How could I possibly be angry? Look . . . okay, it's bad timing, it's definitely not the ideal situation, but everything will be okay. I'll be here for you, and we can figure this out together. I'm not going to let anything bad happen to my child, or to you."

When he says those words out loud—*my child*—I think the gravity of the situation hits me for the first time. I am not ready to have somebody's child.

"Del," I say, trying to calm him, to make him quickly understand how things are going to be, "I'm not going to keep the baby. I have a plan, okay? I'm going to go stay with Renee at the end of the school year. I'm going to live in New York City with her and Bruce—my parents already told me it's okay—and then I'll give the baby up for adoption. Nobody will even have to know there *was* a baby. So you can't tell anyone, all right?"

158

Del frowns. I can tell immediately that he doesn't like the idea. "But it's my baby, too."

I nod. "I know. But it's my body. This is what I have to do."

"Well, I'm not sure I'm okay with that. You know I grew up without a real family. I don't even know where my sister is. Now you're telling me you're gonna take my baby and give it to some strangers, just so you don't have to feel embarrassed that you got pregnant?" His voice is starting to rise, and I'm starting to panic. I didn't expect him to react this way. I don't know what I expected, but certainly not the delusion that we could all become one big happy family. The idea is laughable, and Del should know that.

Maybe he doesn't. "I grew up in foster homes," he continues, and I can tell he's trying to keep his voice steady. "You don't know what it's like not to have a real family. We can't do the same thing to our baby."

"Del, we're *not* doing the same thing. Our baby will have a good home. I'll make sure of it."

He shakes his head. "No. *No!* This is my baby, too, and I'm going to raise it with you."

"Del, shhh!" I grip his arm tightly. "You need to calm down. We can talk about this more. We don't have to make any decisions yet."

He stares at me. "It looks like you've been making decisions without me for quite a while."

"Please don't act this way," I tell him. "I'm so scared."

"There's nothing to be scared about."

He has no idea.

Usually, Del walks me back to my dorm, but not tonight. Tonight I trek across campus by myself, the snow and ice on the ground crunching beneath my feet. Being alone, outside in the cold, feels incredibly lonely and overwhelming.

Once I'm finally standing beneath Stephanie's window, I pack

a tight snowball and toss it as gently as possible at the glass. A few seconds later, her face appears in the window. I can see her sighing. It's late enough that all the doors to the dorm are locked, so I stand in the freezing cold, watching and waiting as Steph takes her time opening the window and unrolling the rope ladder for me to climb up to the quad. I ought to send her father a thank-you card.

I don't get a chance to have nightmares, because I don't sleep all night. The next morning, Del isn't at breakfast, but my father is. He approaches my table, where I'm sitting with my roommates, puts a hand on my shoulder, and squeezes.

I take a bite of my cereal, refusing to look at him. "Hi, Daddy."

"Emily. Sweetie, I want you to come to my office during study hall."

I have third period study hall, right after chorus and French. It's the only class I have with Renee, and I'm dying to tell her what happened last night with Del.

"Can't I come later?"

"Study hall," he says.

I look at him. My vision is blurry, my eyes burning from lack of sleep. "What for?"

"There's something we need to talk about."

"Okay. I'll be there."

"Good." He doesn't smile. "I'll be waiting."

When Del doesn't show up at all for breakfast, I start to worry just a twinge. Usually, he makes an appearance right before it's over and sits with Ethan and a bunch of the other guys from Winchester on the other end of the cafeteria, pretending not to know I'm alive for my father's benefit.

And when he doesn't stroll past my locker before first period, I start to panic. He was irrational last night. What might he have done? I remember my dad warning me about him. But Del is the smartest person I've ever met. He wouldn't do anything stupid, right?

I find out soon enough. When I step into his office, my dad closes the door behind us, and when I get all the way inside I see both my mom and Dr. Miller waiting for me. But no Del. *Oh. Shit.*

Could he have told my parents that I'm pregnant? Could they have found out some other way? It doesn't seem possible; it's *not* possible. My mind flashes to an image of my dad standing with his ear to Del's bedroom door. Oh God. Where *is* that boy?

"Daddy?" I ask, my tone tentative. "What's going on?"

"Emily, there's something your mother and I need to ask you. We really should be having this conversation at home, but at this point it doesn't matter." His tone is almost hopeless. "Does it?"

I glance at Dr. Miller, who gives me a pitiful smile. It's not reassuring at *all*. "What's going on?" I ask.

"Emily, honey. I want you to answer us honestly," my mom says. "And I want you to know that, whatever your answer, we'll deal with it. You aren't going to be in any trouble."

*They know. He told them. Here it comes.*

"Emily," my dad asks, "are you using drugs?"

I'm so relieved that it takes all my effort not to laugh in their faces. "Am I what? What do you mean?" And then it occurs to me that all of my roommates smoke pot, and that I'm certainly *around* drugs enough. But of course, I haven't been using them lately.

"I'm talking about cocaine," my father says. His voice is shaking. "Are you using cocaine?"

"What?" I stare at him, dumbfounded. "I'm sorry, did you just

say *cocaine*? Why would you possibly think that?" I stare back and forth at my parents. Then, without any fanfare, my father pulls a tiny bag of white powder from his pocket and drops it on his desk. "Because we found this in Del Sugar's room this morning before breakfast. He's been expelled. His parents picked him up about an hour ago."

And like that, in three brief sentences, the whole world is pulled out from under me. Again.

"Daddy," I say, trying my best not to cry, "this has to be a mistake. Del doesn't do drugs."

"Really?" My father's tone becomes sarcastic. "And how do you know that?"

I stare at him, defiant. "You know how I know."

"Tell me, Emily, have you ever noticed that he has a quick temper, or is easily excitable? Have you ever noticed a strange smell on him? And by that, I'm not talking about the cigarettes and dope that all you kids so routinely smoke practically right out your damn *windows*." He's getting angry now, angrier than I've ever seen him before. "It's a smell more like kerosene."

I feel slapped. I've smelled it on him a thousand times. But I've never even seen cocaine before today, and if my dad hadn't just told me, I wouldn't have known to connect the smell.

It all makes sense, though. All of those long disappearances. His dilated pupils. His constant sniffling. How could I not have realized what he was doing?

"When I talked to Del last night," my father continues, "he told me that you two were in love. He said there was nothing I could do to keep you two apart. And you know, Emily, I almost thought he was right. But I noticed that he kept sniffling while we talked. And that he stunk. You know his IQ is off the charts, right?" My dad slaps his forehead in mock surprise. "Of course you do. I told you myself."

I nod, tears slipping down my face, as my father continues to rant.

"It doesn't even matter how smart he is, because *boy* did he ever screw up! I didn't have to do a damn thing to keep you two apart. Del did it all by himself." He picks up the bag again. "You know, he had this in his sock drawer? He barely even tried to hide it." My dad shakes his head. "We can't have kids like that at Stonybrook."

"So he's gone?" I ask, sobbing now, so panicked that my body feels electric.

"He's gone," my dad finishes. "Just like that."

"Emily," my mother interrupts, and from her tone I can tell she feels sorry for me, "you never actually answered your father's question. Were you using drugs with him?"

"Oh my God, Mom, no! How could you even think that?"

"Because you've been sneaking around with the kid all year!" my dad blurts. "God knows what you've been doing with him, Emily! Have you been sleeping with him?"

"I think we all need to calm down," Dr. Miller interrupts, before I can even think about answering my dad. "Emily, I told your father that I haven't noticed any signs of drug use during our sessions. But I was surprised that you didn't confide in me about your relationship with Del. We've been meeting all year, and you've never even mentioned him."

I glare at her, sniffling through my tears. "It was a secret. That means you don't tell anyone. It's kind of how they work." *Besides that, you would have told my father in a second. Hell, you probably tell him everything else already.* "And to answer your question," I tell my parents, "no, I have not been using drugs. Go ahead and test me if you want. I don't even smoke cigarettes." With my last sentence, I glare at my mother. She doesn't show any signs of comprehension or guilt.

I wipe my eyes. "So that's it. I'm never going to see him again." But that *can't* be it. Del knows where to find me, and I'm confident that he will. It's only a matter of time.

"That's it," my father says.

The four of us sit in silence for a moment. Finally, I ask, "Is this over? Can I go back to study hall?"

He sighs. "Are you sure there isn't anything else you want to tell us?"

I stare at him. "Yes, I'm sure."

He stares right back for what feels like a full minute. "All right, then. Go ahead."

Everyone looks at me when I come into the room, my face streaked with tears. I started crying hard as soon as I left my dad's office, and all I could think about, besides Del, was getting to Renee and telling her what happened.

But she already knows. In true Stonybrook form, everybody already knows. Apparently, Dr. Exley's first period Chem II spent the whole class staring out the window at Winchester Hall, watching Del and his parents pack his belongings into their car. And Ethan, since he's a prefect at Winchester, spoke briefly with my dad this morning about the situation. It makes sense now; he was especially nice to me during chorus.

After school, Renee and I go into my room together. We're alone for the moment. When I tell her about the kerosene smell, she looks just as shocked as I was. "Emily. You didn't know that about him?"

"What do you mean? Of course I didn't know. I never would have—wait, you *knew*?"

"Well, my mother *has* been in rehab like six times. I know

what someone looks like when they've been snorting powder up their nose. And the way he smelled was a dead giveaway. He was probably going into the pier at Groton on the weekends or something. You know, the kerosene smell is a sign of something really low quality, something that's been cut too many times."

I stare at her. "How do you know that?"

She shrugs. "I just do. I'm sorry. I assumed you were okay with it." She lowers her voice. "Emily, did you tell him?"

I nod.

"What did he say?"

I whisper in her ear.

"Wow," she says. "You're lucky he didn't tell your dad this morning."

"I know."

"Well, what are you going to do now?"

I shake my head. I'm trying so hard to calm down and stop crying that my breathing is labored. But I can't stop. All I want is to go back to the first night I ever met Del Sugar and change everything. I've been so stupid.

"I'm going to come home with you this summer."

"And?" She winds a strand of hair around her finger. Her hair is still damp.

I hug her. I close my eyes. "I don't know," I say. "Can you help me?"

Renee nods. Her hair smells like strawberries and cigarette smoke. "Of course."

"Tell me it will be okay."

She pulls away. She sighs. "Everything will be okay," she says.

But we both know that things won't be okay. Not this summer, and maybe not ever again.

What is there to do? Once Renee is gone, I put my head down

on my pillow and cry. Nobody blames me for what has happened to Del; everybody feels sorry for me. Poor Emily Meckler and her broken heart.

If they had any idea what I was really crying about, none of them would even want to look at me. I can barely look at myself anymore. There were so many signs that something was not right with Del, from my father's warnings, to the precalc answers he sent me, to the constant smell of kerosene. How could it have taken me so long to see it? And why was he so careless about his drug habit? He's too smart to have done something so stupid. It almost seems like he wanted to get kicked out. To leave me, alone.

# chapter thirteen

It's called a closed adoption, and Bruce Graham tells me—cocktail in hand, as we stand in his penthouse apartment in Greenwich Village at the beginning of the summer—that he thinks it's my best option.

Bruce Graham is the kind of guy who's always very well dressed and holding a drink more often than not. He smokes constantly, outside on the balcony, and spends more time on the phone with his agent and publicist and assistant—and surprisingly, Renee's mom, although their conversations are more like screaming matches—than you could possibly imagine. I mean, this man is on the phone, drink in hand, at least seven to eight hours a day. I don't know how he has time to do anything else.

Bruce is middle-aged, but he's still pretty movie-star handsome. He's tall and muscled with just the slightest bit of a gut. He has a full head of brown hair and chestnut eyes. On the train to New York City, Renee explained to me that Bruce has legal custody of her, even though he isn't married to her mother anymore.

"How did that happen?" I asked.

We were sitting way in the back of the train. Renee wore an oversized sun hat and glasses so that nobody would recognize her.

"My mother has never been willing to say who my real father is. Probably some producer she had an affair with to get one of her early acting jobs. Anyway, she's a mess, you know?"

I shake my head. "I only know what I've read in magazines."

"Well, what you've read is mostly true. She's been in and out of rehab since I was a little girl. I can remember walking into the living room and seeing Mark Parsons, her first husband, snorting lines of coke off of her naked belly. I was, like, five years old. So my mom straightened out for a while after her split from Mark, and then she met Bruce and they got married. He legally adopted me while they were together, and once they broke up she fought for custody, but it was just for her image. I'm glad I get to live with Bruce."

The apartment is like nothing I've ever seen before. Coming from a place like Stonybrook, where everyone's parents are loaded, that's saying something. I mean, there are *stairs* in this place; it takes up the top three floors of the building. The first story of the apartment is a huge studio space, with an open kitchen and living room, and an inexplicable teepee in the corner. Renee tells me later that the teepee is for Bruce's dog, an enormous German shepherd named Wags, to sleep in.

The second floor is all bedrooms and bathrooms. And the third floor is—I actually gasp when I see it—an indoor swimming pool, hot tub, and exercise room.

I get my own bedroom, bathroom, closet, and *sitting room*. After I've got my stuff unpacked, when Renee and Bruce and I are sitting around talking, he tells me about closed adoptions.

It's basically like this: I'll go to an adoption agency, and they'll find a prescreened couple to adopt my baby. Without ever meeting me, the couple will take care of all my medical expenses. When I have the baby, I can see it if I want, but that's about it; after it's born, I sign away all my parental rights. Seventeen-year-olds

aren't supposed to be able to make decisions like this without parental consent, but thanks to some fudged paperwork courtesy of Bruce, I'm supposedly eighteen.

And then it's like the whole thing never happened. At least on paper.

"The agency that I'm going to recommend you use has a reputation for finding wonderful families," Bruce says to me. "I probably shouldn't tell you this, but I happen to know several high-profile women who have fabricated their pregnancies, and adopted instead."

I gape at him. "What do you mean, fabricated? Like, they faked them?"

Bruce nods. "That's right. It's very common in this industry. Women will do anything to avoid gaining weight." He grins. "Since we're all keeping secrets here, would you like to know some people who have done it?" And he tells me a few names that I can hardly believe. I mean, hiding a pregnancy is one thing, but *faking* a pregnancy and then adopting a baby?

"Why would they do that? Why not just adopt a baby?"

He takes a sip of his drink. "Because pregnancy is very popular right now, Emily. There's nothing better for a woman's career than being able to have a baby, work full time, and be back in a size zero within weeks of giving birth."

"And it's all a fake?"

He shrugs. "Isn't almost everything?"

You'd be surprised how easy it is to hide a pregnancy. At school, I got ahold of some uniforms that were a few sizes too large, wore the shirts loosely tucked, and kept my blazer buttoned. The only tough part was making sure my roommates never saw me without clothes. I took showers early in the morning, before everyone else

was up. I wore loose pj's. And I got lucky; some women get really big when they're pregnant, but by the time school let out for the summer, I'd only gained about thirteen pounds. Because of the baggy clothes I was wearing, there were actually a few people who asked if I was losing weight.

But as the summer wears on, I become visibly with child. Bruce, Renee, and I went to the adoption agency first thing at the beginning of June, and by July there's a couple out there waiting to take custody of my baby after it's born. I don't know anything about them, not their names or where they live, or even what they do for a living. And I'm never going to know. I will deliver my baby. I will sign a sheet of paper. And this will all be over. Even if my child wants to find me someday, he or she will have a difficult time; the records are kept permanently sealed.

I've never been so scared. I don't admit it to anyone, not even Renee. But this is my *baby*. I can feel it kicking inside me every day, doing somersaults in my belly. I feel an undeniable connection to it. And, in less than a few months, I will give it to strangers. I tell myself over and over again that he or she will have a better life without me, and that I'm making the right choice. But when I'm in bed at night, lying on my side because the baby has become too heavy to bear on my back, I often hold my belly and cry. Not because I don't think I'm making the right decision, but because it doesn't seem like there's any decision that will be good enough to make everyone happy. I'm seventeen, and I'm deciding the future for another, helpless life. I don't feel like I have the right, but I certainly don't have a choice anymore.

Then there are the nightmares. Without any of Dr. Miller's pills, they're in full swing. But they're a little bit different now: I hear lullabies sometimes—one in particular. It's the oddest thing. It's the lullaby that I sang to Del, on that first night outside my dorm. *Daisy, Daisy, give me an answer, do . . .*

The song doesn't bring me any comfort; it only makes the nightmares worse. Because I'll never sing to my own child. I'll never lay eyes on him or her; I'll never know what my child ends up doing with his or her life or even if he or she is okay. I don't know why, but I'm certain this is how things have to be. I want things to be *over*. I want my life back. More than anything, though, the more I think about it, I feel certain that I want to forget about Del, to rid myself of every reminder of him and all his lies. And this is one big reminder.

Sometimes it feels vulgar. I'm only seventeen years old, and my body has been surrendered to forces that only grown women should deal with.

So that's how I spend the summer in between my junior and senior year of high school: hanging out with Renee and Bruce Graham, going to doctors' appointments, and watching myself grow, surprisingly slowly.

When Renee is home, we talk about what school will be like in the fall. We talk about how surreal it is that we're managing to pull this off together; how sometimes it feels like we were meant to become friends, how we were drawn to each other despite our differences. And of course, we talk about Del.

"I just feel so betrayed," I tell her one afternoon in the apartment. I'm sitting on the sofa, hands on my eight-and-a-half-month full belly. Renee is in the teepee with Wags, trying to force-feed him a pill for canine arthritis.

"Because of the cocaine?" she asks. "Wags, *sit*. Oh, you stupid dog. Sorry, Emily. Bruce has never given me chores, so I really feel like I should do this a hundred percent." Wags spits out the pill, walks in a tight circle around the inside of the teepee, and gives Renee a smug dog-look.

"*Yes*, because of the cocaine. But it's other things, too. It's, like, once I saw how he reacted to my being pregnant, and after everything fell apart and he got kicked out, I felt so *furious* with him."

"For leaving you behind," she says. "Wags, *come*."

"Yes. He gave me such a convincing argument about how he wanted to be a family and stand by me, and then he goes and gets himself expelled . . . Renee?"

"Hmm?"

"Did you ever think—you know, he almost led my dad straight to his stash—did you ever think that maybe—"

"He got kicked out on purpose?" she asks. "Well, *yeah*. It kind of makes sense, don't you think? He probably freaked out. He's run away from places before, hasn't he?" I've told her all about his life preadoption.

"Yes," I admit. "I just can't believe he'd do something like that to me. He's supposed to love me."

She looks at me. "Obviously, he's got some major issues of his own going on."

Of course, Renee is right. The person who Del seems to care about most, I realize, is himself.

"So you never want to see him again," she finishes. "Wags, you dumb dog, come *here*!"

"Yes." I nod. "I never want to see him again."

But this is a lie. In fact, I think it's the only lie I've ever told Renee. It isn't that I think she'd be upset; I'm actually pretty sure she'd understand my feelings. It's more like I'm trying to convince *myself* that I never want to see him again, and I feel like, if that's what I tell Renee, then it will become the truth.


And then, near the end of July, it happens. I go into labor. Renee and Bruce (is he *ever* actually working?—he even has a drink in

172

the limo) drive me to the hospital, where I'm rushed to a private room and met almost immediately by the adoption agent I've been working with all summer.

They give me a Pitocin IV drip, which is a medicine to speed the labor along. The adoption agent, whose name is Claire, tells me she's notified the family who will adopt my baby. She tells me they're here, in the hospital, already. Every time I see someone passing in the hall, I wonder if it's them. But I'll never know.

When I start to feel serious pain, an anesthesiologist puts a very thin needle in my spine—it's called an epidural—that makes me numb from the chest down.

I don't want to talk much about what happens next. There is pain despite every effort to avoid pain. There is a mess unlike anything I could have anticipated. And there's that cry—the first sound I hear after what feels like an eternity of pushing—the scream that makes me squeeze my eyes shut before I have a chance to see him or her, the odd sensation of the doctor cutting the umbilical cord that connects me to my child. And, of course, once they've ushered the baby from the room to clean it off, I open my eyes a crack, roll my head to the right, and see Bruce Graham sitting in a crisp suit, *drink in hand*, hair perfectly styled.

"Well, well," he says, grinning at me. "That certainly was an adventure like I've never seen before."

I'm so exhausted that I can barely keep my eyes open. The only thing I can think to say is, "You obviously own a blow-dryer, don't you?"


They send me home a day later. From the nursery down the hall, I could hear the babies crying sometimes, and once in a while I'd wonder which one was mine before I'd realize that none of them belonged to me. All it took was a signature.

And then things are back to normal. Sort of. Almost. There's a hollow feeling inside me, the feeling like I've lost a part of myself. I find myself thinking more and more of Del, wondering where he is and if he's okay, thinking that maybe I can steal his file when I get back to campus, if my dad even bothered to keep it. He probably burned it the moment Del left.

Two days before we're supposed to go back to school, Renee drops her bombshell.

We're sitting in Bruce's apartment, all three of us drinking vodka and soda like it's no big deal. Bruce and Renee are both smoking cigarettes. More than anything, even though he's been generous and accommodating and all that good stuff, Bruce seems grateful to have his apartment back, instead of constantly having to remember that he's around a pregnant woman who can't be exposed to smoke. He's been so nice to me, I don't want to tell him how much it bothers me.

"Let me tell you something, Emily," he says, giving me a wink as he talks, exhaling gracefully into the air. "I know this has been a difficult summer, but you did the right thing. You did the best thing possible under the circumstances."

"Lying to almost everyone I know was the best thing possible?"

He doesn't blink. "Yes. Sometimes it's necessary to lie. Imagine the mess you would have been in if you'd told everyone the truth. Trust me. This is right for all parties involved."

"Bruce," Renee says, "I should tell her now."

I give her a hesitant look. I'm not sure how much more drama I can handle. "Tell me what?"

Renee and Bruce exchange one of their private glances that I've become so used to over the summer.

"Okay," Bruce says. "So tell her."

"Emily, I'm not coming back to Stonybrook."

I don't want to believe what she's saying. I can't imagine life without Renee now. I've barely even talked to my other friends all summer, except for some awkward conversations and vague e-mails with Stephanie, and I know that she's beyond irritated that I decided to spend my vacation with Renee instead of coming to visit her in Colorado.

"Why not?" I demand.

"It's, um, I got in trouble. I got kicked out. Your dad waited until a few weeks ago to tell me."

*My father.* This is no accident. It took everything I had, plus a huge donation and personal phone call from Bruce, to convince my parents to let me stay the summer with Renee. They don't like her. And lately, ironically enough, her mother has been in the news again for another trip to rehab and another broken marriage. At least Stephanie will believe me about *that*.

"What for? How can they kick you out when you haven't been on campus in three months?"

Renee glances at Bruce again. He nods, urging her to continue. It's not even six p.m. and he's already in a tux.

She puts her head down. She won't look at me. "I'm so sorry, Emily. Hillary found Madeline's file. I hid it under our dresser, and one day she went to move it, and . . . there it was. She took it to your dad right away."

"They're kicking you out for *that*? After all the money Bruce donated? There wasn't even anything interesting in it! And you didn't steal it. I gave it to you!"

"Emily, that's not exactly true."

"What do you mean?"

"I don't think it's because he thought I took Madeline's folder. I think it has more to do with you. See, a couple of days after you and Del stole those folders, Del kind of approached me privately."

I raise my eyebrows. "He did, did he?"

"Did you know he stole your file that night, too?"

I shake my head. "I knew he stole some other files to make it look less obvious that we were after Madeline's. But I didn't know he took mine." I pause. "Why would he do that?"

"He did more than that," Renee says. "He gave it to me. He showed me something in particular. It was something he said you had a right to know. See, Emily, there was a note in your folder that didn't make a lot of sense."

"In my folder?" It would never even occur to me to look at my folder. How could there be anything in it that I don't already know? And why would Del take it? Wouldn't it make it all the more obvious that I was involved with the theft somehow?

"Something that didn't make sense," I repeat. "Okay. What was it? Do you still have it?"

"Yes. I saved the paper." Renee reaches into the back pocket of her jeans. She pulls out a paper that's been folded half a dozen times and is worn at the creases. She's obviously been carrying it around all summer.

I stare at it. It's just a basic demographic sheet with your usual info: name, address, age, all that good stuff. "There's nothing weird here," I say, confused.

"Look at the bottom." Renee swallows. "Look at the emergency contacts."

First there's my mom and dad, obviously. It seems absurd that they would even have a page like this for me. After my mom and dad, there's Dr. Miller's personal cell and office numbers. My grandparents on both sides are dead. I don't have any aunts or uncles or cousins that I know of. For my entire life, it's just been me and my parents.

But right there, in my father's handwriting at the very bottom of the page, there's an asterisk. Beside it, he's written:

ICE: SANDY GRAY. MARYLAND?

I close my eyes and see fire. It's suddenly hard to breathe. I've never seen the name before in my life until this moment. So why the fire? Why now? And why do I feel like I've been punched in the gut?

Bruce and Renee look at me, waiting for me to respond.

"Who the hell is Sandy Gray? And what does ICE mean?"

"ICE means 'in case of emergency,'" Renee says. "And I don't know who Sandy Gray is, Emily . . . but I think you need to find out."

part three

# chapter fourteen

At the beginning of my senior year, I find myself back in the quad with Stephanie, Franny, and Grace. Things are so different now: Del is gone, Renee is gone, and I've just had a baby that almost nobody knows about. But when I'm alone with my roommates, I can almost convince myself that everything is the same as it's always been.

Over the summer, I've only kept in touch with Steph, and even that's been on and off. It's normal for kids at Stonybrook to take a kind of hiatus from each other over summer breaks; everyone goes home, back to their other friends and their family and alternate lives, and we come back in the fall and pick up where we left off.

My tummy is flat again, thanks to a trainer who came highly recommended from Bruce Graham. "I don't use him," Bruce had said, "because I enjoy my bearlike physique." He was holding a tumbler of scotch and wearing a red silk bathrobe and slippers when he told me this. It was something like two in the afternoon. "But I've heard he can really whip a person into shape."

My trainer's name was Colby. I never learned his last name. We worked out five days a week for an hour and a half, all on Bruce's dime. Most of the workouts left me in tears. Sometimes

I was so sore that Renee had to help me sit on the toilet and do other, basic things, like pulling a shirt over my head. But by the end of the summer, I'm in the best shape of my life. I almost have a six-pack.

Everything's the same; everything is different. I am still having nightmares. I feel an emptiness in my body, the absence of all the experiences with my child that I will never know—even though I don't exactly want to know them—and the absence of Del making me feel hollowed somehow, so much so that I ache inside. I don't know why I think about him so much. I'm so angry with him for everything he did to me, and all the lies he told me, that I've convinced myself I don't want to see him again. Maybe it's because we left things so unfinished. Maybe it's because, deep down, there is a part of me that still cares for him, and worries that he's okay, wherever he is. How can I not? He used to mean everything to me, and then, all of a sudden, he was gone.

But it's Renee I miss more than anyone. She is the only person now who truly knows me, who shares all of my secrets. I realize it's possible that, for the rest of my life, she will be the only one. It's a lot to deal with alone, without her: there's the secret that seems to still be breathing inside me, the nightmares that come fast and frequent, and this new mystery that only Renee and I (and Bruce, and Del) know about: who is Sandy Gray, and why was her name in my file?

I know I should just ask my parents, but I have my doubts about whether or not they'll tell me the truth. So I go to the second-best source: Dr. Miller.

"Have you been taking your medication all summer?" she asks during our first session together.

"Yes," I lie.

"And are you still having the nightmares?"

"Yep." I'm sitting on the sofa in her office, staring at her across

the desk. The mood in the room is palpably tense as I wait for the right moment to ask her. I realize I'm almost glaring. All these secrets and lies, they start to get to you after a while. My whole body is a lie now, my whole life lived with a secret embedded somewhere within my past, where there was a Sandy Gray who meant something. Maybe she still does.

Since I'm a senior, I'll only be spending one more year under Dr. Miller's psychiatric care, and then it's off to college, where I suppose there will be a mental health center on campus, or something like that. Are all psychiatrists like her, I wonder? Surely some of them are actually *helpful*.

"Well," she muses, leaning back in her chair, "let's talk about your summer. What did you do?"

*Oh, the usual teenage high jinks. Hid out in a celebrity's penthouse while I carried a baby to term. Gave it up for adoption in the middle of the summer. Managed to hide the pregnancy from everyone, even my parents. Nothing new.*

Now seems as good a time as any to change the subject.

"Dr. Miller," I say, "you know how Renee got kicked out for stealing those files?"

She nods. "She's lucky your parents didn't press charges. That's breaking and entering, you know. It's larceny. She was fortunate that all she got was expelled."

"She didn't really steal them," I say.

Dr. Miller blinks coolly at me. "Then who did?"

"Del."

"Ah, but Madeline's file was in Renee's room, wasn't it? She was involved somehow." Dr. Miller pauses. "You know, there were no signs of a break-in at your parents' house. They wouldn't even have known the file was missing if Hillary hadn't found it." She narrows her eyes. "Emily? Do you know more about this than you're telling me?"

I ignore her. "Anyway," I continue, "Del took my file, too. Did you know that?"

Dr. Miller tries to act nonchalant, but I can tell she's thrilled to be getting the information. "I had an idea of something like that, yes." She sure pays close attention to all of the teenage happenings around here, doesn't she?

"He gave my file to Renee. He said there was something I had a right to know about. And a few weeks ago, she showed me what it was."

Dr. Miller seems genuinely clueless. "Well? What was it?"

"It was a name. Under 'In Case of Emergency.'"

"And what name was that?"

I swallow. "Sandy Gray. Dr. Miller, do you know who she is? Or why her name would be in my file? I've never even heard the name before."

"What did you say the name was?"

"Sandy Gray."

She shakes her head slowly back and forth. "You don't have any aunts? Any close family friends with that name?"

"No. I don't have any close relatives besides my parents. I don't know anyone with that name. So why would it be there? And why would Del think I had a right to know?" For the first time since I've been seeing her, I'm actually interested in her input. "Do you think my parents could be hiding something from me?"

"I can't imagine," she says. "Your parents adore you. If there was something significant about this woman, I don't think they'd be hiding it from you. But still"—she smiles—"it can't hurt to ask them, can it? After all, our sessions are to help you understand yourself better. Obviously, if this woman is an emergency contact, you should probably know why."

"So we can ask them?"

"Certainly."

"Even though the file was stolen?"

"Yes. You still have a right to know. Ask your mother. I'm sure she'll shed some light on it."

"But you don't know anything?"

Dr. Miller gives me a steady, sincere look. "Emily. If I knew anything at all, I would tell you. I will never lie to you. Okay?"

I bite my lip. *Thanks for nothing.* "Okay. But in the meantime, can you tell me what to do?"

"I can tell you to keep writing down your nightmares. Keep taking your medication. And—and that's all."

Over the summer, Ethan has blossomed in a big way. He was always great looking, but Stephanie tells me that, since he made head prefect, he's been lifting weights and studying vocab words like there's no tomorrow, determined to uphold Stonybrook's reputation for excellence, and to get into Stanford.

I giggle. "Does he also want to fly backward around the earth?"

The *Superman* references—everybody makes them—have always annoyed Steph for some reason. I'm starting to realize it's precisely *because* everyone makes them that she doesn't like them, because it's something about him that she has to share with everyone else. If she's changed at all over the summer, she's become even more touchy and bitter.

"Shut up," she says. "You know I hate that."

We're in the library during English class, where we're supposed to be researching an author of our choice for a term paper. In order to avoid doing much work, I've chosen Victor Hugo. I did a junior year English paper on him, and I've seen *Les Misérables*, like, five times.

Grace is sitting with us. She and I exchange a look. "Steph?" Grace asks, her tone casual. "Can I just ask you a question about Ethan?"

"What?"

"Did he spend a lot of time in his Fortress of Solitude this summer?"

I snort. Grace giggles, beaming at me. "That was funny, wasn't it?" She's proud of herself.

"I swear to God, Grace," Stephanie says, "I'll stab you with my pen if you don't shut up."

Grace is wholly unafraid. "My goodness," she says, "you'll get blood all over the library."

Stephanie kicks her under the table.

"Ow! You're assaulting me! I was kidding!"

"It wasn't funny."

"Yes, it was." Grace reaches down to rub her calf. "Emily was laughing. It was funny."

Steph glares at me. "Could we stop talking about my brother?"

"Okay," I say, "I'll change the subject. So, Steph. Where do you want to go to college?"

Stephanie is researching Franz Kafka for her paper. She pretends to be deeply engrossed in the book she's reading. "I don't know. I'm going to try to get into Stanford, too, with Ethan."

"Steph . . ." I let my voice trail off.

"What?" she snaps. "Don't tell me I don't have the grades for it."

"You don't have the grades for it," Grace says. "Does she, Emily?"

I hesitate. I don't say anything else.

Stephanie glares at both of us again. Then she slams her book shut, gathers up her things, and moves two tables over. She's still well within earshot.

"Did somebody say my name?" Ethan is suddenly behind me,

his hands resting lightly on my shoulders like it's the most natural thing in the world. I feel a jolt through my whole body. I remember the Christmas party, the awkward phone call that followed. But that was all before Del left. It feels like a lifetime ago. I haven't talked to Ethan all summer.

"We sure did," Grace says, opening her big mouth. "We're talking about where everyone's going to school next fall, and Steph said she wanted to go to Stanford with you."

"Oh." I can't see Ethan's face, but I sense the hesitation in his tone. "Well, she can apply anywhere she wants. I guess it's, you know, up to the admissions board."

I glance at Stephanie to gauge her expression. She's pretending to stare at her book again, but I can tell she's trying not to cry.

For no reason that I can tell, I find myself thinking of Del. I wonder what he's doing this very moment. I wonder if he's happy, or if he's managed to track down his sister yet. And if he makes it to college—even though he said more than once that he wasn't going—maybe it's possible we'll end up seeing each other again. Maybe things will be different. I don't even know what school he's at.

". . . She's not paying any attention to you," Grace is saying.

"I know. I could probably lean down and say something like, 'Emily Meckler. Can I have your attention, please?'" Ethan's mouth is directly next to my ear, so close that I can feel his warm breath on my skin.

My stomach flutters. "What?"

"I said, do you want to do something tonight after chorus practice?"

I look from Grace to Stephanie. Is Ethan asking me out?

Stephanie scowls, still pretending to read her book. Grace wriggles in her seat, unable to physically contain her excitement.

I should have expected this. I remember everything he said at

the Christmas party last year, and on the phone over Christmas break. In hindsight, it was so obvious. But now that it's actually happening, it's hard for me believe. It occurs to me that Ethan doesn't know who I really am, that he'll probably never know. And if he did, would he still want to have anything to do with me? Is it fair for me to mislead him, to let him think I'm just little Emily Meckler with a pretty voice?

I don't care. I just want life to be normal again—whatever that means.

"Um. Sure. Okay." I can feel myself blushing.

"Okay. Super. Fantastic." His voice is nothing but confident. "We'll get ice cream or something. Sound good?"

Grace looks ready to fall out of her seat. Her grin is so huge that I can see the tops of her gums.

"Okay."

"Okay, then. I'll see you tonight." He takes a deep breath and murmurs, *"Finally."* Then, as quickly as he appeared—he's not even in our English class—he's gone.

"Oh my God," Grace says. "You're going on a date with Ethan Prince. He wants you to be his girlfriend. He likes you." Suddenly, she seems gravely concerned. "Emily. What if he falls in love with you? What if you fall in love with him? Will you go to Stanford? You'll never get into Stanford. Oh my God. You two could get *married. Emily Meckler-Prince.*" She whistles softly. "That sounds *really* classy."

"Grace," I whisper, looking around to make sure he's gone. I can't stop smiling. "He just wants to get ice cream."

"Emily," Grace says, "he's a seventeen-year-old boy. He wants more than ice cream."

In case there was any doubt on my part, Stephanie speaks up. "I wouldn't get too excited, Emily. I think he's just being friendly."

She glares at Grace. "It's not a date. Don't get your hopes up on being a bridesmaid anytime soon, sweetie."

I stare at her. "How do you know what he wants?"

"Because he's my twin brother. We have a connection."

"Oh, really?" I suddenly can't stand her. "Did you know that he called me last Christmas break? After the party?"

Stephanie's expression falls flat. "What?"

"That's right," I say. "He called me up just to tell me merry Christmas." I cross my arms. "What do you think about that?"

She doesn't say anything for a long moment, but she glowers at me and Grace. Finally, her voice cracking, she says, "I think my brother is a really nice guy. And I think he deserves a really nice girl."

She slams her book shut. Then she stands up, shoves her things into her book bag, and walks quickly out of the library.

As I watch her leave, I find myself thinking of Del again, feeling guilty that I'm so excited to go out with Ethan. How would I feel if Del had another girlfriend at his new school?

Del does *not* have another girlfriend. I feel certain. I feel like I would know if he did.

There's a small part of me, I know, that's waiting for him to show up again, anticipating him any day now. But I'm not sure what I expect him to do once he gets here.


In my room, there's a letter for me in a plain white envelope, resting on my pillow, undoubtedly placed there by an already dozing Franny (her underwear says THURSDAY!, even though it's Wednesday). The letter writer was obviously trying to be discreet—there's no return address or anything—but I would recognize the sloppy handwriting anywhere; it's from Renee.

189

I've never gotten a letter from anyone besides colleges and junk mail. I tear it open carefully, like it's an artifact, and sit on top of my covers to read it.

> September 8
> 44 degrees, rainy and overcast
> sore throat
>
>
> Hi Emily,
>     I'm writing to you because I figure nobody would expect us to communicate in such an archaic way. The new school is good. Lots of hippie, artsy kids, which I guess is okay. How are you? Did the trainer (Cory? Colby?) take care of everything for you? Last time I saw, you had killer abs, so I'm betting there are no problems.
>     You should go see Bruce's new movie. The movie itself sucks, but he really liked you. It's worth ten bucks for a ticket to return the favor, right? He and my mother are going to court again to fight over custody of me. I'm seventeen and at boarding school nine months out of the year, so you'd think they'd give it up by now. Especially because I haven't seen my mother since last year sometime.
>     My new address is below. I'd love to have a pen pal. Miss you and all our adventures. Everything's good on your end, yes? Definitely let me know…
>
>     Much love,
>     R.G.

The letter brings tears to my eyes. I'm wiping them away when I hear Grace and Stephanie in the hallway. Before they come in, I shove the letter beneath my mattress.

*I'd love to have a pen pal.*

*Me, too,* I think. There is so much to say that can't be said to anyone else.


After chorus, Ethan strolls over to me, cool as can be, and says, "Well? You ready for some ice cream, sweet thing?"

Oh, yeah. It's a date.

Going to downtown Stonybrook is like stepping back in time. There are soda shops and restaurants along the shore; there's a long pier with mansions stretching on either side of it down the beach as far as we can see. We get our ice cream—hot fudge sundaes for both of us, which I can imagine Grace will find disappointingly boring—and walk to the end of the pier. Ethan reaches for my hand; I flinch.

"Emily? Is this okay?" he asks.

I smile. "Yes." *It's just that I had a secret baby with Del Sugar over the summer, and I'm not sure but I think there's a slight possibility that I still love Del, and I have no idea where he is, and I'm not even ready to start dealing with my feelings about giving the baby up for adoption, so it's not like I'm exactly ready to jump into a serious relationship right now, especially with someone as sweet and normal as you.* "It's great."

He laces his fingers through mine. His hand is cold, the evening cool. He keeps holding my hand as we sit down on a bench. I rest my head on his shoulder. I've done it a million times; until he started acting differently toward me, he was almost like a brother.

At first I feel uncomfortable being so close to a boy again. But then I remind myself: this is Ethan. He's a good person. Ethan Prince would *not* impregnate his girlfriend while secretly abusing cocaine behind her back, and then leave her all alone.

"Emily?" His voice is more nervous than I've ever heard it. "I wanted to tell you something."

It's past dusk on the pier; the sun slips gently into the sea and we're left chilly, almost alone as the tourists start to meander back to their cars.

"I've liked you for a long time," Ethan says.

It's so cold that I can see my breath. I remember Del's red blanket wrapped around my body.

*"It isn't covered in dirt. It's covered in you."*

But Del is gone. Ethan is right here. "I had an idea," I tell him. "I mean, there was the Christmas party."

"I was going to ask you out last year," he explains, "as soon as we got to school. But then everything happened with you and Del, and I didn't get the chance. I wasn't even supposed to talk to you."

"You can talk to me now."

"I know," he says. He smiles. "I don't want to waste any more time."

"I have to tell you, Ethan, this is all kind of hard to believe. I mean, you're my best friend's twin brother."

"I know," he repeats. "I hope you don't think it's too weird."

I pause, taking a moment to think about it. I look at him; I mean, I *really* look at him. Renee was wrong about Ethan; he's not boring. He's kind and concerned and intelligent. He loves music, just like I do. He is honest. He feels calm. He feels safe.

"No," I say, "I don't think it's weird. I think it's kind of wonderful."

He smiles again. "When we got back to school last year, I'd been waiting to ask you out all summer. Then my parents split up, and you and Del got together, and everything got all screwed up." His grin turns into a scowl. "I could have killed Del for what he did. Sneaking off all the time behind your back. Getting kicked out the way he did. I watched you cry, you know? I just wanted to

hug you, to tell you there were better guys out there, but you were so heartbroken, I didn't know what I could possibly say to make you feel better." Then he asks, "Are you over him?"

"Um. God, Ethan, this is a lot of information you're giving me! I mean, what about Stephanie? Have you thought about her? You know she's furious with me, don't you?"

He shrugs. "She's my sister. And you're her best friend. She'll get over it, trust me. She'll be happy for us."

But I'm not so sure. And as worried as I am about what Stephanie might think, all I can *really* think about is DelDelDel. Aboyaboyaboy. My boy. The mess that's been left behind in his absence. The fact that I have no idea where he is feels painful. The fact that we never got to say good-bye, that I never got to tell him how angry I was, and that our child is out there somewhere, is too much to think about right now, sitting on the pier with Ethan.

"We never had any real closure," I explain. "He was just gone."

Ethan seems surprised. "You haven't heard from him at all?"

I shake my head. "No."

"Wow. You'd think Boy Genius would have figured out a way to contact you."

The words sting; he's just said out loud what I've been thinking all summer. Del is the smartest person I've ever met. If he wanted to get in touch with me, I'm sure he would have found a way by now. So that's it. It's over. All I have to do is forget. But is that what I really want? It's all so emotionally messy, so difficult to think about with any clarity. If only a normal boy had fathered my illegitimate child, things would be much easier.

"So come on, Emily," Ethan says. "What do you think?"

The truth is, I've always had a little crush on Ethan. I just never considered it was possible that he'd like me back.

*A boy!* Aboyaboyaboy! "Okay." I smile. "But you have to promise that we can take things slow. I have a lot going on in my head

right now." I feel stupid just saying the words. I'm practically a solid C student, and Ethan is head prefect. I almost expect him to laugh at me—I mean, he must figure, how much could there possibly be going on in my head?

But then, so gently and with such warmth that I shiver, Ethan leans forward, brushes the hair from my eyes, and gives me a soft kiss on the forehead. "I know you do," he says. "That's what I like about you."

"Really?" I ask.

"Really. Emily . . . I'm going to treat you so good, you'll forget all about Del Sugar."

I close my eyes. I let him kiss my forehead again, and then my nose, and finally my lips. All I can think is, *You go ahead and try, Superman.*

# chapter fifteen

The dream is violent: pounding rain, rain so hard that I can barely breathe in it, and I wake up to a weak slap in the face, a brittle arm shaking me, Franny sitting beside me while Grace and Stephanie stare down at me.

I try to gasp. I need air, and nothing is coming.

"What's the matter with her?" Franny asks, her voice almost a shriek. All the lights are on in the quad, my roommates looking disheveled in their pj's, Grace's hair in its usual set of curlers for the night, dots of zit cream in Steph's T-zone, and Franny's cheekbones looking painfully prominent as she leans in and says, "Breathe, Em, breathe!"

I try to gasp again. I feel air rushing into my lungs, and I fall back onto my pillow. Tears come to my eyes, my roommates' faces suddenly blurred. I begin to breathe deeply, frantically, grateful for every breath.

I'm nauseous. My sheets are damp with sweat.

"Franny, scoot over," Steph says. She sits beside me, peers down into my eyes. "Emily." Her tone is worried and serious. "What the hell is the matter with you? You were like something from *The Exorcist*."

"You woke all of us up," Grace says.

"Sweetie, what's the matter? Why are you crying?" Stephanie gazes at me with a peculiar expression, shifting from concern to curiosity. "Did something happen?"

I shake my head, still teary and sick to my stomach, still trying to catch my breath. I feel like, if they hadn't woken me, I could have drowned right there in my bed.

Once I've calmed down, Stephanie says, "Come with me, hon. Let's go downstairs, okay?"

I nod.

"We'll make some tea and watch the *Late Show*," she says, half-smiling.

"Okay."

Downstairs, the dorm is eerily dark, everyone else asleep. From upstairs, I smell cigarette smoke curling down the hallway, its unmistakable stink infiltrating the whole dorm. It's undoubtedly Franny and Grace; I imagine them perched in the windowsill, talking about me.

It's past two in the morning; we're watching a *rerun* of the *Late Show*, sipping tea, my head on Stephanie's shoulder and our bodies tucked together beneath a blanket in the still of the deep night. Aside from the light coming from the television, everything around us is black, senseless, almost surreal.

"Emily," Stephanie says, turning down the television, "what's the matter?"

I take a sip of my tea. "I had a nightmare," I say.

"Worse than usual?" she asks.

"Yes. I couldn't breathe until you woke me up. I felt like I was drowning."

"You weren't. You were making an awful noise like a scream and a gasp all at once." She hesitates. "You should talk to Dr. Miller tomorrow. This isn't normal."

I nod, but don't say anything. Dr. Miller is no help whatsoever. I'm not going to get any real answers until I confront my mom about Sandy Gray. Her name was in my father's handwriting, but my mother *must* know who she is.

"What did you and Ethan do tonight?" she asks.

Her tone is light enough, but the question is out of nowhere.

"We went out for ice cream," I say.

"And? What did he want?"

"Stephanie, you know what he wants."

She sits up straighter. She turns to stare at me in the almost-dark, light from the television hitting her face to illuminate it just enough for me to see her serious expression. She's not thrilled. "He talked about you all summer."

"Did he tell you he liked me?"

"Yes."

"You told me earlier there was no way he wanted to go out," I say.

"I know." She blinks. "I didn't want to think about it. It feels like you and Del just broke up. And, Emily, he's my *brother*."

"So what?"

"What do you mean, *'so what?'* Emily, you've been off the map lately. Things haven't exactly been peachy between you and me. We barely talked all summer. I'm just looking out for him." She pauses. "Have you talked to Del?"

I shake my head.

"Not at all? No e-mail, nothing?"

"Nothing."

"Oh. I thought for sure . . . I mean, you two never really broke up."

I nod. "I know that."

"Don't you feel like you're cheating on him? With my brother?"

"Steph, I didn't do anything with Ethan."

"I don't want to know," she says. "But you have to get yourself under control. I don't want you dating my brother when you're practically waking up the whole dorm with your nightmares." Her tone softens just a bit. "Emily, you can talk to me. You can tell me anything. Don't you know that?"

"Can we just watch TV?" I ask, putting my head back on her shoulder, scooting closer to her beneath the blanket so that our crossed legs overlap. The truth is, I haven't remembered how to talk to Stephanie about anything serious in a long time.

"Sure we can. Drink your tea." And she rests her head against mine, our bodies taking the same familiar position that they have for years, since we were just little girls.

I don't remember falling asleep. But when I wake up, the sun is beginning to shine through the window at dawn. We're still in the common room, still tucked under the blanket together. The local news is on television; aside from that, the dorm is quiet and still.

I shake Stephanie awake and we go upstairs. Instead of getting into my own bed, I crawl into hers and we sleep together for another couple of hours. When I wake up, it's from an elbow to the face; Franny has climbed into bed with us at some point in the morning.

Sometime between last night and now, she's changed her underwear to announce that it's THURSDAY! Except, once again, she's got it wrong—it's a Tuesday. I wonder what the hell is going on with her.

"Franny, my God, you're a bag of bones," I murmur, pinching the skin against her ribs. I sit up, stretching my arms toward the ceiling. The three of us are crammed between the rails of the bunk bed.

"You looked so peaceful," she says, "I just wanted to cuddle."

Her eyes still closed, Stephanie snorts. "It's like cuddling with a coat hanger."

"Shut up." Franny gets out of bed, turning off the alarm before it has a chance to go off.

Above us, Grace stirs. "Did I miss a cuddlepalooza?"

"Mm-hmm," I say.

"Aww, dammit."

"I'm taking a shower," Franny announces, gathering her towel and supplies.

"Can we cuddle again tonight?" Grace pouts. "It's not fair that I missed it."

"Your curlers are too big for comfortable cuddling, Grace," I tell her.

"I won't wear them!"

"There isn't enough *room* for everyone."

"We'll push the beds together! Come on, guys—cuddlefest. Cuddles." Grace stands up, stares at us, her lips curled into an adorable pout.

I yawn, smiling at her. It feels so good to have a normal conversation. This is why I love my roommates. "Maybe," I say.

But as normal and sweet and easy as the conversation feels, there's no forgetting last night, and the feeling of suffocation that took hold of me as I slept.

Once Grace and Franny are both out of the room, Stephanie puts her arm around me. "Are you better now?"

I nod. "Yes. Thanks."

"Anytime." She smiles. "Just let someone help you," she says.

I feel nauseous again, like something is stirring within my gut. There's no way for me to know what's about to happen, but it feels like threads from all over are being tugged within my body, attached to something I can't identify, pulling me apart.

ICE stands for "in case of emergency." I don't know how or why, but I think I can sense one coming.

# chapter sixteen

When I walk into the house, the first thing I hear is my mother playing the piano in the living room. That's how I learned to sing. When I was a little girl, she would play Beatles songs all the time, and one day, without any prompting, I opened my mouth to join her, and out came the voice I'd never realized I had. I remember my father sitting on the sofa, reading a book, and the way he slowly put it down to watch me. I remember how my soft voice grew louder as I heard it and understood that it was something powerful.

She's playing the Beatles' "Let It Be." Sometimes, if I walk in while she's at the piano, I'll go over to her and start singing. She's always liked that.

But I don't do it today. Today, I stand beside the piano with my arms crossed, waiting for her to finish, trying to suppress the feeling of dread at what I'm about to ask.

I've been going over possible scenarios in my mind for how she'll react. Maybe it's no big deal. Maybe Sandy Gray is an aunt I don't know about, and she and my parents are estranged. Maybe she's an old friend of my mom and dad's, and they put her in their will to take care of me if anything ever happened to them. But I don't know *anyone* with the last name Gray, and I've never heard my parents mention it.

My mother stops playing. "Emily. What are you doing here, baby?"

My dad isn't here, which is the way I want things tonight. My mom will be easier to crack if he's not around. If this is something I'm not supposed to know about, or something that has been hidden from me, my dad would want to keep protecting me. And it's not that my mom doesn't *want* to protect me; after all, she's been hiding this woman from me for my entire life. It's just that I know that, if they have a united front, I might not get through to either of them.

I don't know how I'm supposed to start. So I just ask.

"Mom? Who is Sandy Gray?"

The palms of my mother's hands go limp on the piano. "Who—how did you—"

"Del," I explain. "He took my file when he took Madeline's. By the way, Renee got kicked out for no reason. She was just holding the file. She didn't actually steal it."

My mom starts to shake her head, brings her fist to her mouth, but before she can say anything I interrupt with, "Don't lie to me or I'll know. You have to tell me who this woman is. Why is she listed in case of an emergency? I've never heard her name in my life."

My mom takes a deep breath. Her hands are shaking. "We knew we'd have to tell you this eventually," she says, her voice small and sad. "We just didn't know how, baby."

*Oh, shit.* I don't want to know, I don't want to know, I don't want to know. But it's too late; she's going to tell me.

"Emily, sweetie," my mom begins, "I know this is going to be impossible for you to understand, but—oh hell, I guess I should just say it. I mean, it's complicated. There's a long story involved—"

I am officially freaking out. "What do you mean, there's a *story*? Tell me the damn story, then."

She doesn't say anything for a long time. She stares at her hands, at the wall behind me, looking anywhere but at my face. She won't look me in the eye. Finally she says, "Sandy Gray was your father's first wife."

I'm beyond confused. "What do you mean, my father's first wife? Daddy was married before?"

My mom shakes her head. "No. Your daddy wasn't married before." She takes another deep breath. I'm almost worried she's going to hyperventilate. I've never seen her so nervous.

"Then what? Mom, you're not making sense. If Daddy wasn't married before, then what the hell are you talking about?"

She looks me in the eye. "Your father is not your real father. I was married once before, a long time ago." She swallows. "I was married to your real father."

I feel dizzy. I feel hot. But more than anything, I feel confused.

"Let me understand this," I repeat, tears prickling my eyes. "You were married before."

My mother nods.

"I'm your child with your first husband."

For an almost imperceptible moment, she hesitates, as though she's trying to figure out the story for herself. Then she nods again.

"You were married to another man before Daddy, and that man is my real father," I repeat.

"Yes." Her voice sounds far away.

"What was his name? My real father?"

She can't—or won't—look at me again. "Tom. His name was Tom."

"And what happened to Tom?"

"He died." She takes a deep, shaky breath. "We almost all died. Emily, there was a fire. You were three years old. We lived in a

202

small house in New Hampshire. I remember that night so vividly. I can't tell you how often I replay it in my head. You had an ear infection, so I slept in your room, in your bed. When I woke up, there was smoke everywhere. There was a fireman standing in your bedroom. The smoke was so thick that I couldn't even see you. It was horrible."

"And where was my father?" I ask. *Fire. Smoke everywhere. I remember now; I've always remembered.*

She's crying. "He was in our bedroom, asleep. He suffocated from the smoke and died. But, Emily, it was such a strange coincidence that things worked out the way they did. Normally, when you weren't sick, you'd crawl into bed with us at night. The fire started in the living room and came up through the closet in our bedroom." She wipes her eyes, obviously overwhelmed by the memory. "If you hadn't been sick, we might have all been killed. It was a miracle that you and I survived."

All I can think is, *My father is not my father. My daddy* is not who I thought he was. They have been lying to me my whole life.

"How did the fire start?" I ask. "Do you know?"

Her head hangs further. She manages a soft nod. "It was because of me."

My whole body feels cold. "What do you mean?"

Before she tells me, I know the answer. Everything begins to fall into place.

"I was smoking," she says. "I used to smoke."

"You still smoke," I tell her.

She looks startled. "How did you know that?"

"I've seen you outside. I've heard you sneak out late at night." I can't believe what she's telling me. "So you were smoking in our house, and *that's* what caused the fire—and you still smoke?"

"Your father doesn't know," she says. "I only started again a few months ago. When you started seeing Del, and your dreams

got worse. I knew we would have to tell you eventually what had happened. The stress became overwhelming." She shakes her head, wiping tears from her cheeks. "Emily, I'm sorry. You will never know how sorry I am."

But I don't want to hear that she's sorry. All I want to hear is the truth. "So then what?" I demand. "What happened after the fire? After my—my father died?"

"I came to Connecticut. I met your dad—I mean, I met John. We fell in love. We got married. We didn't know how to explain things to you. Your life had been so traumatic already. Once you'd seemed to have forgotten, we thought it would be easier if we didn't tell you. Not right away."

"But I started having nightmares! Do you know what they're like? How could you sit there, through all those sessions with Dr. Miller, and not say anything? How could you do that to me?"

She takes another deep breath. "We planned on telling you after high school. We wanted to wait until you were an adult. Emily," she rushes on, "everything we've done is to protect you. Everything we've done is because we love you."

"You *lied* to me! You let me suffer for all these years." And then it occurs to me that she hasn't even explained the question I came here to have her answer.

"But Sandy Gray? Why is her name in my file?"

My mom nods to herself. "Because she's a connection to your past. She's your real father's first wife, and she has a lot of information about him. We thought that if anything ever happened— if you needed a comprehensive medical history, or anything like that—Sandy might know things about your father that I don't."

My dad is not my dad. He's my *step*father. How am I supposed to react when the world has been pulled out from underneath me? I begin to cry again. "My dreams," I say. "My nightmares. The fire. I remember all of it."

"You were only three," my mom says. "You were in the hospital for two days for smoke inhalation. I didn't let you come to your father's funeral. You were so little. Oh, baby, it was a nightmare, and you must have tucked it away somewhere, and all these years it's been trying to get out." She stands up so we are eye to eye. "I'm sorry we didn't tell you. I wanted to. But you have to understand, Emily, it was important that we wait until you were ready to hear it." She pauses. "I guess you're ready now."

"I guess so." My voice is flat.

"I mean, none of this is exactly—"

"Proper," I finish, bitter.

She nods.

"But I've seen my birth certificate. Your and Daddy's names are on it."

"Emily. Don't hate us," she whispers.

I feel cold. "What? What did you do?"

"Your father has a friend. It's his roommate from college. He did us some favors. He got us paperwork. So then, when it came time for us to do him a favor, we felt like we had no choice."

I shake my head, not comprehending.

"Del's father, honey. He was your dad's college roommate. He's the only other person who knows the truth about your past." She swallows. "Your dad and I are pretty sure that Del had an inkling of it, too. We've always thought that it's a big part of why he was so interested in you."

I feel so stupid. Of *course* it's why he was interested in me. My past is just as sad as his, only I didn't know it.

"You kept this from me my whole life," I say. I'm so furious that I'm trembling. The room feels fuzzy. "The fire was your fault. You started it with your cigarette."

My mother nods.

"But what about the water? In my nightmares?"

For another, almost imperceptible moment, she pauses. Is there something she's still not telling me?

"I don't know," she says. "Maybe you remember all the water that got in the house when they were putting out the fire."

I get the feeling that she's lying. But what she's telling me makes perfect sense; there would have been water everywhere.

I'm so angry and confused and heartbroken all at once that I don't know what to do. None of this feels real. None of it seems possible. My father is not my father. All my life, I've been dreaming of my real father without knowing it. I don't even remember what he looks like.

"Do you still have pictures of my real father?" I ask.

She nods.

"And you swear you were going to tell me when I turned eighteen?"

She nods again.

"Then why did you even put Sandy's name down, if you were going to tell me anyway?"

"I told you. We put her name down because we thought that if anything ever happened to both of us, then you would have to find out the truth, and she would be able to shed some light on it for you. But, Emily," she says, shaking her head, almost as though if she shakes it hard enough she can make all of this go away, "I've never even met Sandy Gray. Your real father told me she had a drug problem; that was why they split up in the first place. To be honest, I don't even know if she's still alive. So it's very odd that you would stumble upon her name, and it would lead you to all of this."

I close my eyes. *Let it be, Let it be, Let it be, Let it be . . .* I should have gone to her side and started singing when I came into the house. I should have left everything alone. This is too much for one girl to hold all by herself.

"You said you wanted to tell me," I say to my mom, "so why didn't you?"

"I didn't know where to begin," she says. "I was afraid you'd be so angry . . . are you?"

"Yes. You lied to me. How am I supposed to look at Daddy now? How am I ever supposed to think of him in the same way?"

"Emily, you have to understand—he *is* your father. He loves you more than anything in the world. He would do anything for you."

All I can think about is my own baby. How will he or she feel someday, knowing that I abandoned my baby? Will my child hate me?

I'll never know. And now that I've talked to my mother, learned the truth about my past, I almost wish I didn't know.

Maybe Bruce Graham was right. Maybe sometimes, it's better to lie.

# chapter seventeen

Almost two weeks go by without any signs from my father that he knows what I've learned. Then, one morning as I'm about to sit down beside Franny in homeroom, my advisor, Dr. Hollinger, shakes his head at me. "Don't even bother," he says. "Your dad wants to see you."

Even though it's been weeks since my mom told me the truth about Sandy Gray, about the fire and my real father, I know immediately what my dad wants to talk to me about, and I can't imagine facing him right now. It is simply too soon. Sure, I've seen him on campus. I've had brief, meaningless conversations with him here and there, but this is going to be a serious talk. I don't know what we might possibly say to each other.

In a way, though, I want to see him more than anything. I need to hear certain things from him: I want to know that I am still his daughter. That I will always be his daughter.

The door to his office is cracked, and I stand outside for a moment, watching him. He's holding a putting club in his hands, knees slightly bent, practicing his swing. I smile a little bit. To practice his putts, he has a tiny machine that spits the golf ball back out and across the room once the ball has been sunk. It was a gift from me a few years ago. For Father's Day.

"Daddy?" I ask, taking a step into the room.

*Clink.* He hits the ball. It goes past the putting machine, too far to the right, and comes to a rolling stop beneath his sofa.

He stands for a moment, staring at the ball until it becomes completely still.

"Emily," he says. He doesn't look at me, just continues to stare downward. "Close the door, would you?"

It appears as though my dad has aged ten years overnight. The lines in his face seem more pronounced, less gentle somehow. How can this man not be my father? He raised me. He has given me everything. Now, though, it feels like I'm no different than Franny or Grace or Steph: just another sad student with nobody else but him to call "Dad."

We take seats on opposite ends of his sofa. "I don't know how to say this," he begins, "so I'm just going to start. I know you talked to your mother. She told me last night."

I can only stare at the carpet. I don't want to cry, but it seems inevitable. I feel like I've done enough crying in the past year for a whole lifetime. Besides that, I feel physically exhausted in a way that I've never experienced before. I'm angry with my parents, of course, but it's more than that—my entire reality has been shattered. In the past weeks I've spent most of my nights wide-awake, thinking about all the things that I've taken for granted up until now, and how almost none of them are real. I feel almost too tired to speak. More than anything, I want to curl up in my parents' arms and have them hold me, to go back to the way things were before I knew anything about my past. I want to be oblivious again. But that's impossible.

"Emily," my dad continues, "I've thought about this day so

many times over the years, and I never knew exactly how it would play out. I never pictured it happening this way."

"Do you know that Mom still smokes?" I ask. It's the only thing I can think of to say.

Of course, I know he doesn't know she's still smoking; she told me herself. I am so, so tired of all the lies. I don't want to keep any more secrets.

Except for the secret about my baby.

*My baby.* I have no right to call it that. At night I've been wondering where he or she is living, wondering if my child is safe. What if somebody leaves a cigarette burning? Or walks away from my baby in a bathtub? Or doesn't keep him or her warm enough in the winter? When I signed away my child, I signed away my rights to know about, or have any control over, his or her happiness. The reality makes me heartsick.

"I didn't know your mom was still smoking," my dad says. His voice is slightly hoarse, so soft that I have to strain to hear it. "Emily," he repeats, "I would give you anything you want. Anything in the world."

I look him in the eye. "I want you to be my real father."

"I am your real father. Maybe not biologically, but in every other way."

"You lied to me."

"I didn't think I had a choice."

"Are there other lies? Other things you're not telling me?"

He doesn't say anything. The silence is enough; I know the answer is *yes.* But I can't even imagine what other secrets my parents might be keeping.

"Tell me what you want at this moment," my father says.

*Oh, Daddy.* All I want—all I *really* want—is to tell him my secrets, for him to tell me the whole truth about my past, and to know for sure that he still loves me. I want to be a family.

But none of that seems possible, so I ask for something I know I can have.

"I want to sleep," I say.

"Okay." My father nods. "We can do that. Do you want to go home for the morning?"

I gaze at him. "Can I sleep here? On your couch?"

He seems surprised. "Really?"

I nod. "Yes."

He doesn't think about it for more than a second. "Okay. Go ahead and lie down."

So I do. There's a throw with the Stonybrook Academy insignia lying across the back of the sofa; I pull it around my body, curl up in a ball, and rest my head against my hands.

My dad turns off the lights in his office. He kneels beside me, tugs the blanket toward my chin, and gives me a kiss on the forehead.

"Sleep," he says. "Take as long as you want."

I look at him, my vision growing blurry through tears. "I love you."

"I have always loved you," he says. "Someday, Emily, these will all be nothing but bad memories."

I know he's wrong; my child will never fade into nothing but a memory from a difficult time. But I can't tell him that, so instead I give him a half smile and say, "I hope so, Daddy."

He brushes the hair from my cheek. "Sweet dreams."

I am unconscious almost before he closes the door on his way out. It is a hard, dreamless sleep that lasts for over two hours.

It feels like I blink and the bell signaling the end of second period is ringing. I hear doors opening, voices in the hallway, and for a moment I consider pulling the blanket more tightly around me and sleeping through the whole morning.

Instead, I get up and go to class, like it's any other day in a normal life.

Every day before chorus, Ethan meets me outside my calculus class (which I'm failing), and we walk to the music room together. And every day, as we swing our arms hand in hand, he asks me the same question:

"So. Do you want to be my girlfriend?"

Every day, I give him the same answer. "I don't know, Ethan. I'm still kind of committed to someone."

I say it real coy, like I'm only kidding. And for all practical purposes, I might as well be. Everyone thinks Ethan and I are a couple.

Today, since I wasn't in calculus, he's waiting for me outside the chorus room. After we go through the same conversation, after I explain that I'm still somewhat committed, he frowns and asks, "Well, how about this?" He gives me a knee-buckling grin. "I'll fly backward around the earth to go back in time so that you never meet Del. We could rewrite history."

We're standing in the hallway beside the big double doors to the music room. It's been almost a month since our evening at the pier.

I'm leaning against the wall. Ethan stands in front of me, a hand on the wall beside me, his hips close to mine. He's a good ten inches taller than I am, so I have to stand on my tiptoes to put my lips close to his ear.

"Okay," I whisper. "You do that, and I'll be your girlfriend." It's amazing how good I'm getting at switching back and forth between chaos and normalcy. If he knew how I'd spent my morning, he might rethink flying backward around the earth for me.

He pulls back a little bit. "What's that supposed to mean?"

Our music director, Mrs. Foster, rushes past us into the room. She gives us a wink as she passes. "Come on, lovebirds. Time to sing."

"I didn't mean anything. It came out wrong," I say.

"Emily, it's been a month and you still won't say you're my girlfriend. You won't say that you'll go to homecoming with me. What do I have to do, track down Del so you can tell him it's officially over? Even though you haven't heard from him or spoken to him in months? Because I have news, Emily. It wouldn't take much for him to get in contact with you. He could pick up a phone. He could send an e-mail. Hell, he could write you a letter. You keep saying you're not sure it's over, and I'm getting tired of it." His tone softens as I try to blink back tears, without success. I should have stayed in my dad's office.

"Hey. Oh, come on, don't cry. Come here." He puts his arms around me. Despite everything I'm feeling that he can't possibly know about, I put my head against his chest and wrap my arms around his waist. He's so good, so kind—so different from Del in every way. I adore Ethan. And he deserves better than what I'm giving him.

"I'm sorry," I say. "There's a lot that went on between me and Del that you don't know about. I don't want him anymore, it's just that—"

"Emily." He's still holding me close. "If you're talking about what I think you're talking about, it's okay. I already know."

I pull back slightly, wiping my eyes, feeling mild alarm rise in goose bumps all over my body. "What do you know?"

He looks at the floor. "I know you slept with him."

"How do you know that?"

"My sister."

*That bitch. Bitch, bitch, bitch.* I don't even remember telling Stephanie that Del and I slept together, not explicitly. But she

213

knew I was sneaking out. She must have just assumed. "Oh. Well, you had a right to know."

"It's okay. I mean, it has to happen sometime, right?"

I nod.

Then he looks at me, his dark blue eyes flashing with sincerity. "I want you to know," he says, "that I haven't been with anyone yet."

"Oh." *Have I told you I'm also a mother? And I'm not who you think I am, either. I don't even know if my name is really Emily. Maybe my parents wanted to reinvent my entire past, to "protect" me from it. Pretty much my whole life up until now has been one big lie.*

When I think about it in those terms—all the lies, everything that has been kept hidden or buried for so long—it makes me want to be free, more than anything. It makes me want something good, something true.

"Ethan," I say, standing on my tiptoes, my mouth close to his, "I don't want to talk about Del anymore. I want to be with you." That reminds me. "Hey," I say, "what happened to your band? Do you still need a singer?"

He shakes his head. "We broke up at the end of last year."

"Why didn't I know that?"

"You were . . . distracted," he says. He's right. I wasn't paying attention to much of anything besides myself by the end of last year.

"You should get back together," I tell him. "I want to sing for you."

He rests his forehead against mine. The first bell rings for class.

"Really?"

"Yes."

His tone is cautious. "And you want to be together? You're sure?"

"I'm sure." And to show him I mean it, I kiss him on the mouth. We step backward until we're both leaning against the wall, ignoring the students rushing past us into the room to avoid the late bell. There's a part of me—a small part, but it's definitely there—that can't help but feel excited that I'm *Ethan Prince's Girlfriend*. Everyone who passes us pauses for a moment to stare.

I'm the princess. It has to be the most undeserved crown in the history of royalty.

There's another letter from Renee waiting for me in my room. In my reply to her, I'd told her all about my mother's news, about my certainty that Del knew what he was doing when he went after me. I'd told her about Ethan, and about how, ever since I found out about my own past, the guilt from my secret was starting to tear me up inside. I told her I thought of my baby every day, wondered where it was and if it was safe and happy. It's a horrible thing, to think of your own child and not even know whether it's a boy or a girl. To know that your child can never really be yours, that the choices you had to make at seventeen will affect multiple lives forever.

> Friday
> unseasonably cool but sunny
> legs v. sore from running the mile in gym class
>
> Emily,
>     I cannot believe you're dating Evan! (Just kidding...
> I know it's Ethan.) What is he like? You two are probably a
> nauseatingly adorable couple—worse than Hillary and Max.
> Do people call you Princess?
>     I wouldn't be so sure that Del's out of the picture. He

loved you, and he was a clever one. Just because you haven't heard from him doesn't mean you're not going to. I feel like he's just biding his time, like he has a plan. I don't think he'd just walk away knowing what he knew.

I'm applying to Yale for the summer. I'm going to take classes there and hopefully I'll get into their drama program next fall. Bruce says I don't need to go to college, and he's right, but I feel like it will keep me grounded, you know? A person has to have an identity that doesn't depend on other people, or else they can just disappear.

Now that you know what your nightmares are about, have they gone away? Have you talked to your father or Dr. Miller?

Can't you sense whether your baby was a boy or a girl? You must know deep inside somewhere, if you were able to hold on to those nightmares all your life. If I were you, I'd decide. Give him or her a name. Imagine how loved that baby is, just like you are. I think it will make you feel better.

xoxo
R.G.

It's funny how Renee knows exactly what to say, even from a distance. It's definitely occurred to me before that Del has some kind of plan, but I can't imagine what it might be. Isn't he afraid that I've stopped caring about him? Or does he know, somehow, that I can never stop caring, never stop thinking of him, because of what we created together?

*Can't you sense whether your baby was a boy or a girl?*

I can. I know, from somewhere deep within my body, that my baby was a girl. She was born July 23. She's ten weeks old.

Ten weeks! It feels like nothing, no time at all. But because of all the hours I spent with my trainer in New York, I can lie back on the bed and feel my abdominal muscles; I can feel the slight hollow between my hip bones. Ten weeks ago I had a baby, and almost nobody knows but me and Renee Graham, daughter to the stars, my secret pen pal. The whole situation seems too bizarre to be real. I tuck the letter under my mattress with the others as I hear my roommates making their way down the hall.

They're practically bumping into each other as they rush through the door.

"Emily," Grace says, clapping her hands together, "you're never going to guess what we have. Wait—ohmygoodness, you are Ethan Prince's *girlfriend*. Everybody saw you two outside the music room, making out like crazy. You can get in trouble for that, you know? Steph! No—Franny—show her what we have."

Franny's backpack, full of books, looks like it's going to knock her over. She hoists it onto her desk, digs through it, and pulls out a huge Ziploc bag of marijuana.

"Guess who we got this from. You'll never guess. Not in a million years." Grace snatches the bag from Franny, opens it, and takes a whiff. "It's called Mexican red hair. It was a thousand dollars."

Leave it to Stonybrook to have a fatally flawed banking system for its students. This is how it works: If you want money, you go to the school store, where there is basically a credit system with no limits. You need books? A new uniform? Fifty bucks for a haircut? A thousand dollars to buy primo dope? It gets put on your account, and your parents get charged at the end of the semester. The bills

217

are itemized, but most people's parents are so rich that nobody asks questions if their kids are taking out excessive amounts of cash—which most of the students do, for one reason or another. Last year, for instance, once I knew I was going to New York with Renee, I started systematically taking out a hundred dollars a week. My parents never batted an eye.

"Let me guess," I say, rolling my eyes, "you got it from Digger."

"WRONG!" Grace shrieks. She pauses. "Although we do have to give him a cut for turning his head the other way. It's a long story— Anyway, we got it from *Mr. Henry*."

My mouth drops. "Mr. Henry? The intern Mr. Henry?"

Stephanie snickers, grabbing the bag to smell it herself. "No, Em. Your dad Mr. Henry. Yes, Mr. Henry the intern." She grins at me. "Can you freaking believe it?"

"Honestly? No." Paul Henry has been my dad's personal intern for the past two years. He lives in the carriage house above our garage. I cross my arms. "How did this happen?"

"Well," Stephanie begins, "maybe we should let Franny tell you that."

"*Franny?*" I stare at my roommate. She gives me a guilty smile, and the pieces start to fall together: The chicken noodle soup we made him last year, and her insistence that she be the one to deliver it to him. The mismatched underwear. Her odd disappearances. I feel my stomach curdle a little bit. "Oh, please. Say it isn't what I'm thinking it is."

"He's only twenty-three," she says defensively.

"Someone's got daddy issues!" Grace shrieks again. Her grin barely fits on her face. "So," she rushes on, "we figure that we're totally safe, because since Franny is screwing around with *Paul*, he can't tell on us."

"We kind of blackmailed him," Stephanie says. "It was in everyone's best interest." She smiles at me. "Let's go for a ride, Em."

I blink at her. "What, now? To smoke?"

She nods.

"I want to come!" says Grace.

"I want to come!" says Franny.

"Why don't we just do it in here?" I ask. "We won't get caught."

"No," Stephanie says, her tone decisive. "I want to go for a ride with my best friend, and I want to go alone." She dangles her keys in my face. "Now."

I look at my roommates. Grace and Franny go quiet. Despite Stephanie's smile, there's a sudden, palpable tension in the room.

"Right now?"

Stephanie nods, still smiling at me, but her gaze is steely. I can tell it's going to be a fun ride.

# chapter eighteen

Normally, students aren't allowed to just drive off campus without permission. But I figure I've got leverage. Even if I didn't, at this point I don't really care. What are my parents going to do about it?

In the car, Stephanie doesn't say much of anything for a while. We make our way down Stonybrook's winding driveway, and I lay my calc book on my lap to start rolling a joint. Then, once it's lit and we're a good few miles from campus, Stephanie starts talking.

"I want to lay some ground rules," she says as we begin heading down Route 1 toward the beach. She drives a black Mercedes— a sixteenth-birthday present from her dad—and out of pure disgust toward him and his new family, she's made it her point to start taking as little care of the car as possible. As a result, it's seen virtually no maintenance in almost a year. The engine makes a funny clicking sound as we drive. Stephanie's solution is to turn on the radio to drown it out.

I've rolled a tiny joint on the surface of my book, which is balanced on my knees. "Some ground rules," I echo, pretending to be oblivious. "Okay. About what?"

She snorts. "Don't play dumb, Emily. You know. About you and Ethan."

"Stephanie." I light the joint and take a hit, pass it to her. For reasons that have recently become obvious, pot smoke has never bothered me as much as cigarette smoke. Still, I've only gotten high a handful of times. It's never been exactly my thing. "You can't do that," I say, holding my breath.

(Stephanie, holding her breath:) "Why can't I?"

"Because it's weird, that's why. Just because he's your brother—"

"He's my *only* brother. My freaking *twin*. Our dad walked out last year"—(passes joint to me)—"and you have no idea how crazy things have been. I have every right to offer some suggestions about how we can all keep this situation civilized."

"You think I have no idea how crazy things have been? I do have an idea. I'm your best friend." I pause. "And I'm his girlfriend now. I've known both of you since seventh grade. And I know a little bit about screwed-up families."

She doesn't take the bait. "Right. Emily Meckler and her perfect parents. You think your family's screwed up because your mom secretly smokes?" She sighs. "Can I just tell you the rules? There are only three of them. I've been working on them for, like, forever."

"And you're finally getting to impose them on someone, now that your brother is dating one of your friends?"

She shrugs. "Something like that."

I figure, what does it matter? Let her think she has some control. "Okay, fine," I say. "Lay 'em on me."

"Okay." (Puff, puff, pass.) "First of all, no more making out in the hallways like you were this afternoon. It was disgusting. From now on, I don't want to see any physical displays of affection beyond hand-holding."

"We weren't even making out." (Puff, puff, pass.)

"Second of all," she continues, ignoring me, "you can't have

him for any of the holidays. We already have to alternate between my mom's and dad's houses, and he's not coming to campus to visit you."

They live in Colorado. It's not exactly a short commute. "Steph. Fine. You can have your brother for holidays. I'm sure I'll manage without him."

"Okay." (Puff, puff, pass.) "Third. And this is the big one, Emily."

*I can hardly wait.*

"You can't have sex with him. I totally forbid you."

She's gone completely berserk. I've *never* had such a strange conversation with someone—and I've had some odd ones lately.

"No sex with Ethan," I repeat. "You know we've only been an official couple for like a day, right?"

She throws the roach out the window, leans over to fumble through the glove box for her cigarettes. "Yeah, I know that—oh, there was one other rule! I forgot." Her tone remains stern. "You can't break up with him."

"Why can't I break up with him?" I ask. "I thought you'd be happy if I broke up with him. Then you'd have—um—you'd have him back."

The *absurdity* of it all. The *nerve* she has, telling me what I can and can't do with her brother! Not only is it insane, but it's also gross. How would she know if we had sex? Does she expect a play-by-play of every date? If I had a brother—which, who the hell knows at this point, maybe I do somewhere—I certainly wouldn't want to know about his sex life, let alone write the rules for it.

"If things don't work out, that's fine. But I just mean that you can't hurt him. No cheating, no dumping, no flirting with other boys. That kind of thing."

"That sounds like more than three rules. That's, like, four rules plus a bunch of addenda to the rules."

"Just tell me you'll follow them." She looks at her cigarette

with distaste, flicks it out the window as she does a U-turn at a red light. "I don't want you to hurt him, that's all."

"Fine," I say. Then, "Maybe you should write them down and post them on my wall. You know, in case I forget one."

Stephanie giggles. The tension is broken. "I know you think it's weird," she says, "but I'm serious."

"Okay." What she doesn't know is that I have no plans to sleep with Ethan, and I don't think I'll be breaking up with him any-time soon. Unless . . .

*Boysboysboys*. Del's face flashes in my mind. I try to picture the face of a baby, the baby I carried for nine months. *Our* baby. But nothing comes. I can't imagine her. I don't even know what a ten-week-old *looks* like, or what they can do. Do they sit up? Drink from a bottle? Sleep through the night? How would I know? I'm just a kid. She might have come from my body, but I'm not her mother. Not since the second I signed her away, without even looking at her face.

But I remember the sound of her crying. I remember the feeling of achy despair as she was whisked away to the nursery, the way the nurses looked at me the whole time I was in the hospital. They were all cool, detached, and acted like I'd done something terribly wrong.

We make it back to campus just in time for dinner. We throw on our uniforms, spray ourselves with plenty of perfume, and put Visine in our eyes.

On the way up to dinner, I see Ethan waiting for me outside Winchester.

"Let's sit at Mr. Henry's table tonight," I tell him. I feel foggy and sort of gross. I've never really liked smoking pot; it always makes me self-conscious.

But I have some ideas about Paul Henry and Franny. Mostly, I

just want it to stop. She's a *victim*, for God's sake, and she doesn't even realize how pathological she's being.

Paul Henry graduated from Harvard after Stonybrook, and my father adores him. I know for a fact that he wants to give Paul a permanent place on the faculty next fall.

Ethan and I sit at the end of the table farthest from Mr. Henry.

Ethan squints at me as he reaches for the mashed potatoes. "You're acting weird, Emily."

Stephanie is sitting beside me. We've been giggly since we sat down. I put a hand beside my mouth to keep Mr. Henry from seeing and give Ethan the universal sign for getting high, pressing my thumb and index finger together against my lips. Then I give him an apologetic grin, batting my eyelashes.

"Oh." He's obviously surprised. "Really?"

I nod. "Your sister made me do it."

"Well, in that case—here you go." And he begins to pile mashed potatoes onto my plate, one spoonful after the next.

"Stop!" Stephanie screeches, laughing. "You don't want a fat girlfriend."

"Her, too?" Ethan asks.

"Yes," I say. He picks up the serving dish of mixed vegetables and starts dishing them generously onto his sister's plate.

We're practically holding on to each other to stay in our chairs, laughing, when Mr. Henry scowls at us and says, "Hey, girls. Calm down."

"Ohhh," Stephanie says, under her breath, "look who's in charge. Hey, Mr. Henry—what's your girlfriend's name again?"

He glares at her. For the rest of dinner, he doesn't say a word to us.

\* \* \*

Later that night, after study hall but before lights out, I walk across campus to the carriage house above my parents' garage and bang on Mr. Henry's door.

It takes him forever to answer. When he finally does, it's obvious he's just gotten out of the shower: his hair is damp, a T-shirt and jeans thrown on.

"Emily," he says, "what are you doing here?"

"I want to talk to you."

He keeps the door almost closed. "About what?"

"You know what." I cross my arms. "And if you don't let me in, my dad's gonna know all about it, too."

He looks around, checking to see if anyone can see me. There's nobody; besides, it's almost dark. "Okay," he says, "come in."

He doesn't offer me a seat, but I take one on the sofa anyway. "Thanks for getting us our smoke," I say, sarcastic.

He blinks at me. "I have no idea what you're talking about."

"Oh, no? You don't remember getting an ounce of high-grade reefer for your girlfriend? Hm."

His look turns stony. "You've got it all wrong."

I remember when Paul was at Stonybrook, which makes the whole thing with Franny all the more creepy. Was he ogling her when she was in eighth grade and he was a senior?

"Well, then, let's talk about something we both know about," I say. "Franny."

Paul starts to open his mouth, but I don't let him get a word in. "You know she had a stepfather who—" I stop myself. I bite my lip. I feel like it's none of my business to be telling him this. Even worse, I'm afraid that telling him might only make him want her more. This is the last thing Franny needs right now.

"A stepfather who what?" he asks, obviously interested.

"Never mind. But listen, Paul."

225

He smirks. "That's Mr. Henry, please, Emily."

"I said listen, *Paul*. I don't want you screwing around with her anymore."

He looks at me in disbelief. "And you're telling me this because you're what? Her keeper?" He pauses. "She's eighteen, Emily. It's not illegal."

"But it's enough to get you fired."

"You wouldn't do that," he says. "Come on. I've known you since you were a kid." He gives me a smug grin. "Besides, I don't think Daddy would like it very much if he knew his little girl was a stoner."

"I am not a stoner. I didn't have anything to do with that, um, transaction. But you know, Paul, for someone who went to Harvard, you're not being very smart. What are you going to do, go to my dad and say, 'I might be sleeping with a student, but you should know that I sold her roommates a felony's worth of weed'? How does that help your case?"

He opens his mouth, closes it, opens it again. "Okay. What do you want?"

"I already told you, I want you to stop screwing around with Franny." It's not lost on me that I'm doing pretty much the same thing to Paul that Stephanie just did to me. But it's different with Franny. Franny can't protect herself. She needs someone to help her.

"Emily. You have to understand, it's not just a thing with us." He hesitates. "I know a little bit about her stepfather. She's been seeing Dr. Miller. I think it's helping. Have you noticed she hasn't been pulling her hair out lately?"

I hadn't. I've been too preoccupied with my own problems. But now that he mentions it, I realize that he's right.

"Emily," he says, "I'll be honest with you. I think I'm in love with her."

"Oh, for God's sake."

"I'm serious! She's an incredible person. You don't even see her, do you?" He crosses his arms. "If you're going to cause trouble, we'll just wait until after she graduates." And he rolls his eyes. "But you ought to know that you're being ridiculous."

"Shut up. You're just an intern, you know. I know for a fact that my dad is leaning toward not hiring you in the fall," I lie.

He frowns. "He's not? But he told me—"

"I don't care what he told you. I'm his daughter." *Except that I'm not.* "But I could put in a good word. If . . ."

"If what? Anything to get you out of here."

"If you do two small favors for me."

"What?"

"Find out what happened to Madeline Moon-Park." This one's for Renee, mostly. "You remember her, don't you?"

He shrugs. "Not really. She was in your class?"

"She was a year behind me. And she didn't come back last year. She was here since seventh grade, and nobody has heard *anything* from her. So do some digging, ask my dad, whatever. Find out everything you can."

Paul nods. "Okay. I can do that. What's the second favor?"

I hesitate. "There was a boy here last year," I say. "He wasn't here long. You might remember him."

Of *course* he remembers him. How could he not? People like Del come along once in a lifetime.

Paul's lips curl into a slow grin. "Let me guess. His name was Del Sugar?"

"Yes," I say.

"I remember him, all right. I remember him well. You want to know where he went?"

"Do you know?"

"I do," he says. "Your father still talks to his parents, you

know. And for someone who thinks she's so clever, you shouldn't have to blackmail me to find out what happened to him. He was a coke fiend. He went to rehab."

*Of course! Rehab! That's why I haven't* . . .

"But rehab only lasts for, what, a few months?" I ask.

Paul shrugs. "It depends."

"So is he still there?"

He takes a moment to stare at me. "I shouldn't tell you," he murmurs.

"Tell me what?" I can feel my pulse quicken. "What happened to him? Where is he?"

"It's time for you to go," Paul says.

"I'm not leaving this room until you tell me what happened to Del."

"Nobody knows," he says, heading toward the door. I get up and follow him.

"What do you mean, nobody knows?"

Paul opens the door. He leans against the frame, clearly enjoying how agitated I've become. "He went to rehab for three months," he tells me, "and then he went home. After that, he ran away. Nobody's heard from him in months. Not even his parents."

# chapter nineteen

I'm in Dr. Miller's office with my mom and "dad." The first five minutes is nothing but weary silence. Last night, my mother showed up at my dorm room to tell me that, together, she and my father had gone to Dr. Miller and explained the entire situation, and that we were meeting in her office first thing in the morning, during my study hall.

So here we are.

Dr. Miller's hands are folded on her desk. "Well," she begins, "Emily, we're here for you, after all. Would you like to start?"

Where am I supposed to begin? What does she expect me to say? What do any of them expect me to say?

"I don't know what you want to hear," I tell them. "I live the same life for almost eighteen years, never knowing anything different, and then I find out that I'm not even your real child, Daddy. How do you think I feel? I'm pissed." I pause. "I'm just like Franny and Grace and Steph, calling you 'Dad.' I'm not any different now."

"You're pissed," Dr. Miller repeats. "Okay. That's good. That's healthy."

I want to smack her across her accredited face. How can she possibly know how I feel? How can she sit here with my parents, pretending to be an impartial mediator, knowing that we've wasted session after session trying to work to the bottom of something that my parents could have explained in one conversation?

We sit in her office for what feels like hours; when I glance at the clock, I see that it's only been about twenty minutes. Forty to go. My mom has just finished retelling the story of how she and my father have been deceiving me my entire life—which Dr. Miller interrupts to make sure I understand was all "in my best interest"—when my dad sits up a little straighter beside me. Until now, he's been silent and stiff, although there are tears in his eyes. He's gripping the arm of Dr. Miller's sofa so tightly that his knuckles are white.

"We haven't talked about Del," he says to my mother.

Her face goes whitish. I can smell smoke on her. Of everything I've learned recently, the fact that she's still smoking—or rather, smoking again—hurts in an especially sad way. Her smoking led to my father's death, and it almost killed me. And she can't stop? It's sickening. I never, *ever* want to let an addiction rule me like that.

"What about Del?" I ask. "I already know that he knew everything about me."

"Del's missing," my father tells me.

So much for blackmailing Mr. Henry.

"Yeah? So what?" I want to hurt my parents more than anything right now, and I have the ammunition to do it. I could tell them about all the times I snuck out to be with Del after my father had forbidden me to see him, how I fell in love with him. I could tell them we slept together. I could tell them about the baby.

But I won't. It already hurts too badly; hurting my parents will only make things worse. In my nightmares, sometimes, I hear my baby's cry as she's taken away from me, wanting—what? Of course I know what she wanted. She wanted me.

"His parents think that Del went to find his sister," my father continues, "and that's a definite possibility." He stares at the Oriental rug on the floor in front of him. He either can't or won't look at me. "But I think he may come looking for you."

"Why?" I ask.

"Because he knows about your past." My dad starts to tap his fingers nervously against the leather arm of the sofa. "Del is a very intelligent boy, and he knows how to get information. His father called me a few nights ago. His parents are worried sick. They haven't heard from him in months, and he didn't have any money when he left. But his father told me that Del had heard them talk about you before, long before they sent him here. They never used your name, but he must have put two and two together. Emily, honey—that's why I wanted you to stay away from him. He wanted you *because* of what happened to you. You see, Del is fascinated by people who are like him—people with incomplete histories, from broken families. He must have believed that you two belonged together somehow."

For just a second, I lose my breath. The room seems to shrink a little. The bell rings.

"You think he'll come to get me?" I ask. But, knowing what I know now, I'm *certain* he'll come to get me, even though I'm not sure I want to see him. I don't know what I want anymore. I want a normal life, but what's normal? I left "normal" behind a long time ago, the first night I met Del in Winchester.

And I don't know what I expect to happen when he shows up. We can't go anywhere together. I have things to do like apply to colleges and take the SATs. The idea of normalcy seems bizarre when I compare it to the reality of my life right now.

"You can miss class," my father says. "I want us to talk about this."

The late bell rings.

231

"No." I shake my head. I get up, and my parents try to physically push me back onto the sofa.

"Emily, baby," my mom says, "we did all of this because we love you. Don't you understand that?"

All I imagine is trying to tell my own child the same thing someday.

I shove them away. I rush out of the room and hurry to the nearest bathroom to compose myself. I stand in front of the mirror, touch up my makeup, and wait until my eyes don't look so puffy. I smooth out my uniform and take a deep breath. Then I go to chemistry class.

It's like I'm living two different lives. Stephanie, Ethan, and Franny are all in my chem class. Stephanie and Ethan are lab partners; it was another one of her rules. She's been making addenda to the original three rules on a pretty much daily basis. I'm not allowed to be his lab partner, or his partner for any reason in any classes that the three of us are in together. I've been letting everything slide, mostly because I'm so preoccupied with the mess that my life has become, and I can barely devote any thought to having a normal senior year, but I'm starting to get tired of it. I smile at Ethan from across the room, where the contents of his test tube have turned the correct shade of blue. Franny and I are partners; our tube is purple, and it's giving off a foul smell.

"I know what you did," Franny murmurs, dumping some white powder into the tube, which turns the contents almost black. The smell gets worse.

"What did I do?" I ask innocently.

"I know you talked to Paul. He told me everything."

"Oh, did he? Franny, what he's doing is wrong. He's taking advantage of you."

"We love each other!" she insists. "And besides, I don't think you have any right to talk."

"What's that supposed to mean?"

"You know exactly what it means. I'm talking about you and Del, last year. Everyone knew you were sneaking out to sleep with him at night. You're not exactly pure as the fallen snow, and he was no angel, so maybe you should mind your own business." Then she rifles through her book bag—our test tube contents beginning to bubble and smoke, which is *definitely* not supposed to happen—and pulls out a plain white envelope. "Here," she whispers. "I'm supposed to give this to you."

I blink at the envelope. "What is it?"

"It's from Paul."

Since I know nobody knows where Del is—there's no way *Paul* could have figured it out—the envelope must have the information about Madeline.

"Did you open this?" I ask.

She shakes her head. "He told me not to. He told me to tell you to handle the contents delicately. He said you'd understand." She's curious, though. "What is it?"

I shake my head. "It's nothing. Just some stuff about Del that I wanted him to get for me."

"Oh? I thought you were over Del Sugar. After all," she smirks, "you're the Princess now."

"I *am* over Del," I say. "It's just, you know, information is always a good thing."

"Whatever." She glares at me. "Now you have what you wanted. Happy?"

I nod, tucking the envelope into my chem notebook. I don't know why Franny's so upset with me; I'm only trying to protect her. She's been much more assertive lately, though. I suppose it's good for her to stand up for herself.

"Good. Then leave us alone, Emily. You don't know what it's like to love somebody who you're not supposed to have."

I almost laugh out loud.

I rush back to the dorms after school before anybody else has a chance to get there, dig into my backpack, and find the envelope. Inside, there are two pieces of paper: a note from Paul, and a photocopy of a newspaper clipping.

> Emily,
>
> I hope you'll understand how important it is to keep this quiet. It was hard to get, and from what I understand, Madeline was a nice girl. Even though she's not here anymore, that doesn't mean this getting out wouldn't hurt her. There's a thing called Karma.
>
> P.
>
> P.S. She's at a boarding school in West Virginia now called Woodsdale Academy. If she hasn't contacted you, it's probably because she wants it that way. Can you blame her? But since you were so insistent, here's her phone number: (304) 555-8547.

The clipping is obviously from Madeline's hometown paper. The article takes up two full columns of print. The details are grisly.

Madeline's mother died. But it's so much more than that. It's more than I ever could have imagined. I shudder as I read the entire article, and when I'm finished, I immediately read it again. I can hardly believe what I'm learning. My heart breaks for Madeline.

There's only one other person who deserves to know what happened. I find a new envelope and stuff Paul's note and the photocopied article inside. Then I write a short note of my own.

Renee,
    Here's what I learned about Madeline. You can do what you want. It might help for her to hear from someone who loves her regardless. But knowing what we know now, don't you think it's obvious she wanted to disappear?
    Destroy this letter after reading.

    I miss you. I love you.
    E.

I seal the envelope, put a stamp on it, and take it straight down to the campus mailbox. I make a silent promise to myself that, aside from Renee, I'll never tell another soul what I've just learned.

Less than three days later, I get a reply from her. The note is short and to the point.

Thursday
cold and sunny
heartbroken

Emily,
   Oh my God.
   Shhhh.
   I'm going to call her. Even if she won't talk—I need to hear her voice.

   More to come. I love you, too.
   R.G.

236

# chapter twenty

Over the next few months, I get pretty good at pretending that things are normal in my life. Ethan and I go out together most weekends. He is different from Del in every way imaginable. Last year, at a Halloween party off campus, Del and I went dressed as Adam and Eve. The apple tattoo on his arm was a nice touch. This year, Ethan and I stay on campus for Halloween and go to the homecoming dance dressed as—who else?—Clark Kent and Lois Lane.

But it's not just the physical differences, Del's wiry build and blond hair compared to Ethan in all his muscled, tall-dark-and-handsome glory. There are so many personality differences that it's hard to believe I've dated both of them. It's hard to believe how much I care for both of them. Del was sneaky and brilliant to the point where even I didn't actually know him. And the more I get to know Ethan as his girlfriend, the more I realize that he is genuinely kind and honest and compassionate. He rarely drinks; he isn't exactly the greatest at holding his liquor. He'd never dream of smoking.

We are together all the time, but things are progressing slowly. When we're alone, I'm always afraid of him getting too close. The idea of sex feels vulgar to me. I've been pregnant and had a child;

my body does not feel like a teenager's so much as it does a woman's. I remember what it's like to carry a baby and to give birth. I have had physical experiences that none of my peers can even imagine. They were experiences I never wanted or asked for, but I can't get them out of my head.

Since we've been dating more than four months, the topic of sex has naturally come up. I told him that I wasn't comfortable with it. I told him that what happened with Del was a mistake that I regret more than anything. True to form, Ethan respected my decision. He didn't ask questions.

I try not to think about Del. But sometimes at night, when I'm taking out my contact lenses before bed, I slide them to the side and stand in front of the mirror, willing myself not to blink them back into place, just to remember how it felt that first night.

*Can you see me?*

*No.*

*I can see you.*

I know now what he was really talking about. He saw so much more of me than I knew.

Since I've been dating Ethan, things between me and Stephanie have been fine. I'm following all of her rules, even though they're ridiculous, and life has been relatively calm. There are the nightmares that I'm still having, not only about my childhood and the father I never knew, but now about my own baby, the sound of her cries as she was taken away from me. And there's the worry that eats away at me from not knowing where Del is, whether or not he's safe, or if he will ever show up to see me. And if he does— what then? There's the fact that I can barely even look at my father, who isn't really my father. There's the fact that I'm still haunted by so many questions that there aren't answers for. What about

the water in my dreams? My mother's response just didn't seem to cut it.

By January, after a brutally awkward winter break at home with my parents, Connecticut has a constant blanket of snow covering everything in sight. All of the students are used to the intense cold; we trudge up to school in boots and coats lined with down; we sleep with three blankets to keep warm in the drafty old buildings; we carry premium lip balm and moisturizer pretty much everywhere and stay indoors as much as possible and get used to being shocked on a regular basis from all the dry friction.

But just after we get back from winter break, there's a brief warm snap. It lasts only about a week. By "warm" I mean that the temperature climbs into the fifties. All the snow melts; you can actually *feel* the sun as you're walking to school. So, figuring we should seize the day while we still can, the seniors decide to have a beach party in Groton, at—where else—Amanda Stream's family's summer house.

Amanda's parents are, of course, not in town. With no supervision all weekend, things get a little crazy. There is a huge bonfire on the beach. Inside the house, someone has somehow (I suspect Franny through Mr. Henry, who she's *still* seeing) gotten ahold of four kegs. By midnight, the house and the private beach behind it are both full of drunken teenagers.

Ethan and I have been inseparable all night. I feel so comfortable and calm around him. He is so much safer than Del, so much softer in a way. I love that he is genuine and sweet and giving. I love that he does not keep secrets from me. There are times when I feel like I could tell him anything, and he would understand. But, of course, there are plenty of things that I'll never tell anyone.

We are perched in a lawn chair beside the bonfire. I'm sitting on Ethan's lap; a huge plaid blanket is wrapped around both of us, and my head is resting on his shoulder as we alternately sip from

the same beer. When it's gone, Ethan nudges me. "Want to go for a walk?"

"Sure," I say.

With the blanket still wrapped around our bodies, arms around each other's waists, we walk to the edge of the property. It's a beautiful night, cool but not too cold. The moon looks nearly full, and reflects off the dark water to illuminate a clear sky full of fat, glowing stars.

"Can you believe this?" Ethan asks, taking a seat in the sand, tugging me beside him. "Look at the ocean."

"It seems endless."

He knows about my supposedly inexplicable fear of water. He pulls me closer. "I'm right here," he says. "I've got you."

"Yes, you do." I kiss him.

"I'm so glad." He kisses me back. Before I know it, we're both on the sand, the blanket on top of us, out of sight from the rest of the party.

Things go from warm to hot in a matter of moments. We are both tipsy, sloppy, loving the feel of each other's bodies.

"Ethan," I murmur, "we need to stop."

"I know." He kisses my neck, slides his hands up the back of my shirt to unclasp my bra. "Believe me, Em, I know."

I pull back slightly. "Does it bother you?"

He shakes his head. "I told you, I'll respect whatever you want to do. Whenever you're ready."

*But what if I'm never ready*? The thought hasn't occurred to me until now. Things with Ethan are fantastic; they're definitely serious. Won't it have to happen sometime?

"I'm not on any birth control," I say.

He pauses in his effort to remove my shirt. "What?"

The shirt is halfway over my head. "Hm?"

He tugs it all the way off, pulls me even closer so that there's

almost no space between our bodies. He's already taken his shirt off. We are pressed together close as can be.

He puts his mouth against my ear. "Does this mean you're thinking about getting on birth control?"

"I didn't say that. Ethan, just kiss me."

So he does. As things grow hotter, as his fumbling becomes more deliberate, he murmurs, "I want to tell you something."

"What?"

"I love you."

"I know that." I hesitate only for a moment before responding. I know it's true. Maybe not the same way it was with Del, but true nevertheless. "I love you, too."

He's almost *crying.* "I've loved you for so long, Emily."

I pause. "You have?"

"Yes. And there's something I want you to know. I don't want you to feel pressured. But I just think you should know about it, for whenever the time is right."

He's slurring his words a little bit, fumbling drunkenly with the button on my pants.

"Okay."

"I carry a condom with me. All the time. Every time we're together. So you don't have to worry too much about birth control. I've got it covered. Whenever you're ready."

"Good to know," I murmur, gently tugging his hands away from my pants, holding them in mine.

"Ethan?"

"Yes?"

"We're drunk. I don't want to do it tonight. Not like this."

He sighs, half-yawning. "You're such a good girl." The irony to his statement makes me hate myself a little bit. Then he asks, "Em?"

"Yeah?"

"When do you think it will be time?"

"I don't know."

He takes a long, deep breath. "All right."

"I'm sorry."

"It's okay. Really, it's fine. I do love you."

"I love you, too."

"Emily?"

"What is it, Ethan?"

"I think I have to throw up."

The next morning, Ethan realizes that he lost his watch at some point in the evening. We look for it in the sand, but can't find it anywhere.

Ethan is the kind of guy who *needs* to wear a watch. He can't stand not being on time, not being on top of life in general. So I decide to buy him one for his birthday, which is coming up on January 15.

Of course, it's also Stephanie's birthday. On the evening of the fifteenth, she comes into my room and asks, "What did you get my brother?"

Without looking up, I say, "I'm going to sleep with him. That's his present. Wild sex."

"Not funny," she says. "Seriously, I just got back from the mall with his present. I want to compare gifts."

I show her the watch I bought him. I'm excited about it; it's almost identical to the old one, except I've had it engraved on the back: it says, "*To E.P. with love, E.M.*"

I smile at her. "What do you think? He'll love it, right?"

Stephanie frowns. "No. I don't think so, Emily." When she looks at me, she's practically glaring.

I'm confused. "Why not? He just lost his watch last week. I was *with him* when he lost it. He needs—"

"I know he just lost his watch. That's why I bought him *this*." And she pulls her gift for him out of its bag.

It's the same watch. I'm not kidding: the same exact watch from the same store.

"It wasn't just me," she says. "My mom and I picked it out together. She's over at Winchester right now, and the *three* of us are going out to dinner tonight." She gives me a matter-of-fact look. "I guess you'll be taking that back, won't you?"

"Steph, no." I shake my head. "It's engraved." And I show her.

She snorts. "Well, that was stupid of you. I mean, that's even more of a reason why I should give him this one instead. What's he going to do after you two break up, Emily? He's not going to want a watch with your initials on it."

I can feel my cheeks growing warm. "Who said anything about us breaking up? And you know, he invited me to dinner tonight."

She looks like she wants to smack me. "I said no holidays!"

"It's your *birthday*, not freaking Christmas! Besides, you're going to be there, too!"

"You're taking that watch back."

I shake my head. "No. I'm not."

"You're not coming to dinner with us."

"Yes, I am. I was *invited*."

"Well, as the birthday girl, I'm officially uninviting you."

"I don't think the birthday *boy* will be too happy about that."

Stephanie stands up. "You know what? Fine, Emily. How about this? I go to dinner with my mother and brother for our *family* birthday dinner. My mom and I give Ethan the watch that *we* bought him. Then, later on tonight, you can give him the watch *you* bought. And we'll see which one he wants to keep."

We are glaring at each other; it's the first real fight we've had since I started dating Ethan. Considering how ridiculous she's been, I'm surprised there haven't been more problems before now.

But I know Ethan, and I know he'll love the watch. *My* watch. So I say, "Fine. That sounds like an excellent plan."

"Fine."

"Good."

"*Good*." She stands up, clutching the watch she bought tightly to her chest. "I'm going over to Winchester now. I'll see you later."


Every time it's somebody's birthday, the school makes a cake for the birthday boy or girl to pick up after dinner and take back to the dorm. Since Stephanie and Ethan aren't here, my room-mates and I pick up their cakes for them. I drop Ethan's off at his dorm, and then Grace and Franny and I walk back to the quad with Stephanie's.

There's a faculty meeting up at the school tonight, so the dorms are pretty much deserted. It makes it tough to do home-work knowing that nobody's going to pop a head into your door-way (which has to be open during study hall) to make sure you're getting things done. As a result, after something like forty-five minutes of work, Grace and Franny and I make a collective deci-sion to stop working and give each other manicures.

I'm leaning against the edge of Stephanie's bed, filing Franny's brittle nails while she pages through an issue of *Cosmo* with her free hand. "I'm pissed at Steph," I say.

"Really?" Franny asks, looking up from the magazine. "Why?"

I tell them briefly what happened with the watches. When I'm finished, Grace says, "Let me see the watch."

I go into my room and get the box.

When I open it up to show them, I almost can't believe what I'm looking at. I blink and blink, making sure my contacts are in place. The face of the watch is smashed. Glass broken, time-telling ability defunct.

"It's *broken*, Emily," Grace tells me, suddenly standing at my side. She's obviously excited, shaking a bottle of purple nail polish, grinning like a maniac.

"Is it? I thought it was supposed to look this way." I glare at her. "You know who did this?"

Franny gasps. "You think Steph would have?"

"It's been in my desk drawer since we left for dinner. She left to go over to Winchester . . . but she could have come back once she saw me leave." I'm so furious, I can barely think straight. "She's the only person who knew I bought him this watch. Besides, who else would want to break it?"

"I know, but Emily. That's so . . . insane."

I am fuming. The watch was expensive, but that's not the point; *my best friend broke my boyfriend's watch*. It's just a watch, and she couldn't stand the idea of *me* giving it to him.

"I don't think Steph would have done that," Franny says.

I want to slap her for being so naive. "We're talking about Stephanie. She's obsessed."

"You should beat her up!" Grace shrieks.

"I'm not going to beat her up," I say. I realize that my voice is shaking.

My roommates both look at me with expectation. "You have to do *something*," Franny says.

My eyes fall on Stephanie's cake. It's a double-layer devil's food with "Happy Birthday Stephanie!" written in careful cursive icing, surrounded by red and white flowers.

"I know," I murmur. "I have an idea."

They both look at me, following my gaze.

"You could poison it," Grace offers.

"Grace," Franny says, "where would she get *poison*?"

"I don't know. The chem lab?"

They start talking like I'm not even there.

"What kind of poison? She's not going to kill her."

"I don't know, Franny. It was just an idea."

"You know how bad Emily is in chem." Franny shakes her head, as if the idea were ever actually a possibility. "Poison is definitely *not* the way to go. Emily could get arrested."

"Would you two be quiet?" I snap. "This is what I'm doing. And you two are going to help me."

I glance from the broken watch to the cake, back to the watch. Then I take a few steps across the room and, with my bare hand, grab a fistful of cake and shove it into my mouth.

Franny and Grace stand there, gaping at me, both of them on the verge of . . . *something*. Either laughter or outrage.

"Look at that watch," I say, my mouth full. "It looks like she took a freaking hammer to it. We are going to eat this *entire* cake. Right now."

Franny picks up the watch to take a better look. When she does, shards of glass from the face fall out onto the ground.

She bites her lip. "I shouldn't. It's so much sugar."

"Oh, right," Grace says, "you really shouldn't. You wouldn't want to be a size zero, fatty."

I take another handful of cake and rush across the room to Franny, shoving it into her mouth. "You like that? It's good, right?"

"Stop!" Grace shrieks, doubled over laughing. "Wait, wait, I want some. Wait for me."

We don't have any silverware, just our hands. The three of us sit in Stephanie and Grace's room together, in a semicircle around the cake, and shovel it in, bite by bite, until the last crumb is gone.

Three girls, one cake, two crimes. Again and again, it occurs to me how wonderfully, absurdly *ordinary* all of this is compared to the secret truths I'm living with.

"I can't believe we ate the whole thing," Grace says. Her tone is somber as she stares at the cardboard platter and box.

"Stephanie's going to wonder," Franny murmurs. "She's going to expect her cake, and when it's not here, she's going to want to know what happened to it."

"We'll tell her it never came," I say. I still don't know how I'm going to confront her about the watch. What will Ethan think? He'll definitely be angry with her, but will it make him realize how much she's intruding in our relationship? I wonder what he would do if he knew she'd forbidden us to have sex. The fact that she smashed the watch almost makes me want to do it with him, just to *show* her.

Franny shakes her head. "People saw us coming back from dinner with it. She's going to know it was here."

"Okay," I say, thinking. "We have to destroy the evidence." And I take the box, crumple it up into the tiniest ball possible, and stuff it in my coat pocket. "I'll be right back."

I go out to the Dumpster behind our dorm. I stand on my tip-toes and toss in the handful of crushed cardboard. When I get back to my room, the three of us go to the bathroom together and brush our teeth. Then we wait.


Stephanie comes back around eight thirty.

"You guys are supposed to be working," she says, giving me a fresh scowl. "We have midterms coming up. Em, you're going to fail everything."

I stand up. "Oh, like that's your concern right now." I *do* want to beat her up. I want to hit her, to pull her hair, to punch her in her smug birthday-girl face. "Come on," I say, stepping close to her. "We are officially in a fight."

She smiles innocently. "Why?"

"You know why! Don't play stupid." And I show her the watch.

She covers her mouth with a hand; I can tell she's trying not to laugh. "Oh my God. Emily, I swear to you, I did not do that."

"Right." And I take my index finger and poke her right in the center of the chest. "Don't bother, okay? It was obviously you. Just wait until I tell your brother."

She narrows her eyes at me. "You aren't going to do that."

"I'm not? I'm putting my shoes on right now. I'm going over to Winchester to tell him. How are you gonna stop me?"

Stephanie doesn't move. She doesn't seem alarmed or upset in the slightest. Her tone remains calm and collected. "Franny? Grace? Can Em and I be alone for a minute?"

The two of them rush from the room.

Stephanie takes a moment to stare at me. Then she goes to our bedroom door, opens it to find Grace and Franny pressed against it, listening, and says, "I mean it. This is serious. Emily and I need to talk alone."

They scurry downstairs. When she's sure it's just the two of us, she says, "Sit down, Emily."

"We ate your cake," I say. "We ate the whole freaking thing with our bare hands. It was delicious."

She crosses her arms and says, as cool as can be, "I don't give a damn about my cake."

Not the reaction I was anticipating.

The tension in the room is almost enough to make me dizzy. Still eerily calm, Stephanie takes a seat on my bottom bunk.

"It was me. I smashed the watch," she says. "But not because I didn't want you to give it to my brother."

"Really?" I ask. "Then why?"

"Because," she says, deadly serious, "you don't deserve to give it to him. You don't deserve to have anything to do with him."

"And what makes you say that?"

"I was looking for the watch. I was going to hide it somewhere so you couldn't find it. And then I looked under your mattress and I found an envelope."

My whole body goes cold. I keep Renee's letters in a huge manila envelope under my mattress. I never dreamed that anyone would go rifling through my stuff, let alone looking under my bed.

"And what did you do with the envelope?"

She shrugs. "I opened it. I read some of the letters." Stephanie licks her lips. She stares at me for a long time before speaking. Even though I already know what she's going to say, I could almost pass out when she says the words out loud. "Del Sugar got you pregnant last year."

To hear her say it feels devastating in a way I almost can't explain. It makes it more real than anything has before, because now it's out there, broken into the world I'm trying to function normally in—and who knows what Stephanie is going to do with the information?

"Steph," I say, trying to stay calm, even though I've started to shake, "I wanted to tell you. You don't understand."

"I understand perfectly. You're a liar, and I shouldn't believe a word that comes out of your mouth. What happened to the baby, Emily? Did you get an abortion? Tell. Me. The. Truth."

I can't look at her. "I gave her up for adoption."

"You *hid* a pregnancy?"

"Yes." I stare at the floor.

"You told Renee and not me," she says.

"Yes."

"Do your parents even know?"

I shake my head.

"Nobody else knows?"

"Del knew."

"Emily," she says, "I'm telling Ethan."

"Oh, Steph, please don't do that! I'm begging you. I'll do anything you want me to."

She nods. "Okay. Then break up with him."

I don't say anything. Ethan is a huge part of my life. He's a huge part of what makes my life almost *normal*. If I break up with him for no discernible reason, I'll be losing my boyfriend and best friend in one punch.

"I can't do that," I say. "Why are you doing this to me?"

"What does it even matter? It's not like we can be friends anymore, not after you lied to me all year."

"But how could I tell you? How could I tell anyone?"

She shakes her head. "You told Renee. You could have told me. I would have understood."

"You would have? Like you're understanding me right now?"

"This is different."

"No, it isn't. Look, Stephanie, just give me a day. Just think about it for a while. Think about how you would feel. Please? Take some time before you ruin everything. You don't know the whole story."

She bites her lip. "One day."

I let out my breath; I hadn't even realized I'd been holding it. "And then we'll talk."

"Then we'll talk. But I don't think I'm going to change my mind."

"Tomorrow," I say, knowing it will be here way too soon.

She stands up. "Tomorrow."

I stare at her as she leaves the room. "Where are you going?"

"To tell on you for eating my effing cake."

# chapter twenty-one

I can't sleep. Even two of Dr. Miller's pills don't do anything to help me calm down. After she came back from telling on us—apparently she walked all the way up to school and caught my dad coming out of the faculty meeting—Stephanie marched into our room to inform us that we were all supposed to be in the headmaster's office before breakfast the following day.

I couldn't care less about the cake. It will mean a couple of work details at the worst; Stephanie knows that. And now she knows about the baby, too. I can't imagine what people will do if they find out. I'm sure that girls have gotten pregnant at Stonybrook before, but there haven't been any that I've known about—and certainly none of them have been the headmaster's daughter.

Above me, Franny snores softly, her concave belly full of cake, probably the fullest it's been in months. It's a little past one in the morning. It's been a tense evening in our room, for sure, but before she fell asleep, Franny said to me, "Don't worry so much, Emily. Everything will be okay in the morning. We'll get in trouble and then it will be over."

But for me, it feels like it will never be over. My baby would be seven months old now. What do seven-month-old babies do? A quick Google search told me more than I wanted to know. They sit up, roll over, and babble. They sleep through the night if you're lucky. They start to get teeth. Some of them even start crawling. They begin to develop a preference for certain people, in particular their mothers.

I sit up in bed and kick the sheets off my legs. I'm wearing thick flannel pajamas that my parents bought me for Christmas. Outside, it's so cold that there's frost forming on the insides of the windows in our room. Digger rarely stays out this late when it's this deep into winter.

I get up, still not knowing for sure what I'm going to do. All I know are facts. Fact one: my life is a mess. Fact two: I don't want to lose Ethan. Fact three: if anyone will understand, maybe it's him.

So I pull my boots and coat on over my pj's, and I sneak quietly into Steph and Grace's room. I retrieve the rope ladder from under Stephanie's bed and am gone before she has a chance to wake up. Then I trek all the way over to Winchester, and knock at Ethan's window with burning cold knuckles until he wakes up and lets me in.


It's funny how you remember things. As I'm crawling through his window, I remember the night I came over here with Stephanie, the very first time I met Del Sugar. I remember the feeling of electric excitement when Ethan hugged me that night in the hallway. He's told me since he liked me even then, and in hindsight, it was obvious. If I had realized, or even if Del hadn't been up watching TV that night, everything might be different.

When I put my arms around him now, he slides his hands inside my coat and kisses me on the neck.

"Happy birthday," I murmur, knowing I'm going to start crying any second now.

"It's past midnight," he says. "Not my birthday anymore."

"Oh."

"Why didn't you come to dinner? Steph said you weren't feeling well."

I pull back and look at him. He was obviously asleep; his hair is disheveled, and he's squinting in such a way that I know he's not wearing his contact lenses.

He gazes down at my pj's as I shrug off my coat and let it fall onto his floor. "If this is a striptease, you might want to reconsider your outfit."

All he's wearing is a pair of red boxer shorts. "Aren't you cold?" I ask.

"I have a good blanket," he says. "Come on, lie down with me."

We crawl into his bed together. We lie there on our sides for a few minutes, quietly, before I start to cry.

"Emily," he says, "something's wrong. I can tell."

Still on my side, I notice that Ethan is wearing his new watch—the one he got from his sister and mother.

"I like your watch," I say, ignoring his worry.

"Do you? Steph and Mom bought it for me. It's nice."

"I bought you the same watch."

He pauses. "You did?"

"Mm-hmm. When your sister found out, she smashed it into bits and told me I wasn't allowed to go to dinner with you."

Ethan sits up straight. "You're kidding me. God, Stephanie did that?" He shakes his head. He's getting angry. "She's jealous, you know. She doesn't want anyone else to have my attention. It's all because of our parents' divorce. Look, Emily, I'll have a talk with her. I mean, it would have been enough for you to just take the watch back, you know?"

I pause. I literally *stop breathing* for a moment. Then, sitting up to look at him, I ask, "What do you mean?"

"Well, if you both bought me the same watch, then one of you would have to take it back, right? You could always get me something else."

"I got it engraved," I say.

"Oh." He lowers his gaze. "Emily . . . they're my family. I don't mean to be ungrateful, but—well, what does it matter? Steph overreacted, and I'm going to talk to her. I'll get her to pay you back for the watch."

I shake my head. "Don't bother. That's not why I came here."

He gives me an awkward grin. "You didn't come for a striptease either, did you? Because I'm not really into crying strippers." And he puts his arm around me. "Just tell me what's wrong, Em."

I should know better than to say anything. I should break up with him, graduate and go to whatever college will have me, and forget that this entire nightmare ever happened.

But I have to tell someone. And I want it to be Ethan.

I close my eyes and force myself to say it. "Last year, when I was with Del, something happened." I pause. "I got pregnant."

He doesn't say anything for a long time. I open my eyes to look at him. He reaches for his nightstand, picks up his glasses, and puts them on. *There he is. Clark Kent.*

"You got pregnant," he repeats.

I nod. "Yes."

"And what—what happened? Did you have an abortion?"

I shake my head. "I couldn't have done that. I thought about it, but there was no way."

"Then what did you do?"

"I got pregnant near the end of October. So during the school year, I didn't show very much. I wore baggy clothes. People didn't even notice."

He stares at me. "Oh my God," he whispers. "How could people not notice?"

"They didn't know what they were looking for," I say. "It was easier than you might think. After school was over, I spent the summer with Renee Graham. You know that. Del found out right before he got expelled. But nobody else knew, Ethan. Not my parents. Not any of my other friends. It was terrible keeping a secret like that—you can't imagine how terrible. Anyway, Renee and I have been writing letters back and forth. When your sister was looking for your watch tonight—when she was *going through my stuff*—she found the letters and read them. And now she knows everything about last year, and about the baby. And she told me that if I didn't break up with you, she'd tell you everything."

We sit on the bed, both of us cross-legged and staring at each other. I'm crying.

Finally, Ethan asks, "Is that all?"

I wish it were. But for him, it's enough. "Yes," I say. "That's all."

For a long time, he appears to be thinking. Then he says, "So you came over here tonight to tell me that my sister broke the watch you bought me for my birthday. And you also came over to preemptively tell me that last year you got pregnant and kept it a secret from everyone." He pauses. "Even me. Even after we started dating. You lied to everyone." He shakes his head. "Even your *parents*."

"Ethan, I didn't lie. I just wanted you to know the truth before your sister—"

"If I don't know the truth already, then it's because you lied."

"I didn't think you'd understand! You don't know what this has been like for me!"

"So what did you think? Let me guess, okay? You thought that I'd be so pissed off at Stephanie for breaking my stupid watch that I'd just *forgive* you for keeping such a huge secret from me?"

Never in a million years would I have expected a reaction like this.

"Ethan," I say, wiping the tears from my face, "please understand."

He is completely still. "I don't know how to feel right now, Emily. You need to give me some time."

"Some time? But what about . . . what about us?"

He bites his bottom lip. He straightens the glasses on his face. Then, like a punch to the stomach, he says, "I don't want there to be an *'us'* anymore. At least not right now."

I'm sobbing. "But, Ethan, I *love* you—"

"I don't even know who you are, Emily!"

*Funny*, I think, *neither do I.*

"Stephanie was right," he says. "It was a mistake for us to get involved in the first place."

"Stephanie," I blurt, "is your sister. Did you ever think your relationship with her is a little bit, I don't know, *weird*?"

He glares at me. "We're twins. Twins are always close."

"Uh-huh. Were you born holding hands or something? Because I've met other twins, and they're not like you two."

His glare turns into a scowl. I'm not sure I've ever seen Ethan this angry before.

"Get out," he says. "Just leave my room, right now. We'll talk later."


I cry all the way back to my dorm. I crawl into bed with Franny—she never minds a bit—and stay close to her while I cry myself to sleep. If Stephanie is awake on the other side of the quad, I'm sure she's quite pleased with herself.

It isn't even light outside when I feel someone shaking me awake, softly. Before I open my eyes, I know. I've been waiting for so long. Finally, he's here. I can smell him. He doesn't smell like kerosene anymore, but it's still unmistakably Del.

I open my eyes a little bit. "There you are," I whisper.

Franny is still snoring softly. I have no idea how Del got into the dorm. I get the feeling he can do just about anything he puts his mind to.

"What are you doing here?" I ask, still whispering.

He smiles. "I'm here for you."

"What will we do?"

"Leave," he says.

"Why?"

"Why not?" His hand is on my arm. His fingers feel rough and callused. He looks dirty.

And as much as I want to resist him—as angry as I still am, as much as I want to hate him, to leave him behind—his blue eyes still pierce right through me.

"I found her," he says, keeping his voice low and calm.

I sit up. "You what?"

"I found our baby. She's a little girl."

So I was right. I knew it.

"A family in New Hampshire adopted her." He pauses. "I want to take you with me. I have to see her. I have to make sure she's all right."

"Del, we aren't allowed to do that. It's a closed adoption. It's illegal."

"They never saw you, did they? They won't know it's you. Emily, come on. I have to know she's okay."

I know exactly how he feels.

"I should pack," I tell him, still whispering.

"I've got a green pickup parked in the off-campus lot," he says. "You'll see it. Why don't you get ready and meet me there before this place starts to wake up?"

I shake my head. "Del, I don't know. You're talking about running away."

"Why not?" he demands. "What do you have that's keeping you here?"

I think about it for a second. I think about Stephanie and Ethan, my parents and the whole mess that life has become. There is no *normal* anymore. He's right; there's no reason for me to stay.

"Okay," I tell him. "Give me fifteen minutes."

He squeezes my arm. "I can't wait." Then he leans forward and kisses me on the forehead. I close my eyes and remember everything: how it felt to be with him, how I loved him, how devastated I was when I lost him. And now he's back. Deep down, I always knew he would be.

I hurry up and get dressed, stuffing as much as I can into my backpack. I gather up the money I have, put on my coat and gloves, and am about to leave the room when I realize I should probably leave a note.

What is there to say? Nothing. I'm leaving, and I don't know when I'm coming back. I'm leaving because I have no other choice; I have to see my baby.

I find a piece of paper and a black felt-tipped pen. On my desk, I leave a note that says:

GOTTA GO
—EMILY

I know my parents will be horrified when they find out that I'm gone, but I don't care. In fact, there's a part of me that feels satisfied they'll be so upset. They've lied to me and hidden so much; they *deserve* to be upset.

I tiptoe out of the dark room, into Stephanie's room again, down the rope ladder again, where the dark is waiting for me. I

hurry off campus to the parking lot. Del is waiting in an old green pickup truck.

"Where did you get this?" I ask. God, I hope he didn't steal it.

"I borrowed it," he says, starting the truck, "from my sister."

"Your sister?"

"That's right. I went to find her. And then I came for you."

He reaches over and squeezes my hand. "Are you sure you want to do this?"

I nod, flinching a little bit at his touch. I realize I don't feel much of anything for him. But I have to go.

"Del, it's freezing in here. Turn on the heat."

"I can't. The heat doesn't work."

I stare at him. "How are we supposed to drive all the way to New Hampshire, in the middle of the winter, with no heat? We'll freeze."

"No, we won't. I brought you something." And he reaches behind my seat.

It's the same red blanket we used to lie on together all the time. Carefully, Del unfolds it and spreads it out across my body. It smells like him. He pulls it all the way to my chin. "There," he says. "Now you'll be warm."

I don't say anything. I only nod.

"Okay, then. Ready?" He puts the truck into drive.

I take a deep breath, stare at the morning sunlight that's beginning to illuminate campus. "Ready."

And we pull out of the parking lot, down the road and onto the highway, heading north.

# chapter twenty-two

It's only a few hours to New Hampshire. For a while, I can't think of anything to say, and the inside of the truck is almost silent, the only noises the whirring of the engine and the murmur of low talk radio, which neither of us is listening to.

Finally, I say, "So you found your sister. That's great."

He nods. "It sure is."

"Where was she? How did you find her?"

He shrugs. "I've told you. You got a computer, that's pretty much all you need to find someone nowadays." He's quiet for a minute. "That reminds me. Did you ever find that girl you were looking for? Madeline?"

"No," I say, "we didn't." Renee and I agreed that we wouldn't tell anyone else what we learned about Madeline; that includes Del.

He shakes his head. "It's so strange. You girls talked about her all the time, but I've never seen her. I've never even seen any evidence that she's real. It's almost like she's a figment of your imaginations." He adds, "You know—like Columbo's wife."

I can't help but smile, thinking of the first night I met him.

"I don't know why you're having such a hard time," he continues. "It's easy to track people down."

"Maybe for a boy genius."

"I'm serious," he says. "There's information everywhere, just waiting for people to take it."

I hesitate. Then I say, "I know that you knew about me when you came here."

He stares straight ahead. He doesn't say anything, until finally, "Yeah. So what?"

"So that's why you liked me, isn't it? You knew all about the fire. You knew I lost my dad and didn't even belong to my family the way I thought. You knew, and I didn't, and you were supposed to love me and you never even told me. You knew that I had nightmares, and you knew what they were about, and you never told me any of it. Why not? Why would you keep that a secret from me when you knew I was suffering?"

"You weren't ready. I didn't want to hurt you." He glances at me. "Trust me, Emily. I know how things like that can hurt."

"How noble of you," I say, sarcastic.

He tries to keep his tone casual. "So you found out you were in the fire?"

I nod.

"You were in a fire with your parents," he repeats. "Right?"

"Del, you already know all of this. Yes."

"And your father died. And you almost died."

"Uh-huh. That's why I have the nightmares, you know—fire and water. I was still in bed when a fireman saved me. There was fire and water everywhere. It all makes perfect sense."

"Uh-huh," Del says. "Did your mother tell you that?"

"Yes. Del, why are you being weird?"

"My sister," he begins, obviously trying to change the subject, "she's all grown up now. You should have seen the two of us together. I stayed with her for a while, while I looked for the baby. Mel has this boyfriend—guess what his name is?"

I roll my eyes. "What?"

"*Cola*. He's this big silent black guy named *Cola*. Honest to God."

"That's weird."

He shrugs. "Well, Mellie's always been attracted to the odd ones. Comes with the territory, I guess."

We fall into silence again.

"So," I say, almost afraid to ask. "Tell me about our baby. Where is she in New Hampshire?"

"In this little town called Saltsburg." He pauses. "I've got the address. Something Foster Street. That's all I know."

"I knew it was a girl," I murmur.

"Is that so?" He swings into a highway rest stop. We've been driving for about forty minutes. The sun is all the way up. By now, my roommates will realize I'm gone. It's only a matter of time before my parents put two and two together, and then they'll be looking for us. I feel terrified, exhilarated, but most of all I feel like I have no choice but to go see my baby. I have to know that she's all right.

We go into the rest stop to use the bathroom and get some breakfast. It's one of those new buildings with a food court and souvenir shop and shiny bathrooms.

As I'm washing my hands, a middle-aged woman approaches me. She stands a few feet away, staring, and I start to get paranoid that she's with the police. But they couldn't have reported me missing already, could they?

"You look lost, sweetheart," she says. "Can I help you?"

"Oh." I smile. "I'm not lost. I know exactly where I'm going."

She takes a step closer. "Do you? Do you really know, honey? What's your name?"

"Emily," I say, without thinking. I should walk away, but she's got me cornered. She holds out a pamphlet. "Emily, my name is

Mary. I'm from the Church of the Open Door, and I have a gift for recognizing people who are in trouble. I can see people who need guidance."

"That's okay—really," I tell her, trying to edge around her body. "I'm not from around here. I couldn't come to your church, anyway."

As I'm rushing out of the bathroom, she *shouts* after me, "God is watching you! He can help you, Emily!"

When I jump back into the truck, I'm shaking. "Oh my God," I tell Del, "that was so bizarre."

"What?"

And I tell him all about the woman in the bathroom—how she seemed to know that something was going on, that something was wrong with me. Del only laughs.

"There was a guy in the men's bathroom, too! Here." He hands me a muffin and coffee. "He was from the same church. I think they follow a script or something, because he said almost exactly the same thing to me."

"He did?" I'm still shaking. I force myself to sip my coffee and take a bite of my muffin. "What did you say?"

Del grins. "I said, 'You're from the Church of the Open Door?' And he goes, 'Yes, Robert, I am.' I told him my name was Robert, by the way."

I nod.

"And so I go, 'Well, sir, I'm from the Church of the Closed Door.' And I crumple up the pamphlet and toss it in the trash and walk away."

We're on our way again. I gasp. "No, you didn't!"

"I did. What business does he have, coming up to me in the bathroom? It's crazy." He glances at me. "I don't want to talk about that. I want to talk about you."

"Okay. What do you want to know?"

"Everything. Tell me what you've been up to since I left."

I shrug. "Oh, you know. It's been a totally normal senior year. Friends, homecoming, that kind of thing." And then I add—just to hurt him, to let him know that I don't belong to him—"I have a boyfriend, too."

"Boyfriend," he says, frowning. "Let me guess. Ethan Prince."

I nod. "Until about six hours ago."

"Oh, yeah? Why is that?"

I give him a brief synopsis of the circumstances surrounding our breakup. Considering what Del and I are doing, the fact that I've just run away, that we're going to find our *child*, and how empty I feel when it comes to Del, the whole situation with Stephanie and Ethan—the watch, the cake, all the stupid rules—seems incredibly petty and mundane.

"So right now, your roommates are in your dad's office, getting work details for eating cake." He snorts. "That's freaking hilarious."

I pause. "Actually, they're probably in his office, showing him the note I left. He's probably calling the police right now."

Del gives me a sideways glance. "You're eighteen, Emily. The police can't declare you missing for twenty-four hours."

"Maybe not officially. But my dad knows them. Stonybrook is a tiny town. Trust me, if they're not looking for us now, they will be soon."

"We'll be crossing the state line," he says. "Don't worry about it." Then, in a tone that's way too casual for the question, he says, "So tell me more about you and Ethan. Do you love him?"

I close my eyes for a second. Just for a moment, I imagine that, when I open them, I'll be back at the dorm, waking up to find the whole previous night was only a dream.

But I'm not so lucky. "Yes," I say, "I think so."

"Oh, really? So you're sleeping with him, then?"

I shake my head. "Del, just because you love a person doesn't mean you have to sleep with them." I add, "And no. I couldn't."

"Why not?"

"Because of you. Because of the baby." I swallow. "It just felt wrong. But, Del, you and I, it doesn't feel right. Not anymore."

"It doesn't matter if it feels right, it *is* right," he insists. "Emily, don't you understand? We're the same. Look at what we're doing. We've run away together, and we're on our way to find the baby that we *made* together. From the first time I saw you, knowing what I knew, I was positive that we should be together. Now, whether you stay or go is up to you, but we're going to go look at that baby together. We're going to see her. And then you'll realize."

"Realize what?" I ask.

"You'll realize how things should be. Some things are meant to be."

I shake my head. "Del, no. It's over."

"Ethan doesn't care about you the way I do. Nobody will ever care about you the way I do. What do you think Ethan would do if he knew about your dad? You think he'd be head over heels for you? I guarantee, he'd be running for the closest debutante in a second."

"This isn't about Ethan. It's about me. Besides, that's not true. You don't know him."

"It isn't true? He dumped you when he found out about the baby, didn't he?"

"He was shocked. Who wouldn't be? He felt betrayed, and rightly so. I'm not going to talk about this with you. You don't have any right to tell me how to live my life." It feels exhilarating to stand up to him. I should have done it a long time ago.

He shakes his head. "You just don't want to see. You aren't like

them. You might look like them and know how to act like them—
hell, so do I. But deep down we're the same. You've gotta understand that, Emily."

But I don't. And I don't think I ever will.

"Just drive," I tell him.

"I think we need to talk," he says.

"Oh yeah? About what?"

"We're going to make more than one stop. We'll drive up to
New Hampshire, and then we'll drive to Rhode Island. There's
someone there I want you to meet."

"God," I murmur, rolling my eyes.

He grins. "Nope. Not God."

In the short time we've been in the truck together, I've become
almost homesick for my old life. I don't care anymore if my dad
isn't technically my dad; my parents just did what they thought
was best, didn't they? I figure we're stopping to see Melody in
Rhode Island—who else could it be?—and I don't want to. I want
to see my baby and make sure she's all right. Then I want to go
home. I want to tell everything to Stephanie and Ethan—to get rid
of all the secrets and have everything out in the open.

I want to see our baby. There's a part of me that feels like I
have to see her. But after today, I think, I never want to see Del
Sugar again. He's like poison, like a cancer that I can feel growing inside me. I may never be able to get rid of the memories we
have—and I'm not sure that I want to—yet I know that, if I stay
with him, nothing good will come of it. But as I look at him, so
focused as he drives, his fingers probably numb around the steer-
ing wheel, his breath visible in the cold air inside the truck, I don't
get the feeling that he has any plans to calmly walk away.

# chapter twenty-three

"Their names," Del says, shortly after we cross the New Hampshire line, "are Ron and Melinda Zimmerman. They don't have any other kids."

"Del," I say, shaking my head, "how do you *know* all this?"

He shrugs. "I told you, all you need's a computer."

"That's not true! It's a closed adoption."

"Don't worry about it, Emily. Just prepare yourself. You can't go falling apart once we get there."

"What are we going to do?" I imagine knocking at their front door, saying, "Hi, I'm Emily Meckler, and this is Del Sugar. We're the parents of your baby." Then I imagine the police showing up in about fifteen seconds to haul us away.

"We'll pretend to be going door-to-door. Before I crumpled that one up, I got a few extra pamphlets from the guy in the bathroom."

"We're going to pretend to be *Bible-thumpers*? That's your big idea?"

He smirks. "You got a better one? What, take the baby and run? You know how long you'd end up in jail, for that?"

"I don't want to take the baby," I say. "I just want to see her."

He pauses. "I know that. I'm sorry. I just thought it would be an easy way to get inside the door, you know? I can be persuasive."

I snort. "So I've noticed. But what if the baby's not there?"

"She'll be there. It's the middle of the day."

"What if she's sleeping?"

"Then you ask to use the bathroom, you sneak into her room, and you wake her up. While I'm talking to the Mrs. about God, you can do that, you know? Then she'll have to go get the baby, and we can see it. I mean her." He hesitates. "I don't have any other ideas. I don't want to break in. I don't want to scare them."

I nod. "Okay. All right. How far are we?"

"Not far. Ten minutes, maybe."

As soon as he says it, the fact that this is really happening begins to overwhelm me. Up until now, I have never seen my baby. Like my real father, she's almost an abstraction, something I've been missing constantly these past few months while knowing there's nothing in the world I can ever do about it. Except now I really *am* going to see her. What is that going to accomplish? I almost tell Del to turn around and forget about the whole thing. But I can't. I want this more than anything.

"Look," I tell him, taking a deep breath. "We're going to do this, okay? I know that. I want that. But, Del, I *swear*, if you try anything crazy, I will run away so fast and leave you behind and get to the nearest pay phone to call my parents."

His mouth drops a little. "Is that so?"

"Yes," I say, my voice growing stronger. "I came with you willingly. This is *our* baby, and it's *my* life, but things aren't going to get crazy."

He raises an eyebrow at me. "Look at you. All grown up and bossing me around."

I don't say anything. I pull the blanket more tightly around my body. It is *freezing* in the truck.

We turn onto a narrow street lined with middle-class houses.

"Is this it? Is this their street?" I ask.

Del nods.

"It's not nice." It's true; the houses are all small, brick ranches, not your usual New England architecture. It's obviously a lower-middle-class neighborhood. The lawns are all snow covered; some of them have crooked, lumpy snowmen in the front yards.

"It's 1168 Foster Street," he murmurs. "1100 . . . 1122 . . . it's gonna be on the left up here, Emily."

In spite of the confidence I've shown, I couldn't be more nervous. "There it is," I say, trying to keep my voice calm. "I see it."

He pulls the truck over to park in front of a tiny ranch house with almost no front yard. Somebody is home; there's a rusted blue pickup truck in the driveway, along with a maroon sedan. Del hands me a pamphlet. "Come on. Don't worry, I'll do most of the talking. Just follow my lead."

When I glare at him, he quickly adds, "I know what I'm doing, Emily. I promise, things will be okay."


A woman answers the front door. She doesn't peer through a crack like any sane person would if two strange teenagers rang their doorbell; she opens the door wide and says, "Hi, there. Can I help you?"

She's pretty in a kind of plain way. Behind her, on the sofa, sits what I assume is her husband.

He's holding a baby. The baby has wispy red hair. When she sees us, she smiles. I feel my knees start to buckle.

Before I have a chance to answer her, Del interrupts with, "Yes, ma'am. My name is Steven."

I swallow. "My name is Emily," I say. I can't lie to this woman. I won't.

"We're from the Church of the Open Door," Del continues. He hands her a pamphlet. "We're expanding our congregation here in New Hampshire, and, why, we just thought maybe you'd be interested in having a conversation about Jesus for a minute or two."

Man, he's good. The woman glances back at her husband, who gives her a reluctant shrug.

"Well . . ." She hesitates. "I'm not sure that we're interested, but at least come on in out of the snow. What did you say your names were?"

"Steven," Del says, reaching out to shake the woman's hand. "And this is my friend Emily."

"Emily, Steven, I'm Melinda. This is my husband, Ron." And with a big smile, she says, "And coincidentally enough, this is our new little girl, Emily."

I freeze. I feel like crying, but I know that I can't, that it would ruin everything and they'd probably put two and two together and call the police. But I can't help myself from asking. I say, "You named your daughter Emily?"

Ron and Melinda glance at each other again. "Yes," Ron says. He bounces my daughter lightly on his knee. "You see . . . well, never mind."

"It's okay, sweetie. You can go ahead and tell them," Melinda says. She beams at me. "We're new parents. We can't help but gush over her."

"She's adopted," Ron says, "and we never got to know the birth mother. But we were so grateful for the gift she'd given us, that that's who we named our baby after."

"Someday," Melinda says, "we'll tell our daughter that we named her after the woman who loved her so much that she did everything she could to make sure she would have a happy life."

It takes all of my energy not to cry. I blink back the tears.

"Emily?" Melinda peers at me, concerned. "Are you all right?"

"Yes." I nod, doing my best to come up with a quick explanation. "It's just that I'm adopted, too . . . and that's such a beautiful story. You didn't have to do that. It was so thoughtful of you."

Melinda smiles. "We just knew it was the right thing. Didn't we, Ron?"

Even Del seems at a loss for words. I realize that he wasn't planning to surprise me with this. He didn't want to throw me off guard; he genuinely didn't know our baby's name.

"You can sit down if you want," Melinda offers. "Would either of you like something to drink?" She smiles. "Maybe some hot cocoa?"

I can hardly talk. "Uh . . . sure."

"That would be great," Del breathes, staring at Emily. At *our* Emily.

The Zimmermans are friendly. With almost no prompting from me or Del, they explain that Melinda is a night-shift nurse, while Ron shovels snow in the winter and paves driveways in the summer. Since the current snowfall has been frozen for the past few days with no new precipitation, Ron hasn't had much to do but stay home and help out with the baby.

"It changes you forever, you know," he tells us. "You kids are way too young for babies, but let me tell you—adopted or no, there's just nothing more incredible than feeling the love for your own child."

I can't stop staring at Emily. "I can't imagine," I say.

"Ron and I tried to get pregnant for years and years," Melinda explains, putting two mugs of hot cocoa in front of me and Del on a stained, chipped coffee table. "Emily here is the second baby we thought we'd be getting. But the first one . . . it was a little boy . . . his mother changed her mind at the last minute."

Why are they telling us this? I don't need to know their story. I don't think I really *want* to know. But maybe they need to tell it.

"We were heartbroken," Ron continues. "Especially Melinda. It was the mother's right, though . . . we knew what we were getting into when we decided to pursue a domestic adoption."

"Ron," Melinda says, "these kids don't want to hear all of this."

"I'm sorry. But now we have Emily, and she's just . . . well, she's just the most perfect, happiest little thing you've ever seen in your life. I know she was meant for us." He gives her a kiss on the cheek. "Now, what did you kids want to talk to us about? Church?"

And just like that, I can't lie to them again. I can't sit in their house, across from *their* baby, without telling them who I really am.

Beside me, I can sense Del tensing up. "We wanted to talk to you about . . . uh, well, have a look at the pamphlet, sir."

"Wait," I blurt.

"Emily, be quiet," he says, still smiling.

"No," I say. "We're not here because of church."

Ron and Melinda exchange a hesitant glance. I notice that Ron holds Emily a little tighter. "Then what are you here for?"

But as much as I want to, I can't tell them the whole truth, either. In a swift moment, I remember what my life was like before I met Del Sugar, before I got pregnant and learned that my father is not my father. Looking at this family, looking at *my* baby—who will never really be my baby—I realize that I wish I'd never seen her. There are some things that should be left alone.

Swallowing hard, unable to take my eyes off Emily, I say, "We were going to try to sell you something."

"Oh. *Oh.*" Ron stands up. "Well, it wasn't right for you kids to do this. What are you selling?"

"We're taking donations, really," Del rushes. "For our church. But you're right—we should have been honest."

There is a long pause. I notice that Melinda is staring at me, as I continue to hold back the tears that will come, hard and fast, as soon as I walk out the door.

"I, uh, I don't have any cash. I'm sorry," Ron says.

"Then I guess we should leave," I say, putting down my hot cocoa. I still can't take my eyes off Emily.

We go to the front door. There are so many things I could do—shout the truth, turn around and grab her . . . but I don't do anything. I just walk, my hands shaking, Del's arm wrapped tightly around my waist.

Melinda has followed us to the door. She still appears to be studying my face. "You kids . . . stay warm," she says.

I nod. "We will."

Then, looking me in the eye, she asks, "Emily. What did you say your last name was?" Before I can answer her, she says, "I'll bet people tell you all the time that you have such beautiful red hair. I just love redheads."

And in an instant, right there: I know that she knows. Like I knew that Emily was a girl, even though I'd never laid eyes on her. And I know that Emily belongs to Ron and Melinda. I know that it's how it should be.

"I didn't," I say. "But it's Emily Meckler."

"Emily Meckler," she repeats. "And this is your boyfriend?"

My voice is so soft, so strained, that I almost can't speak. "He used to be. Last year."

"And where do you live, Emily Meckler?"

"I live in Stonybrook, Connecticut," I say.

She nods. "You're a long way from home."

We stand there for what feels like an eternity. Ron walks away, down the hallway and out of sight, carrying Emily with him. I know I'll never see her again. It's okay. I know that she's loved, that she's safe. That's all I needed.

"You two go home now, okay?" Melinda says, her voice cracking. "Go back to Connecticut."

Del tugs me closer to the door. I feel the cold wind in my face,

the sudden cruelty of the reality that we've created, such a contrast to the warmth inside the happy Zimmerman home.

We get in the truck. Melinda stands, watching us from the front door, until we drive away.

Once we're back on the highway, Del asks, "Emily, why did you do that? They could have called the police."

"I don't know," I say, crying. "They deserved better than a bunch of lies."

"They knew. At least, she knew."

"I know."

It is unusual to see Del so flustered. "Do you think she'll do anything about it?"

"No."

"You're sure? She could call the cops, or the adoption agency, and tell them what we did."

"She won't do that," I say. "I'm sure of it. But she'll remember my name forever."

# chapter twenty-four

Del won't tell my why we're going to Rhode Island. We drive for a few hours in a kind of hostile silence. Then, just when I think we have to be there already, he pulls into a motel called the Sunny Side Inn. The name is ironic at best; the place looks like the Bates Motel.

"What are we doing here?" I ask. "You're crazy if you think I'm—"

"We have to stay overnight. Your parents are looking for us. The police might be looking for us. We have to lie low."

"Aren't we going to see your sister? Honestly, Del, I don't even care. I just want to go home. It's enough already."

He opens his door. "You're not going home yet."

"Why not?" I demand. "What's so important that you have to keep me here overnight? If you think I'm *doing* anything with you, then you have another thing—"

"It's not that," he interrupts. He sighs and turns off the engine. "Emily, there's something I have to tell you before we go to Rhode Island tomorrow."

What has he done now? "And what's that?" I ask.

He stares at me, his gaze somehow loving and lost and defiant all at once. "The truth. I'm going to tell you the truth."

I'm almost afraid to ask. "The truth about what?"

"About everything."

So here we are, at the Sunny Side Inn, sharing a room with one full-sized bed, living out of our backpacks, sharing a delivery pizza that tastes like cardboard.

We eat in almost total silence. Things are, to say the least, not the same between me and Del. I don't have the same electric feelings toward him; all of my fantasies that he would come rescue me and take me away from Stonybrook—to what? to be a family?—are gone. Our child is safe. She has a good life. Now that I know that, I'm not sure what I'm doing here with Del.

All I want is to go home. I want to see my parents. I want to clear things up with Ethan and Stephanie. I want my life back.

After we've eaten, Del and I sit on the bed together and I say to him, "Okay, Del. What's the big secret you have to tell me? I already know everything, I told you that. I know that my real father died in a fire when I was a little girl. I know that my dad legally adopted me when he married my mother. What else could there possibly be?"

He shakes his head. "You're so naive, Emily. People tell you things and you just believe them."

"And you think I shouldn't?" I'm starting to get angry. "You know, people are always telling me how naive I am. I had a *baby* that I hid from everyone. I just met her. I've dealt with the fact that my father isn't my father, I've lived through night after night of horrible dreams . . . I'm sick of being called naive. Just because my life hasn't been as difficult as yours doesn't mean I can't take care of myself as well as anyone else."

"Do you remember the night we stole those files?" he interrupts.

"Yes. Do you? Or were you so coked up that it's just a blur?"

"That's low, Emily. I went to rehab. I'm clean. I'm done with all that." He pauses. "And I'm sorry you didn't know. But that's what I mean. You're too naive for your own good."

I glare at him. "It's not my fault that you lied to me when I trusted you more than anyone else. Why should I believe anything you tell me now?" Before he can answer, I rush on. "Listen, there's something I need to know. It's important."

"Okay. What is it?"

"Did you do it on purpose? Did you mean to get kicked out?"

He seems startled by the question. He stares at the ugly paisley comforter on our bed and doesn't say anything.

"Del?" I snap my fingers beneath his face. "Answer me."

He rubs his tattoo. He says, "I didn't mean for things to turn out this way."

The answer makes me feel sick to my stomach. "I should have listened to my dad," I murmur. "I never should have had anything to do with you."

"It's too late to be sorry," he says. He's *smiling*. I want to punch him.

"I have something important to tell you," he continues. "Are you going to listen?"

"Why should I?"

"Because it's the truth," he says simply. "And I'm the only one who's going to share it with you. So do you want to know, or do you want to know?"

I'm not sure anymore. I'm starting to believe that ignorance truly is bliss; at least, it was before my life opened up and all these secrets came pouring out.

But before then, there were the nightmares. And they still

277

haven't gone away. Why not? If I know everything there is to know, then what is it my dreams are still trying to tell me?

"Okay," I say, reluctantly. "What is it?"

"You remember the night we stole those files," he repeats.

"Of course I remember."

"When I handed yours over to Renee, I was hoping that she'd read it. I was hoping she'd tell you about something inside."

"If this is about Sandy," I tell him, "I already know."

He seems shocked. "You do?"

"Yes. She's my real father's first wife. My parents didn't want me to know about her, obviously, because I didn't know about my real father. Del, is this the big reveal you've been waiting to tell me about?"

"Your father's first wife," he repeats.

"Yes," I say, impatient. "Sandy Gray. It's old news."

He shakes his head. "Emily, no."

There it is again: that cool, almost electric feeling of dread that I've become so used to.

"What do you mean, *no*? My parents told me—"

"Your parents lied to you."

"They didn't."

"They *did*. Emily."

"..."

"..."

When he finally speaks again, I feel like the whole world splits apart. "She's your mother."


I sit there listening, not wanting to believe, as Del explains everything to me in his calm, collected way, and I can't deny that all the pieces are falling together. It all makes sense. Finally.

"My dad and your dad were college roommates—you already knew that," he says. "And when your dad—I mean Dr. Meckler—met your mom—I mean his wife now—he called my dad to help him solve a problem."

The room feels *fuzzy*. I keep listening, afraid that if I make any sudden movements the room might tilt off its axis and send me spinning into hysterics.

"What was the problem?" I ask, even though I already know.

"You," Del says. "Your dad and mom, the Mecklers, had fallen in love. They wanted to get married. But then your mother explained that the four-year-old she was raising wasn't exactly hers."

"What do you mean, not *exactly*?"

"You were her stepdaughter, and her husband had died. She'd never legally adopted you, so she didn't have any legal claim to you. But she didn't want to give you back to your mother. Apparently the lady was a real mess. So your dad called my dad for a favor."

"What's that?"

He shrugs. "Paperwork. A plausible explanation. It was kidnapping, Emily, no matter how you try to rationalize it or explain it. They kept you when they had no right to. Maybe if they'd gone to your birth mother and gotten her to relinquish her parental rights—"

"But why didn't she look for me in the first place? I mean, after my father died? If Sandy Gray is my mother, how come I'm eighteen and I've just learned her *name* this year?"

"Because she didn't come looking for you," Del says. "When she and your father split up, she let him have you."

"So it isn't kidnapping, then. If my mother didn't even—"

"Emily, *no*. It doesn't matter what your mother did. Sandy had a right to know that your father died. She had a right to know that

you were okay, and she definitely had a right to change her mind about leaving you."

"No," I say, shaking my head so hard that my hair whips against my face, "my parents did not kidnap me. That's not possible."

"Maybe they didn't snatch you from a strip mall, Emily. But you don't belong to them." He pauses. "Well, you're eighteen now. So none of it matters in a practical way—you can do what you want. But there could be consequences, if you wanted them."

"Consequences? For whom?"

"For your parents. For your birth mother."

I stare at him. "And you've known this the whole time?"

"Yes," he says. "Before I got sent to Stonybrook, there was this family my dad talked about sometimes. He didn't tell me a lot of details, but it was kind of like an urban legend within our household—you know, that my dad had forged this paperwork to help out an old friend. When I told him that it was kidnapping, and asked him how he could justify that to himself, he said to me, 'Del, there's an old Native American expression that I like to use. "Two dogs live within me. The one that grows the largest is the one I feed the most." She might not have started out as their daughter, but she is now. She's loved. She's safe. And as she gets older, that love will grow and grow until any inkling she has of the past just disappears.'"

"You knew it was me when you met me," I say, feeling sick.

He nods. "Emily, it made me love you. We're the same, you know? And I've always believed, for as long as I've known about you, that you had a right to know where you came from. You had a right to know the whole truth. No matter how much it hurts, we all have a right to know the truth."

He's right, I realize. If everyone had told the truth from the

beginning, none of this would be happening. "What's in Rhode Island?"

Del leans closer to me. He puts his arms around my neck, threads his callused, warm fingers through my hair, and holds me close.

"Your mother," he says. "And tomorrow, we'll go see her."

I make Del sleep on the floor that night. I don't even want to look at him, not after everything he's told me. How am I supposed to handle the news that *both of* my parents are not my parents? How should I feel about the fact that my mother continued to lie to me, even as she was supposedly telling me the "truth" about my past? And do I even want to see my real mother, when she walked away from me and never looked back?

In the morning, Del sits up on the floor, looks at me with sleepy eyes, and asks, "Are you ready?"

I've been thinking about it almost all night. I nod. "Yes."

"You're sure you can go through with it?"

I nod again, this time with more confidence. I know now that I don't have a choice, just like I didn't have a choice to go see my baby. It isn't that Del is forcing me; it's that I'm forcing myself. There has to be a way to find truth. There has to be a way to get closure. Otherwise, my life is nothing but secret upon secret, lie after lie.

Today feels like an inverse of yesterday, exactly the same but somehow entirely different. Yesterday, I went to find my child; today, I am going to see the mother who I never knew existed. I

don't know what I'll say to her, if I'll say anything at all. Maybe I just want to see her, to see if she looks like me, if she's living a good life. There are some things I have to know.

From the motel in New Hampshire to where we're going in Rhode Island, it takes about two hours. We are quiet for most of the ride. Finally, I can't stand the silence anymore.

"So you found your sister," I say, even though we've talked about it a little bit already.

He nods. "I told you, she's good."

"What's she doing with herself?"

He hesitates. Then, unexpectedly, it's like I've reached over and unlocked a door in his heart. He gets tears in his eyes; I'm worried he won't be able to see the road to drive as we go speeding down the highway, which is covered in icy snow.

"You know people get paid to have foster kids," he begins.

I nod. "I know."

"Can you imagine anything more screwed up? Nobody pays you to have kids of your own . . . but there's this financial incentive for foster parents."

"Well, it kind of makes sense. There has to be some kind of incentive to take in another child that doesn't belong to you, doesn't there?" As soon as the words are out of my mouth, I can tell I've made a mistake.

"What about love?" he snaps. "What about giving a kid whose own parents were too cracked out to take care of him, whose parents split up and whose mother had man after man after man in the house, most of whom were more interested in him and his *sister* . . . what about giving them a chance?"

"Del, I'm so sorry. I didn't mean—"

"When you sang me that song—*Daisy, Daisy*—I thought, 'Here is the girl I've been looking for.' It all felt like it came together, Emily. And I fell in love with you—I truly did."

"But you fell in love with me because of my circumstances," I say. "Not because of who I really am."

He shakes his head. "That's not true."

"It's not? Who am I, then? What do you *really* know about me, aside from my past?"

He hesitates. "You had a right to know the truth."

"I know. You're right. But I'm telling you, after this is over, we're done. I don't want to see you again. I don't want to talk to you again."

He snorts. "What do you want me to do? Drop you off back at Stonybrook? Let you walk into the headmaster's office and explain what you've been doing for the past two days?"

I consider. "Yes. That's exactly what I want you to do. You're the one who's always saying I had a right to know the truth. Well, I'm sick of lying. I'm not going to hide things from anyone, not anymore."

He slows the car. He makes a left-hand turn onto an icy dirt road, leaning over to consult a set of printed directions.

"We'll talk about it later," he says. "We're here."

# chapter twenty-five

We're at the entrance to a development of new homes—big houses, almost mansions, each one of them bigger than my house back in Stonybrook.

"She lives here?" I ask.

"Yes." Del pauses. "You're surprised."

"Well, yeah. I guess I am."

"Why?"

I don't have a good answer for him, not at first. Then I remember.

"I had a dream last night," I say.

"Like your other dreams?"

I nod. "Yes. I dreamed of rain, like I usually do. But this time it was more vivid. I was sitting in a car with my mother. Not Sandy—my mom. And I was a little girl, and we were parked on this dirt road in the middle of nowhere, except . . . I think we were in a trailer court. And we sat there in the car, in the rain, for a long time. I was crying. My mom kept telling me that we had to go, and that she would carry me and we'd run very fast to the porch, but I was so afraid. And then we saw another car pull up, and this woman got out. In my dream, it was my real mother. It was Sandy. My mom kept saying, "Let's go, baby," and I was crying, and she was crying, and . . . that's it. We were just sitting there in the car, crying together. I was terrified." I shudder. "So I guess I thought I remembered where my real mom lived. I guess I thought . . ."

"She lived in a trailer," Del says. "And that would make things better?"

I nod. "I guess so."

I can tell he's irritated. "Why, Emily?"

"Because if she felt the need to abandon me in the first place, I guess I'd assumed that her life was too miserable to support a child. Maybe I thought she was too poor to take care of me, or that she didn't want to bring me up under those circumstances." I know I sound like a snob. "Then again," I finish, "I guess some people just don't want babies. Maybe she just didn't *want* me."

"She was only twenty when she had you," Del says. "She dropped out of college to marry your father."

"That doesn't make me feel better."

"All right," Del says, pulling the truck slowly down the cul-de-sac. "It's this one. On the left."

He pulls the truck onto the curb, next to the mailbox of one of the most beautiful homes I've ever seen. It's a contemporary salt-box, very New England, with what looks like a small vineyard in its backyard. The whole scene is blanketed in snow, giving it a peaceful, idyllic look.

He takes the Church of the Open Door pamphlets out of his pocket. Handing me one, he asks, "Are we going to do the same thing?"

I grab his arm. "Wait. Look."

The front door is opening. There's a minivan parked out front, not fifteen feet away from us. A woman emerges from the house

carrying a bundled-up baby in her arms. She's also holding a toddler by the hand.

Two little girls and their mommy. My mommy. Except not. I don't have to think about it. I don't have to wonder or speculate. I feel like, even if I were walking down a crowded street and passed her by, even if I didn't know anything about the source of my dreams or the truth of my past, I would know that, somehow, this woman and I belong to each other.

I get out of the car. I don't take any pamphlets with me. I walk down the sidewalk, toward her and her girls.

When I get close to her, I stare her right in the eyes.

"Hello," I say, smiling.

She looks like me. Her *children* look like me, with the same red hair and the freckles that I've always hated so much.

This is my mother, living a good life with her kids. This is my mother who did not want me in her life. It's enough to make any girl cry.

Except that I don't. I'm done crying for now. I want to hear her speak to me. I want to see if I recognize her voice. I know now that it was her, so many years ago, singing *Daisy, Daisy.*

She stands there staring at me, holding on to her babies in the cold, for a few seconds. The look on her face is confused at first—and then it shifts. She seems startled. She stands there, half-frozen, staring at me.

I'm wearing my winter coat with my hair pulled back in a ponytail and the hood pulled tightly around my face. While she's still watching me, I lower the hood. I pull my hair free, and let my red waves fall over my shoulders. Then I look my mother in the eye again.

But she doesn't react the way I hope. There is no glimmer of recognition, at least not that I can tell. Instead, she says, "Hello. Cold enough for you?"

Her voice gives me a fresh chill. Even though I haven't heard it in years, I recognize it.

Before I have a chance to say anything else, she rushes to the car with her children, glancing back at me just one more time. There's a look of fear in her eyes.

And then I realize: of course. A truck like Del's, in this neighborhood . . . she's *scared* of us.

I walk back to Del's truck and climb inside, rubbing my hands together beneath the red blanket.

"What was that?" Del asks. "You barely said anything! Don't you want to confront her?"

I shake my head.

"Why not? Emily, go tell her who you are! This is what we came here for. You're about to miss your opportunity." He pauses. "She's your *mother*, Emily, and she abandoned you. Doesn't that make you angry?"

I nod.

"Don't you want her to be sorry? What kind of person abandons her baby? It makes her a monster, Emily. Em—look at her. She's a monster."

I watch while she helps her little girls into the car, leans over to buckle their seat belts for them. Then she gives us one last glance, climbs into the driver's seat, starts the car, and pulls away.

"She's gone," Del says.

"She's not a monster," I say.

"What?" he asks, irritated.

"I said, she's not a monster."

He pauses. "Then what is she? What kind of woman does what she did, and then goes on to live a life like this?"

"Any woman," I say. "Del, she's just a person. She's not my mother, not anymore."

"Yes, she is! Emily, I have paperwork, I can prove it to you—"

"My mother lives in Connecticut," I tell him firmly. "And I want you to take me to her. I want to go home."

When we get close to campus, Del says, "I'm sure the police are waiting."

I'm sure they are, too. There's no way my parents haven't put two and two together and called them.

"Maybe you should drop me off here," I tell him. "I'll walk the rest of the way." I pause. "Are you going home after this?"

"That depends on your definition of home."

"Where are you going?"

"I'm gonna return this truck to my sister. Maybe stay there for a few days." He hesitates. "I'm eighteen, you know. I have plans. I'm not going to college. There's no reason for me to go back to the Marshalls' house."

"Maybe not, but you owe it to them to let them know you're safe. They love you. They adopted you. You can't just *leave*."

He's pulled into a parking lot. From where we sit, I can almost make out my parents' house.

"I suppose that, even if I don't go home, you can just tell your parents who you were with, and they'll call up Doug and Sharon," he says.

"Well, sure."

"And that's what you're going to do?"

I nod.

He puts his hand over mine. "Are you sure you don't want to come with me? Emily, we could be good together. We *are* good together." He swallows. "I really do love you."

I know he means it. But my feelings for him are gone. "I have to go home now," I tell him.

He looks like he wants to cry. "I don't want you to go."

"There's nothing left for us to do," I say. "It's over, Del."

Finally, it seems, he understands. He nods. His eyes are wet. "Okay."

"I'll stall everyone for a while. I'll give you a chance to get away."

He gives me the tiniest grin. "Don't worry about me. I'll be all right."

I know he will. I give him a hug. He puts his arms around me, and we sit together in his truck that way for several moments. As I replay the events of the past forty-eight hours in my head, I realize I have no idea what I'm going home to.

I pull away from him. As I feel his hands sliding from my body, I know it will probably be the last time he ever touches me. I feel a sense of bittersweet relief. "Be good," I tell him. Like he'll ever listen to me.

His blue eyes glisten. "I don't want to make any promises I can't keep." Then, just as I'm about to walk away, he says, "Wait. Emily?"

"What is it?"

"Here." He holds out the blanket. "I want you to keep this."

For a second, I almost say no. But his look is pleading, and without thinking about it, I reach out and take the blanket from his hands.

"Don't lose it," he says. "It's special."

"Don't worry," I tell him. I tuck it under my arm. "I'll keep it safe."

Then I get out of the car; the afternoon is so cold that the wind feels almost sinister. I watch him pull out of the parking lot, watch as he heads down the road toward the interchange for the highway.

Then, once he's out of sight, I walk back to campus, heading for my parents' house. The door is unlocked. They're waiting for me.

# chapter twenty-six

I'm not sure exactly what I expect, but it's not this. I was anticipating cops, but there aren't any. Instead, once I make my way to the voices in my dad's study, I walk into the room to see my parents, along with Stephanie and Ethan.

I stand in the doorway. They all look at me, stunned.

"Hi," I say. Then, in the awkward silence that stretches between us, I add, "I'm home."

My mother leaps off the couch and runs across the room to me. She holds me so tightly that I almost can't breathe.

"Emily," she says, "baby." Then, over and over again, she says, "Baby baby baby. My baby."

And here in this moment, I know that it's true. I put my arms around her, waiting for her to calm down. My father comes over to fold me into another hug. The three of us stand there together, everyone shaking and crying, until we finally pull apart.

"Emily, do you know how worried we were? We thought we'd never see you again," my dad says.

I look past him, at Ethan and Steph. Even though it's a school day, both of them are in street clothes.

"Why would you think that?" I ask.

"Because of your note. We figured you'd run off with Del. We didn't have any idea where you were . . ."

"I'm sorry," I tell them. "I had to go."

"Yeah, it was a nice note," Steph says, her tone cautious and quiet. "Not exactly the most descriptive good-bye."

"I'm sorry," I repeat. Then, looking at the four of them, I realize that I'm in a room surrounded by people who love me. Beyond that, I quickly learn that they're all people who know about the baby. In my absence—they felt they had no other choice—Steph and Ethan have filled in all the blanks for my parents. I know there will be plenty of discussion later on, but for now, my mom and dad are nothing but relieved to see me. Looking around at all of them, it becomes clear: this is love.

So I tell them where we went. I tell them that I saw Emily. "I had to know she was all right," I say. "I had to know she was loved and safe. Otherwise . . . I don't know. So when Del showed up and said that he'd found her, I just—"

"Had to go," Ethan finishes.

"Yes," I say. I glance down at his arm. He's wearing the watch that Stephanie and his mother gave him. Some things, I realize, are not going to change.


Once Stephanie and Ethan have both hugged me, once we've talked some more and everyone is slightly more calm, my father says, "Well, you two, I suppose you ought to get back to class where you belong."

They both look at me, reluctant.

"It's okay," I say. "I'll be there soon."

Once they're gone, my father shuts the door behind him, and

the three of us sit in the warm silence of the room. My mother and I are on the sofa, sitting close to each other, holding hands. Del's red blanket rests at my side.

My dad leans against his desk. "We called the police, you know," he says. "If you weren't eighteen yet, you could have gotten in real trouble. But you left a note, and we *knew* you were with Del . . . we just didn't know where."

"I didn't tell you everything," I say.

Both of my parents pause. "What?" my mother asks. "What else is there to tell us?"

"I went to see Sandy Gray," I say.

There is silence. It lasts for a long time. There is an underlying tone of something—call it terror—in my mother's voice. "Did you speak to her?" she asks.

I shake my head. "I didn't want to. I didn't have to. I know who she is, and I know what you did."

"Baby, you have to understand—"

"It's okay, Mom. She has a good life, I have a good life . . . there's no reason to go digging into the past." I pause. "But there's just one thing I want to know."

My mom nods. "Okay. What is it?"

"Why did you do it? You were a widow. I didn't belong to you. Why didn't you take me back to her? Why didn't you take me home?"

She shakes her head. "Oh, baby . . . I *did* take you back." My mom swallows hard. "You were three. It was a few weeks after your father died, and I didn't know what to do with you, but I knew where your mother lived. So we drove to her house together. It was pouring down rain—no wonder you've always been afraid of water. It was raining so hard that I could barely see the road, and I told you that I was taking you home, and you were crying.

You said you didn't want to leave me. I was the only mother you knew. And then we got there, and she lived—"

"In a trailer court," I finish.

"Yes. How did you know that?"

"My dreams. I remember now. We watched her come home, and she didn't look good, did she?"

My mom shakes her head. "No. She'd had a drug problem when she was married to your father. It was why they split up. She couldn't handle the responsibility of a child, not as far as I knew. She couldn't even take care of herself. She was a mess. And once we got there, once I saw her . . . Emily, you were my baby. As much as I knew it was the right thing to do, in my heart I couldn't let you go. It was obvious she was still using, that her life was no life for a little girl to be living, and I just couldn't do it."

I don't know how to tell her that I understand. So I don't say anything. I stare at my hands. My father crosses the room, sits on the other side of me, and wraps his arms around the two of us. As we hold each other in near silence, I know this won't be the last conversation we have about this, not by far. But for right now, it's enough. What else is there to say? I'm home. We are all safe. That's all that matters, at least in this moment.

And then, it seems, everything is over. For the time being, anyway. After we talk for a while longer, after I watch my father pick up the phone and call Del's parents, letting them know what has happened, he sends me back to class.

Before I can go up to school, I have to put on my uniform. Stephanie is still in her room, getting dressed.

We stand alone in the quad, quiet.

Finally, Stephanie says, "I'm sorry, Emily." She looks at the carpet. "I know I can't imagine how hard this has been for you."

"Right," I say bitterly. "You're such a sympathetic friend that you did everything possible to sabotage my relationship with Ethan." I glare at her, pulling on my tights. "You were so jealous of me you couldn't even see straight. Why don't you just admit it?"

Her voice is soft. "Emily, he's all I have."

"He's your brother!"

"Exactly! He's my only brother, and lately I've felt like he's the only person who really cares about me. My family has fallen apart. My own father barely sees his kids anymore. And then you swoop into his life, and he goes crazy for you . . . of course I was jealous. How could I not be? He's the most precious thing in the world to me."

I take a deep breath. I'm tired of fighting: with Del, with Stephanie, with anyone.

"Is he still mad at me?" I ask.

She gives me a blank look. "What do you think?"

"I honestly don't know. He was pretty upset a few days ago. I mean, I kept a huge secret from him. I kept it from all of you."

"You didn't have a choice," Steph says. "I get it. I might have done the same thing in your position."

"You might have?"

She nods. "I don't know. Probably. I can't imagine what it must have been like."

I'm more than a little surprised by her reaction. I never expected that she would forgive me. But before I can say anything at all, she explains a little further.

"When I found the note, I knew you were with Del. I got *so* scared, Emily. Everybody knew he was bad news. We didn't know if he'd taken you, if you'd gone with him willingly—we didn't know anything."

I take a step closer to her. I have known this girl since we were twelve years old, both of us still in braces. We've had a thousand sleepovers together as roommates and best friends. We've seen the worst of each other, over and over again. And I love her so much, regardless of anything. After all, we're all in it together here. All of us boarding students, alone in the world, our parents off living their lives with only an occasional thought of their own children. Now, more than ever, it seems sickening. We don't belong to anybody, do we? How can I possibly hold a grudge, when she and I have lived such similar lives, when you really get down to the heart of the matter?

I hug her. She feels so familiar, so warm. We stand in my room and cry together. After a few moments, I pull away and say, "I'm sorry things have changed so much between us. I didn't mean for any of this to happen, you know."

She nods. "I know. Neither did I. And . . . I'm sorry, too. For telling you what to do with Ethan, for breaking his watch . . . for everything. I was awful."

I nod. "Yes. You were."

" . . ."

" . . ."

"We don't have a lot of time," she says. "I don't want to fight anymore."

"Me, neither."

She reaches out again, like she wants to touch me. But at the last moment she lets her arm slip back to her side. We stand there looking at each other.

"You never answered my question," I say.

"About what?"

"About Ethan. Is he still angry with me?"

"He's upset," she says. "It was a big secret to keep. But come on, Em—you know him almost as well as I do. Ethan can't stay

mad at someone to save his life." She pauses. Then she almost giggles. "Well, except maybe Del. I think he'll be holding a grudge against him for quite a while."

"He shouldn't blame Del," I say. "Del was just doing the only thing he knows how to do."

Steph shrugs. "Well, he's gone now. That's good."

I nod.

"And Ethan will forgive you."

"Steph?"

"Yes?"

"What about us?"

"What do you mean, *us*?"

"I mean you and me," I tell her. "Everything is different." I look around the room, so warm and familiar, and I know that it will not last. Things are changing. There's nothing we can do.

"We're still friends," she says. "Aren't we?"

"Yes." Then, thinking out loud, I say, "School will be over soon."

"We'll keep in touch." She hesitates. "Right?"

I try to smile. "Of course." But we both know it isn't true.

I've finished getting dressed. I can't believe I'm going to go back up to school, as though nothing ever happened. And then it occurs to me—

"Steph?"

"What?"

"Did you tell everyone? About the baby?"

She gives me a long, hard look. Then she takes her thumb and index finger, zips them across her lips, locks them shut, and tosses an invisible key out the window.

"Thank you," I whisper.

"It's okay." She pauses. "There's something else, Emily. Something came for you yesterday." She goes into her room, returns with an unopened letter. It's from Renee.

17 April
mild and sunny
2:30 afternoon
stuck in boring study hall


Emily,

I called Madeline. She is in West Virginia like we thought. I caught her after school one day and we talked for a long time. She goes by Mazzie Moon now, not Madeline Moon-Park—that's why it was so hard for us to find her. And it's funny...we didn't talk about her mother, or anything that happened. Just how she's doing and what she's been up to. She's different now. Just from her voice, I can tell she's been through so much.

I am going to Yale this summer. Madeline's roommate, a girl named Katie Kitrell, is also going. Guess what I did? I put her down as my roommate choice at Yale. She won't know who I am, or that I know Madeline, but I feel like it will be a way for me to watch over Madeline. I just want to be close to her, even if it's only through another person.

How are your nightmares? Are they calming down? Have you heard from Del yet?


Write soon. Much love.
R.G.


I smile as I fold the letter and put it back into the envelope. Renee and I have a lot of catching up to do.

But there's one thing I can't wait to tell her: I can't be sure yet, but I think the nightmares will be gone for good now. What is there left to be afraid of? Nothing. There are no more secrets, no more lies, no mysteries left to figure out.

\* \* \*

Once I'm dressed and Steph and I have gathered our book bags, we head up to school. Steph doesn't ask about the letter, but I know I'll fill her in on the details eventually. After all, she's my friend. For now.

On the way to school, Ethan joins us as we pass Winchester. He puts his arm around me, and the three of us are quiet for the rest of the walk.

# chapter twenty-seven

People know I've been missing for two days, and pretty much everyone figures that I've been with Del. But they don't know anything beyond that—not where we went, or why we ran away together. More than anything, they seem surprised that I'm still with Ethan.

Ethan and I haven't talked much all day. After school, he walks me back to my dorm and we sit outside in the cold air, in the same place where I once sang a nursery rhyme to Del. Looking back, it's amazing how I never could have dreamed what significance that evening would come to have someday.

"So," he finally says, "this was some day, wasn't it?"

"It sure was." And without thinking about what I'm doing, I rest my head on his shoulder. I feel him flinch, just a little, but it's enough.

"Ethan," I ask, "is this okay?"

He doesn't say anything.

"I'll understand," I tell him. I don't have to explain beyond that.

But instead of pulling farther away, he reaches out to hold my hand. He takes his thumb and rubs it over mine. I get chills.

"We've reassembled the band," he tells me, changing the subject. "We're going to start practicing again tomorrow after school."

"That's great," I tell him. "Do you . . ."

"Do we still want you to sing?" He nods. "Yes."

"You're sure?"

"Of course I'm sure." And he squeezes my hand. "It won't work without you, Emily."

I feel like I'm going to cry. I blink, trying to force back tears. "Is there anything else I missed while I was gone?"

"Actually," he says, "yes. I got into Stanford."

"Oh yeah?" I swallow, doing my best to be enthusiastic. "That's great."

He nods. "I know. But Steph got rejected."

It's no big surprise; she's practically as bad a student as I am. I don't suppose the Stanford admissions board gives a free pass to anyone just because they're someone like Ethan's twin.

"Is she upset?" I ask.

"What do you think?"

There's a long pause.

"It's better this way," he says. "She needs to learn to be more independent."

"Uh-huh." I can't help but glance down at his watch.

"We've all been through so much this year . . . and last year. College will be a fresh start for everyone."

Is this what's happening? Is he trying to break up with me? In spite of everything that's happened in the past few days—all the fighting, all the information that I couldn't possibly have prepared myself for—I find myself focused on only one thing: *Don't do it. It will make for some awfully awkward band practices.*

"Please don't," I whisper.

"Don't what?"

"Don't break up with me."

"Is that what you think is happening?"

I nod, gripping his hand more tightly, not daring to let go, afraid it will be the last time I'm close to him.

"I don't want to break up, Emily. At first I did. I was so angry with you. I couldn't believe you would hide something so huge from everyone. I felt like I couldn't possibly know the real you, not when you'd kept a secret like that."

I start to open my mouth, to try and explain, but he interrupts me.

"But then I started thinking," he says, "about what I would do if I were in the same position as you. Of course, it's impossible—I mean, the whole pregnancy thing is impossible to even imagine—but once I tried to put myself in your shoes, I realized I couldn't possibly understand how you felt. I realized how scared you must have been. And then when you went off with Del . . . I felt responsible, you know? I felt so guilty for rejecting you without even thinking about it. It was a knee-jerk reaction, and I'm sorry."

I can't believe he's apologizing to *me*. But that's Ethan.

"Ethan, I want you to know that nothing happened with Del. I had to go find my baby. There was so much that I needed to know. It wasn't your fault. It had to happen this way."

"I know," he says. "It's a little humiliating, though. People at school, they think you ran off with Del to have some kind of tryst or something, and they'll never know the truth."

"I'm sorry."

He sighs. "It's okay. I mean, it's hard. I could feel everyone looking at me today, like they were feeling sorry for me, wondering what the hell I was still doing with you. But you know what? I don't care." He squeezes my hand more tightly. "I really do love you. I have for years. I meant it when I said it. And you don't just turn your back on someone you love. It's impossible."

*Don't I know it.*

"So. I'm going to Stanford in the fall. And you're going . . . where *are* you going?"

The idea of contemplating college seems insane after what I've been through. "Well, I got into a few state schools. And my dad pulled a few strings, which got me into Sarah Lawrence despite my grades, since I actually did pretty well on my SATs. So I'm thinking Sarah Lawrence. We'll see."

"So . . . East Coast," he finishes.

"Yes."

"Where's Renee going?"

I smile. "She has one more year of high school, you know. But after that . . . she wants to go to Sarah Lawrence."

He sighs again. "I guess I'm not really up for a cross-country relationship. Are you?"

*This is it. Here we go.*

"I guess not, no."

"But we still have a few months of school left," he says. "We'll have the band. And then there's the summer."

I hesitate. Then I say, "Well, technically, I'm not allowed to have you for the summer. You know—it's one of Stephanie's rules . . ."

"She'll make an exception," he says. "Trust me."

"You're sure?" I giggle.

"I'm sure."

"So, what are we doing, Ethan?"

He pulls me closer. He kisses me on the top of the head. I feel calm. I feel normal. Everything from my past has come to light; I've been through more than I could imagine, and I've made it to the other side. Now what?

He keeps his arms around me for a few minutes more, quietly, the two of us sitting together, just enjoying the moment of calm. Then, pulling away slightly, Ethan says, "I don't know what's going to happen. But I know I don't want to let you go yet."

I bite my lip. "Me, neither."

"Okay, then." He smiles. "What if we start with the prom?"

*The prom.* It hadn't even crossed my mind. But when he says it, it sounds wonderful—so ordinary and sweet and safe.

"I would love that," I tell him.

"Really?"

"Yes." I smile. "It sounds perfect."

# epilogue

My mother. My father. The words have whole different meanings now. I don't remember my real father at all. Now that I know the truth, will the memories ever surface? Will I see him before the fire, when I was two, three years old? My mother told me she has pictures somewhere; will they trigger any recollection? And what about Sandy Gray? Will I want to go back someday and tell her who I am? In my heart, I know she'll want to know that I'm healthy, happy, safe. Maybe she couldn't be a mother when I was a baby, but she looked like a good one when I saw her. People change. They make mistakes. They have regrets that haunt them for their entire lives.

Even though it's a school night, I sleep at home tonight instead of at my dorm. There is simply too much left to be said for me to walk away. After such a surreal day at school—chemistry, Ethan, his invitation to the prom—I want to be at home. Even though it's not my home, not really. It's funny; I've always considered myself somehow different from all of the boarding students here at Stonybrook, because my parents were so much more present. I was the headmaster's daughter. I could go home whenever I wanted. But now, it seems that I'm more like them than I could ever have imagined. I can't *really* go home—not ever. I don't know where home is. It's something that existed, for me, fifteen years ago for a brief period of time. Then it went up in flames.

I'm grateful that, for once, my parents haven't recruited Dr. Miller to mediate our time together this evening. They have nearly finished a bottle of wine by the time I arrive. We order a pizza and sit around the kitchen table. There's one thing I want them to understand; it's the most important thing of all, really.

"I want you to know that I'm not angry anymore about what you did," I tell them.

"I kidnapped you," my mother says. She holds her wineglass by its stem, twisting it back and forth between her thumb and middle finger, staring at the reflective contents. "I had no right to do it, but I couldn't stop myself. I couldn't let you stay with that woman. It felt like feeding you to the wolves."

"Mom—Mommy—it's okay," I tell her. "I've been thinking about her all day. After I saw my baby"—my mom flinches at the mention of *my baby*—"I understood why you did what you did."

"It was illegal," she says.

"Not really," my dad interrupts. "It's a gray area. Sandy relinquished her parental rights to Emily. Legally, she wasn't her guardian anymore. And we have the adoption papers to *prove* that she's ours—"

"The adoption papers we had forged for us! The birth certificate we had *altered* when she was four years old. What if she applies for a passport, and they notice something's wrong? What then?" My mom shudders. "I had no choice but to do the wrong thing. I don't know how to explain it beyond that." She looks at me. "You wanted me, Emily. You only knew me as your mother. You'd just lost your father. You have to understand."

"I do understand," I tell her. "I just want to know . . . I guess I just want to know why my real mother didn't want me in the first place."

"She was very young," my mom says. "After you were born, she developed a drug problem, like I told you. Amphetamines. When she and your father split up, she knew there was no chance that she'd get custody of you, and to tell the truth, I think she was probably so overwhelmed by the idea of what a mess her life had become that she was grateful to run away from everything."

My father has opened another bottle of wine. He refills my mother's glass.

"I can tell you something, though, Emily. I never met your mother. I never saw her, aside from that one time outside her trailer. But I know this much." My mom takes a big swallow of wine. "I know that she loves you. I know that she did what she thought was best. And I guarantee, there's not a day that goes by that she doesn't think of you. I'm just as sure of that as I am of my own love for you."

I know she's right. I look at my father. Here is the man who raised me, who put his own neck on the line to make me legally *his*, who treated me like his own child for almost my entire life. I've never felt, not for a second, that I don't belong to him.

"Well," he says, looking at me, "you're eighteen now. If you wanted to, you could go back to your mother and tell her what happened."

"No," I say, "I won't do that." I pause. "But I was thinking of writing her a letter. Maybe someday. Not to reach out and get to know her—just to tell her that I'm safe, and I understand, and I want the best for her."

They both stare at me. "Emily," my father says, "you've really grown into quite a young woman."

"Yeah, well, it's been a broadening couple of years."

And then my father does what I least expect him to do. He stares at me for a few seconds. Then he laughs. My mother follows.

All I can do is sit there, half-smiling, relieved to have even the slightest release in tension.

"Broadening," he says, wiping his eyes. "That's rich." He takes another sip of wine. It's dark outside; there are no lights on in the kitchen except for a lone track light above the sink. We are all shadows and breath and the light stink of booze. Things become silent.

"Well," my father finally says, "what now?"

My mother studies her glass. "Maybe it's time we finally redecorated your room, Emily." She looks at me. "You're not a little girl anymore."

"No. I guess I'm not."

"..."

"..."

"I've decided to go to Sarah Lawrence," I tell them. "And I'm going to the prom with Ethan."

My father looks at me. "Sarah Lawrence? You're staying on the East Coast?"

I nod.

"You're sure you don't want to go to UConn? Maybe something a little less . . ."

"Challenging? No." I shake my head. "I'll work hard. It will be okay."

My mother closes her eyes for a moment. I can tell she's trying not to cry. I can't imagine she has any tears left inside her; I know I don't.

"Mom?" I ask. "Are you okay?"

She nods, her eyes still closed. "It's just that, I remember when you were small, I used to dread the idea of your going to the prom someday."

"Really? Why?"

"Oh . . . I was afraid you'd end up with the wrong boy. I was afraid you'd get into some kind of trouble. You know—just the usual mother's worries."

"But not now," I say. My voice is almost a whisper.

"No," she says. "Not now. Not anymore."

My father puts down his wineglass. He reaches out, takes my hand, takes my mother's hand, and then I reach for my mother, and the three of us sit around the table together, the light slipping away into darkness, a silent family holding itself tightly together, with nothing left to say for the night.

# acknowledgments

I want to thank my family for their continued encouragement and support as they endured all of my late nights and weekends spent working on this book. I simply could not have done it without their patience, understanding, and repeated willingness to order takeout in lieu of a home-cooked meal.

I can't possibly express my gratitude to my editor, Stacy Cantor, who is an absolute joy to work with. You are an amazing cheerleader and a fabulous editor whose perception and support are invaluable. Your energy and enthusiasm are contagious and consistently inspire me to do my best.

None of this would be possible without my agent, Andrea Somberg, who has been with me since the very beginning and whose support has been unwavering. I simply can't thank you enough for all that you've done. I'll never forget getting my first phone call from you when I was twenty-three years old and feeling so excited to be talking to someone from New York City! Never in a million years could I have imagined what was in store.

Catherine M. LoChiatto

**jessica warman** is also the author of the critically acclaimed *Breathless*. She has an MA in creative writing and studied at prep school and Yale. When she isn't writing, she likes to run, read, and spend time with her husband and two daughters. Jessica lives in Pittsburgh, Pennsylvania.

www.jessicawarman.com

There were six people on the boat that night . . .
and when they awoke, there were five.

Read on for a sneak peek
at Jessica Warman's darkly romantic
and deeply haunting new novel.

It's a little after two a.m. Outside the *Elizabeth*, things are relatively quiet. Boats—yachts, really—are tied to the docks, clean white buoys protecting their fiberglass and porcelain exteriors from the wood. The *slosh* of the Long Island Sound, water beating against boats and shore, is a constant in the background. In most of the other boats—with names like *Well Deserved, Privacy, Good Life*—there is peace.

But inside the *Elizabeth*, there is persistent unrest. The boat is a sixty-four-foot cruiser, equipped with a full kitchen, two baths, two bedrooms, and enough extra space to sleep a total of twenty people. Tonight there are only six, though. It's a small party—my parents wouldn't have let me throw a big one. Everybody is asleep, I think, except for me.

I've been staring at the clock for twenty minutes now, listening to this annoying *thump, thump, thump* against the hull. It's late August. The air outside is already cool, and the water is undoubtedly frigid. Connecticut's like that; the water gets warm for a month or so in July, but near the end of the summer it's already cold again. Sometimes it seems like there are only two seasons around here: winter and almost winter.

Regardless of the water's temperature, I'm pretty certain there's a fish out there, stuck between the dock and the boat, pounding against the fiberglass, trying to free itself. The noise has been going on for what feels like forever. It woke me up at exactly 1:57 a.m., and it's starting to drive me nuts.

I finally can't take it anymore. *Thump. Thump-thump.* If it's a fish, it's a *stupid* fish.

"Hey? Do you hear that?" I say to my best friend and stepsister, Josie, who's sleeping beside me on the fold-out couch in the front of the boat, her highlighted dirty-blond hair plastered against the side of her face. She doesn't respond, just continues to snore softly, passed out since a little after midnight from an alcohol-marijuana combination that sent us all to bed before the late show came to an end. That's the last thing I remember before falling asleep: trying to keep my eyes open, mumbling to Josie that we had to wait for 1:37 a.m., which is exactly when I was born, before we fell asleep. Nobody made it. At least, I know I didn't.

I stand up in the near darkness. The only light in the boat is coming from the TV, where there's an infomercial for the SuperMop! running with the sound turned off.

"Anyone awake?" I ask, still keeping my voice low. The boat rocks against the waves coming in from the Long Island Sound. *Thud-thud-thud*. There it is again.

I look at the clock. It's 2:18. I smile to myself; I've officially been eighteen for over a half hour.

If it weren't for the thumping, the rocking of the boat would feel like being tucked inside a lullaby. This is just about my favorite place in the world. Being here with my friends makes it even better, if that's possible. Everything seems peaceful and calm. The stillness of the evening feels almost magical tonight.

*Thump.*

"I'm going outside to liberate a fish," I announce. "Somebody please come with me."

But nobody—not one of them—even stirs.

"Bunch of selfish drunks," I murmur. But I'm only kidding. And anyway, I can go outside by myself. I'm a big girl. There's nothing to be scared of.

I know it sounds hypocritical, since we've been drinking and smoking, but it's true: we're good kids. This is a safe town. Everyone onboard has grown up together in Noank, Connecticut. Our families are friends. We love each other. Looking around at all of them—Josie in the front of the boat, Mera, Caroline, Topher, and Richie in sleeping bags on the floor in the back—life inside the *Elizabeth* feels like a hazy dream.

Elizabeth Valchar. That's me; my parents named this

boat after me when I was six years old. But that was a life-time ago. A few years before we lost my mother, before my dad married Josie's mom. My dad got rid of a lot of my mom's stuff after she died, but he was always adamant about keeping the boat. See, we have so many happy memories here. I always felt safe here. My mom would have wanted it this way.

Still, it can be eerie so late at night, especially outside. Other than the sloshing of the waves, the dull thumping against the hull, the night is dark and silent. The smell of ocean salt water, algae dried onto all the thick rock formations this close to shore, is so overwhelming that, if the wind catches it the right way, it can almost make me nauseated.

I'm not particularly keen on trying to figure out where the mystery noise is coming from all by myself, even though I'm almost certain it's just a fish. So I give Josie one more try. "Hey," I say louder, "wake up. I need your help." I reach out to touch her, but something stops me. It's the oddest feeling— like I shouldn't be disturbing her. For a minute, I think that I must still be drunk. Everything feels kind of fuzzy.

Her eyelids flutter. "Liz?" she murmurs. She's confused, obviously still asleep. For a second there's a flash of something—is it fear? Am I freaking her out?—in her gaze. And then she's out again, and I'm standing by myself, the only person awake. *Thud-thud-thud.*

The docks are like a wooden jigsaw puzzle. Waves break in from the ocean, and by the time they reach the Sound they're usually gentle enough, but tonight they seem stronger than normal, rocking us all to sleep like a bunch of babies. Despite my attempts to be brave, I feel small and afraid as I tiptoe out the open sliding glass door, my shoes making light *clacking* sounds against the fiberglass deck of the boat. Each arm of the docks has only two overhead lights: one at the middle and another at the very end. There is no visible moon. The air is so chilly that I shudder, thinking what the water must feel like. Goose bumps rise on my exposed flesh.

I stand on deck, frozen, listening. Maybe the noise will go away.

*Thump.* Nope.

It's coming from the stern, between the dock and the boat, like something heavy and alive, persistent, stuck. We're the last boat on this arm of the dock, which means the back of the *Elizabeth* is almost fully illuminated by the light. I don't know why I feel the need to be so quiet. The noise from my shoes against the deck is jarring, every footstep making me cringe, no matter how carefully I step. I make my way along the side of the boat, holding tightly to the railing. Once the sound is directly beneath me, I look down.

*Wet.* It's the first word that comes to mind before I scream.

*Soaked. Waterlogged. Facedown.* Oh, shit.

It isn't a fish; it's a person. A girl. Her hair is long and so blond that it's almost white, the pretty, natural color shimmering beneath the water. The wavy strands, moving back and forth like algae, reach almost to her waist. She's wearing jeans and a short-sleeved pink sweater.

But that's not what's making the noise. It's her feet; her boots, actually. She's wearing a pair of white cowgirl boots, encrusted with gemstones, steel-toed decadence.

I scream again, loud enough to wake everyone for a mile around. But I get the feeling nobody can hear me.

# DON'T MISS
## Jessica Warman's stunning debut novel

"Poignantly honest and real."
—Todd Strasser, bestselling author of *Give a Boy a Gun*

# breathless

Some secrets are best kept
beneath the surface.

j e s s i c a  w a r m a n

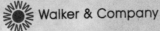

Walker & Company